HIDDEN

EVE KENIN

LOVE SPELL **NEW YORK CITY**

To Imke, because we're good enough friends that she put her usual tact and reserve aside to ask why I hadn't dedicated a book to her yet. And to Lisa and Anne, because they're laughing themselves sick as they read that.

LOVE SPELL®

July 2008

Published by

Dorchester Publishing Co., Inc.
200 Madison Avenue
New York, NY 10016

ISBN 10: 0-505-52761-8
ISBN 13: 978-0-505-52761-5

Printed in the United States of America.

10 9 8 7 6 5 4 3 2 1

Visit us on the web at www.dorchesterpub.com.

ACKNOWLEDGMENTS

I thank my editor, Leah Hultenschmidt, who makes my stories better and who has never held the unfortunate clear Lucite stiletto heel incident against me.

Thank you to my agent, Sha-Shana Crichton, who remains unfazed no matter what I pull out of my hat.

Special thanks to my parents, my brothers and sisters-in-law, and my nieces and nephews for their wonderful enthusiasm and support.

To Nancy and Brenda, I offer my deepest gratitude for critiques, camaraderie and the gift of friendship.

Dylan, my light; Sheridan, my joy; and Henning, my forever love—I thank you for so much more than I can ever express.

PROLOGUE

Sub-basement, Janson Transport Head Office, Port Uranium
January 2088

Blood had its own scent. Metallic, sharp. Faintly sweet.

Tatiana raised her hand to her cheek. She was beyond pain, almost beyond thought. There would be more. With Duncan Bane, there was always more.

To make you stronger. To make you invincible. Bane's justification. And the simple truth. But Tatiana wasn't like Wizard or Yuriko. She didn't recover as quickly as her siblings. She bruised easier. Her bones broke where Wizard's and Yuriko's bent to absorb the force.

And Bane had been particularly brutal this session.

"Because you are soon to go on your first mission," he explained in a soft, soft, cultured voice, pacing a straight line before the three of them. He paused, touched Tatiana on the shoulder. She shuddered, but knew better than to pull away. "This will ensure that you are ready, that you survive. You"—he spun toward Wizard—"will be the commander, and a commander must be able to make rapid decisions."

Another step and Bane stood in front of Yuriko. Running his finger along her cheek, he smiled as she jerked away.

"So decide now, Wizard. Who will be subjected to ten more minutes?"

Tatiana choked back a plea. *Please. I can't. I can't—*

She shook her head, struggled to focus. The room felt too big, too bright, and this all felt so familiar, like she had been here many times before. She knew what Wizard would say even before the words left his lips.

"Me. I will take the ten minutes."

She let out a dry sob. Wizard. Her brother, so logical even in this. He would take the blows because he was the strongest. He would stand before her and take them in her stead.

Yuriko was like him. Clean and linear in thought and action.

But Tatiana . . .

Bane laughed as he stared at Wizard, the sound hollow, echoing off the bare walls, echoing in her darkest dreams.

Yes, just a dream. It must be.

"You are the commander," he said. "The fastest. The strongest. You have the best chance of finishing your mission. I may send you out tonight, before you have time to heal. Choose the weakest, Wizard. A good commander knows when to calculate the odds, when to sacrifice for the good of the mission."

"Wizard . . . save her. Please. She has a chance." Yuriko's normally cool tone was laced with despair, with pain, and Tatiana's heart shattered as it did each time the nightmares sank her to this place, to the deep dark of her soul, the coldest part of her memories. Because in begging Wizard to save Tatiana, Yuriko had doomed herself.

Bane would set loose his brutality on her.

Trembling, Tatiana swayed on her feet, her swollen lips working as she tried to form the words . . . what words?

Did she mean to offer herself to Bane's fists, or to sacrifice her sister?

Again came the eerie, frightening sensation of familiarity and the terrifying knowledge that she had lived these moments again and again, that the outcome was always the same.

The walls around her shimmered and danced, and she heard voices, saw lights. They were wrong. They had no place here.

She had no place here. None of it was real.

Heart racing, palms damp, Tatiana began to run, her feet pounding against the cold stone floor, hard, fast. Only she didn't move at all. Her limbs pumped as hard and as fast as they could, and still she stayed in one place, trapped in the past.

She needed only to pull free, come awake, and they would be gone—the pain, the memories, the horror. But neither the bonds of sleep nor the terrors that dwelled in her memories eased to set her free. They held her in tight tendrils that dragged her back and pulled her into a place she had no wish to be.

Wizard . . . save her. Please. She has a chance.

Yuriko's voice, low, urgent.

Bound in the barbed web of events that had played out long ago, Tatiana thrashed and flailed. A dream. A dream. It was only a dream.

"Calculate the odds," Bane ordered.

Tatiana's breath came in short, huffing pants. She couldn't push any sound past the lump in her throat. Coward. She was a coward. Weak.

Hazy, unfocused, she shifted her gaze to Wizard. Silently she pleaded for . . . what? What did she want him to do? What could he do?

The outcome was always the same. She had been powerless to change it then, was powerless to change it now.

"Choose." Bane whispered the word against Wizard's ear.

For the first time in her recollection, her brother hesitated.

Choose. Choose. Choose.

And then Bane's face melted like wax in a flame, shifting, changing, until it was a different man who chained her, a different man who stood looking down at her, wanting to master her, to use her, to twist what she was for his own gain.

She had thought Bane the face of purest evil. But she'd been wrong. So wrong.

Gavin Ward. Dr. Gavin Ward.

He was here for her. Her time was up.

Sweating, screaming, Tatiana bolted upright, the dream so real that she smelled the stink of her own fear, felt the sting of the blows on her cheek, her jaw, as though they had landed minutes rather than years past. Felt the pain of knowing that her weakness had cost her sister her life.

Yuriko. Oh, God. Yuriko.

Tatiana wrapped her arms around her knees and lowered her forehead. She closed her eyes, shuddering in the cold and the darkness, fighting the memories, the anguish, the fear.

A nightmare, she told herself. Only a nightmare.

But it wasn't.

Because as she raised her head, she saw him, there, in the shadows, just beyond the bars that caged her. Gavin Ward was there. Watching.

And the light glinted off the scalpel in his hand.

CHAPTER ONE

Northern Waste, 2093

Someone ought to kill him.

Tatiana turned to face the bleak silhouette of the dilapidated shack that housed Abbott's General Store. The entire rickety building listed to one side, shored up by a pile of refuse and scrap nearly as tall as the shack itself. To the back was a yard cordoned off with barbed wire, illuminated by the pallid glow of a single lumilight. The small area was dotted with a half-dozen snowscooters—in diverse stages of disrepair—which Abbott would be happy to sell to the unwary purchaser.

The bitter wind swirled around her, whipping her hair against her cheeks as her gaze cut to her own scooter, a Morgat, sleek, black and brand spanking new, faster than a plascannon shot. Handy in her current line of work. The retrieval business favored those who were proficient at a quick getaway; survival depended on it.

She turned back to the sprawling conglomeration of architectural misfortune that housed the store, and beside that, Abbott's Inn and Pub. Two stories high on one side, not quite one story on the other, the whole building looked like a house of cards patched together from a bunch of mismatched decks. The owner, Boyd Abbott, sold everything from clothing to food to snowscooters. Those who made a special request could purchase women or young girls . . . even young boys. Willing. Unwilling.

Abbott stocked it all. He was a sick, greedy bastard, through and through.

So, yeah, someone ought to kill him.

Tatiana weighed the benefits and detriments, considered whether that someone should be her. Flip a plastitech vidcredit? Heads—just break something. Tails—kill him.

Logic decided against either option. She had a job to complete, and killing Abbott wasn't in the three-step plan. Besides, she couldn't save everyone, and she couldn't simply go around breaking bones every time she ran up against shoddy morals and obsidian black ethics. Two lessons she'd been quick to learn since her bizarre change of circumstance six months past.

For an instant, the thin boundary between present and past blurred. Memories spewed from their dank pit like spittle from a rabid dog. She remembered the acrid stink of human death, the horrific sensation of life sifting through her fingers.

She had killed.

Never again. A vow she knew she would break, over and over.

Some things just . . . *were*.

But killing Abbott senior would only open the door for Abbott junior—a sadistic creature with a distinct aversion to personal hygiene—to step up and take his father's place, a far more vicious master to those in his keeping than ever his father had been.

It had taken her all of a single day's freedom to understand that there were no reliable laws to protect the weak, the innocent. There was no real justice here in the

Northern Waste. The New Government Order postured and pretended, but since Bane's death, the veneer of respectability had worn thin. Worn clean through, in places.

Bane had been a despot, the puppeteer yanking the strings of the president of the New Government Order, and his death had opened the door for every type of slime to crawl out from under every rock, anxious to take his place.

Gavin Ward had simply been able to slither faster than everyone else.

She sighed. If it hadn't been Ward who stepped up, it would have been someone else equally evil. In truth, the Order was just a corrupt serpent holding an entire hemisphere in its venomous jaws. If she yanked out one jagged fang, ten more would just grow in its place.

When she'd first gotten free, she'd done her share of yanking. And that had been just plain dumb, because it had drawn a deadly sort of attention.

Leaving a trail of bodies wasn't a great way to hide from Gavin Ward, the guy who wanted to chain her in a lab and slice her into little, usable genetic bits.

That was another thing she'd learned. Stay at least a step ahead of Dr. Ward. Wasn't she just the quick study?

She crossed the poorly lit lot, noting the snowscooter tucked in the narrow spot by the front door of the general store. Clean, well-maintained, but old technology, at least a decade out of date. Probably belonged to a Northern Waste settler in for supplies.

She pushed open the door and stepped inside, scanning the interior, mentally listing the alternate exits—a boarded up window behind the sales counter, a darkened hallway leading to the back door at the rear of the building, a second window to her left, barred and wired for security. The narrow aisles wending between the stacked shelves were empty, save for one guy about halfway across the store. She figured him for the settler who belonged with the outdated scooter she'd seen on the way in.

Still, she made certain to stay aware of his position as she checked out the remainder of the store. A girl could never be too careful.

Boyd Abbott stood behind the counter, long wisps of sandy hair scraped over his shiny scalp from one side to the other, glistening with the grease he'd used to anchor them in place. She thought he might not have bathed since she'd seen him last, some six weeks past.

He had a leer on his face and a Bolinger plasgun nestled in his shoulder, the barrel pointed at her head.

She spread her hands, palms forward.

"Just looking for information," she said, and couldn't help smiling as he studied her for less time than it took to draw breath before lowering the Bolinger. He stored it on the shelf beneath the counter, an action that was neither cautious nor wise. She could have her knife free and flying, could let it find a nice home smack-dab in the middle of his shriveled heart, before he could manage to pull that gun up again.

The prospect held definite appeal, but she really was here for information. He wasn't much use to her dead.

"Nothing's free," Abbott said, his gaze flicking over her. She knew what he saw: beauty, innocence, female vulnerability. The perfect symmetry of her face, the sculpted cheeks, the lush and sexy mouth. But appearances could lie. In the past six months she had learned that it was always her eyes—translucent gray, pale and eerie, startling against dark lashes—that gave her away, made people call her spooky.

So she rarely looked them in the eye. No reason to offer a warning.

Abbott's gaze paused to linger at her breasts and thighs. She almost laughed. As if he could actually see anything through the puff of her parka.

"Cash or . . . trade?" he asked, widening his leer to show off ground-down stubs of brown teeth.

"Cash." Stalking forward, she carefully set down a short stack of interdollars and used her index finger to push them across the counter.

Abbott reached for them, avaricious bastard, but she slapped her palm down hard, trapping both his hand and the money against the pitted and yellowed Formica countertop. She would have preferred not to touch him, but she wasn't about to let him snag the cash without offering the information she needed first.

His gaze jerked to hers, startled and a little wary.

"You're stronger than you look." He grunted as he tried to pull free.

"So I'm told." She eased the pressure enough that he could pull his hand from beneath hers. But he left the interdollars where she'd put them.

From the corner of her eye, she caught a flicker of movement, and she turned just enough to keep an eye on Abbott as well as the guy meandering along the aisles doing a little shopping. He was tall, draped in layers of tattered thermal gear that obscured both face and form.

It was a typical outfit for a settler or a rebel. They reused whatever they could, slicing up worn garments and patching them together to form draping robes that insulated them against the cold. Strategically placed slits allowed freedom of movement—and amazing opportunities for concealed weaponry.

She did a quick scan from top to toe. No obvious weapons—with *obvious* being the key concept—but if he *was* packing a plasgun, it was a small one. No knife hilt at the top of either boot, so he wasn't carrying there. Maybe a sheath at the small of his back. He had to have a weapon somewhere. In the Waste, you carried or you died.

He didn't appear to be particularly interested in her, which made her only slightly less interested in him. She viewed anyone and everyone as a threat. A half step to the left, and she shifted her position so she could keep both Abbott and the ragged settler in sight.

Sliding the top interdollar off the pile, she eased it across the counter, pulled her hand away, and let it lie there.

Abbott snatched it up and tucked it away.

"Gun truckers. Yasha and Viktor Zhuk," Tatiana said, her voice low. "I heard tell that they usually come by on Tuesdays for a little special entertainment. You expecting them tonight?"

Crawling his fingers forward until they rested against the edge of the stack, Abbott narrowed his eyes. "Who wants to know?"

She pushed the money a little closer to him and forced a smile. "Their baby sister. Can't you see the family resemblance?"

A short huff of laughter carried from her left, and her head jerked up to find the settler studying her from about ten feet away. There wasn't much of him to see. Only his eyes were visible beneath the wrapped layers of his thermal gear. But something about him drew her.

His laugh. She liked the sound of his laughter.

Her gaze locked on his. Blue. His eyes were blue, beautiful, night dark, layered with variegated shades, colder than the depths of the ocean that went on forever beneath the ice.

They were crinkled a little at the corners, so she figured he was smiling. Guess he liked her sense of humor.

An odd combination, the hint of that smile with those cold, cold eyes.

Tatiana drew a breath, tried to read him, opening her senses to the ghosting of electric current that was the basis of thought. She kept her attention divided between him and Abbott, her fingertips resting on the stack of interdollars, but her focus was on the rag-draped stranger.

Opening herself a little wider, she dredged for a whisper of the electrochemical spark that was responsible for neuronal action. But there was nothing, nothing but endless darkness. She couldn't read a damned thing from this guy, and the effort made her skull feel like it would split in two.

Slagging nosy settler.

"This isn't a three-way conversation, asshole," she muttered. "Don't you have something else to occupy your attention?"

It was rare for her to slam up against a wall like that when she tried to grab another's thoughts. It happened. But it was rare. And she didn't like it.

She took a step closer to the counter, aware that the settler tracked her as she moved, that he studied her with more than a little curiosity.

Look away. Dismiss him. There was no reason for her to feel even a whisper of interest in who he was. Some settler come to Abbott's for supplies or—since he was wandering the aisles picking up absolutely nothing—maybe he was here to get laid. Either way, she shouldn't waste a thought on him.

So why was she?

"You expecting them or not?" she asked, turning back to face Abbott. She could just grab the answer from his thoughts. He was as easy to read as a holo-book. Problem was, *his* thoughts were as filthy as the smog over Port

Uranium, and she just did not want to crawl around in all that ooze.

The settler ambled off toward the front of the store, and she was glad of that. Something about him made her nervous. Not a feeling she particularly liked. She shifted slightly to keep him in her sights.

"Yeah, I'm expecting Viktor and Yasha." Abbott snaked another interdollar off the pile, and she let him. "I got in some nice fresh meat, young, just the way they like it." He jerked his chin toward the narrow hallway that led from the store to the inn. "They should be here any minute."

She let him snatch the remaining interdollars and squirrel them away beneath the counter, taking care not to touch him again. It would take an ocean's worth of water to remove the feeling that he'd covered her in slime.

"See? That was an easy way to earn some extra cash." Undoing the zip-seam on her pocket, she reached in and withdrew a large vial of fine white crystals. "Sugar," she said. "The real stuff. Not sim-tose or neo-fructose. Genuine sucrose. A full five hundred milliliters."

Abbott eyes widened and he tracked her every move as she popped the seal, carefully poured a couple of grains into her palm and offered them to him. He shivered with excitement as she transferred them, brushing the sugar off her palm into his, again careful not to contact his skin.

He closed his eyes in ecstasy as he licked the sugar from his palm and the taste melted on his tongue.

"Answer one more question and you can have this." She tipped the vial to catch the light, masking her disgust of him. "Shiny, isn't it?"

A woman's desperate cry echoed from the back hallway, and then the sound of a sharp slap and another, followed by hysterical sobs.

Abbott spun. "Gag her!" he yelled. "I don't wanna hear this shit. Save it for the customers." He turned back toward Tatiana and muttered sullenly, "Fresh meat. They always scream. Then they break, and once they do, there's no more screaming. But guys like Yasha and Viktor don't like 'em broken." He shrugged. "Gotta please the customer, ya know?"

Tatiana strangled the urge to reach across the counter and break his face. Kill him, and his son would only take his place, she reminded herself.

"So what do you want to know? I don't know nothing else about Yasha and Viktor."

"What I want to know about them, I can ask them myself when they get here," Tatiana said, keeping her tone level and her hands low, though what she really wanted to do was wrap them around Abbott's scrawny neck and twist, nice and hard and sharp. Hear the satisfying crack. Now that would be a fine way to end her day. "This little treasure"—she lifted the hand that held the sugar—"is a reward for an entirely different set of right answers." Her tone hardened. "I'm looking for Tolliver. Tell me what you know."

Abbott frowned, the greedy glow in his eyes dimming, and Tatiana's hopes sank.

"Tolliver? A place? A person? A new lock-mech device?" Abbott demanded. "What are you asking?"

"Obviously nothing you know the answer to."

"Maybe I do. Maybe I do. This Tolliver . . . person, place or thing? Give me a hint."

Tatiana blew out a huffing breath. He manifested no physiological changes to suggest he was anything but genuinely stymied.

Clearly, he had no idea, and he was getting testy because

she'd phrased her question in a way that didn't let him offer bullshit as the answer.

She tamped down her disappointment. She'd thought for certain that if anyone would know who Tolliver was, *where* he was, it would be Boyd Abbott. Very little went on in this barren corner of the Waste that he didn't know about. Unfortunately, he apparently had no clue who Tolliver was, no clue about his link to the stolen equipment that the news had been reporting for the past three days over the broadband, and no clue that Ward's top dog had a hidden facility nearby where he vivisected people for jollies.

Tolliver. She didn't even know the bastard's first name. All she knew was that he was a scientist, some sort of genetic and infectious-disease specialist. And he worked for Ward.

She'd already tried Bob's Truck Stop, and Jenny's Whorehouse at Gladow Station. Like them, Abbott knew nothing.

His gaze tracked the vial of sugar, and she took a second to enjoy the sadistic pleasure of letting him think it was beyond his grasp.

But the truth was, she didn't need it, and didn't want to carry it with her. What she did need were supplies.

"Since you can't answer my question"—she gently placed the vial on the counter, but kept her fingers resting lightly on the seal—"I'll take the value of the sugar in supplies."

Abbott rubbed his hands together, his demeanor perking up, and he stated a ridiculously low figure as an opening sally. Her heart wasn't in the exchange, but on principle she haggled the sum up to a more acceptable level.

With the deal done, she quickly gathered what she needed, settled her account, and left the store, shouldering past the rag-swathed settler on her way out. He didn't exactly block her path, but he didn't step out of her way, either. And as she passed him, she was close enough to get a close view of those incredible dark blue eyes.

With a shake of her head, she stepped into the frigid air, barely noticing the slap of it.

What was she doing mooning over the color of some guy's eyes?

Mooning over him. What the hell? Just . . . what the slagging hell?

She stalked to her scooter and stored the supplies she had acquired in the general store, then stepped back, out of the pallid pool of light cast by the single overhead lamp. She shoved her hands in the pockets of her parka and stared into the distance, preferring to wait in the cold for a couple of stinking gun truckers rather than stand in Abbott's warm store choking on the urge to slit his throat or wring his neck.

If she hadn't needed the money from this job, she'd have gotten on her scooter and headed somewhere else. Anywhere else. But you couldn't save the world without a few interdollars in your pocket. A girl had to eat.

Tapping the tips of her fingers against her thigh, she stared out at the flat plane of endless white. She felt bare here, exposed.

Because she hated wide-open, endless space, had yet to get used to anything bigger than a cell with stone walls on three sides and shatterproof plastiglass on the fourth, all surrounded by 5100-volt wires designed to deliver the full charge directly to the human body. An opulent cell, to be sure—walls of cold stone, a bed swathed in layers of the finest cottons and silks, priceless furniture of rare mahogany—but a cell nonetheless.

Impatient now, Tatiana glanced about, letting her gaze slide to the horizon where it blended with the night sky, measuring, assessing.

The vastness gnawed at her composure. The infinite open space was a killer. Welcome to the Northern Waste, a barren and frigid, icy stretch of forever. Perfect hunting ground, because there was next to nowhere to hide.

Too bad she was the prey.

But Gavin Ward had no intention of killing her. Not right away. No, he planned to do things far worse than killing her.

Slag. She did not want to get sucked into this space right now. What she wanted was the two gun truckers, the ring they'd stolen, and an end to this particular job so she could get paid and get on with her three-step program to save herself and save the world.

Well, save the Northern Hemisphere, anyway.

Okay, maybe not the whole hemisphere, but the frozen, slagging Waste.

What could she say? She was a goal-oriented kind of girl.

In the distance, the air shimmered, revealing twin points of light, different from the stars that dotted the night sky. She heard the hum, a faint sound. Seconds ticked past, and the hum grew to a growl, then a roar. Her muscles tensed in anticipation. She had a feeling her boys were about to arrive.

Not long ago, she would have been afraid, but in the past few months, a slew of interesting physical abilities had emerged and been honed to a sharp edge. A lovely, danger-ous edge.

There were days she didn't recognize herself. Sometimes, when she thought back to the girl she had been—chained to a wall in the bowels of the earth—she was glad to see a different person staring back at her in the mirror.

And sometimes, she was more than a little wary of what she was turning into.

The twin points of light closed the distance, growing bigger, brighter. The massive truck tires crunched the snow and ice and spit it up in a glittering arc.

Somewhere behind her she heard the slam of a door, and she flicked a glance back toward the general store. The settler was striding toward his scooter, his steps long and confident. He caught her watching him, inclined his head and walked on.

For some reason, this guy set off all her warning sirens. Wizard had always taught her that the least dangerous guys tried the hardest, screamed the loudest. The most dangerous guys didn't need to.

So was this settler—with his ragged gear and his ancient scooter—so benign that he was beneath notice, or so dangerous that he just didn't care?

The roar of the truck's engine and the spray of ice made her turn.

A filthy rig limped into the lot and parked a short distance away. The truck was massive, taller than Abbott's store. Glimpses of dark blue paint peeked from beneath the layers of grime. There were no company markings, which meant they weren't Janson truckers. No surprise there. Janson Transport had fallen on hard times since Bane's death, and much of the fleet had been sold off or scavenged.

This rig was a run-down wreck, and the protruding front grille had maybe half a dozen bleached skulls wired to it. Both facts suggested this wasn't an indie; independent truckers took far better care of their property and usually didn't favor human remains as ornamentation.

But the lack of plating or scaling on the rig suggested that that the owner wasn't a full-fledged Reaver, either. Not yet, anyway.

Which left one option: gun truckers. Hopefully, *her* gun truckers.

About time, boys. About time.

CHAPTER TWO

Tatiana crossed to the rig, felt the vibration of the engine roll through the ground, through her feet, up her limbs. Head down, she pulled off her thermal glove, reached out and laid her bare hand on the metal of the truck, so cold it ought to have frozen her flesh to the surface. It didn't. It couldn't.

Not anymore. Genetic enhancement was a beautiful thing. Most of the time.

Opening the doorway of her senses a crack wider, she let vestiges of the electric current that ghosted human thought flood through the vibrating molecules of the frigid metal and the liquid medium of her cells and tissues. An electro-chemical event.

Not sight or sound or touch. It was simply *awareness*.

She'd spent over a decade with the voices in her head, always there, the thoughts and pain and terror and tragedy of others a constant, discordant symphony in her mind, until she'd learned to control it, to let the gate open only at her will, a sort of voluntary electrical insulation.

Most people had five senses. She had six.

The first smoky wisps of foreign thoughts wended into her like a poison, bitter and stinking of death and rot.

There were two men in the rig, and she had been right. Not indies or company men.

Their memories assaulted her. Ugly, primitive, buffeting her like a physical force, and then she knew for certain that these men were the ones she sought.

Siberian ice pirates, one tiny step above slime on the evolutionary ladder. Or maybe one step below.

These two were particularly brutal, trying to prove themselves and enter an elite cadre of monsters, Belek-ool's Reavers.

Images and convoluted neural patterns slithered through the conduit of the truck's metal frame, from the two men into her, a thick, oily sludge. *They'd killed a dog for the fun of it, left its carcass on the snow. And a child. They'd been part of a group that butchered Northern Waste settlers, refugees seeking shelter at Gladow Station. One of them had hacked off a man's finger, stolen a ring . . . an heirloom . . . raped his wife while he watched, struggling, struggling. Slit his throat and left him beside his wife's bleeding body.*

Tatiana swallowed. The price she'd paid for that information was a dull throb at the base of her skull, a burning nausea in her belly, and a little more darkness to blot her soul.

She jerked her hand from the cold metal of the truck, slammed shut the portal to their thoughts. The driver was the man she sought. She wanted no further knowledge of who he was or what he had done. He wore the ring she'd been commissioned to retrieve on the second finger of his left hand, a gruesome trophy, and she had every intention of collecting it and returning it to the old man who'd hired her.

As if a loop of two hundred-year-old gold worn by generations of fathers and sons could give him comfort.

Made no difference to her. *Money*. She was doing this for the money.

If she told herself that often enough, maybe she would believe it.

Damned ice pirates.

Anticipation ramped through her as she waited for them to exit the vehicle, the sensation both foreign and familiar. In the past months, she had come to recognize that she *changed* when she was faced with confrontation. Her senses sharpened. Her breathing slowed and deepened. She became both exceptionally calm and incredibly edgy at the same time. It was an odd feeling, but she was learning to trust it.

Tipping her head back, she stared up at the night sky, a canvas of deep-ocean black alive with streaks of a brilliant, bloody hue. Waves and folds of color danced and shimmered, bruised purple, incandescent green, but tonight the aurora was mostly red.

Red like blood and pain and rage. Definitely not her favorite color.

She glanced down at her bare hands. She'd yet to pull on her gloves. Up until a few months ago, she would have watched her fingers turn blue, then white, the cells freezing, slowly dying. Just like anyone else, she would have been susceptible to frostbite. Then, for reasons that escaped her, something had changed, her dormant genetic enhancements blooming exponentially day by day.

Guess that made her a late bloomer.

Unfortunate. Had she come into her own a little earlier, she could have ripped off her titanium shackle, killed Ward, and saved herself and the rest of the Waste from his plans.

Yanked out the fang.

Watched a dozen more grow in its place.

Just as Ward had taken Bane's place.

Sensing movement in the cab of the rig, she waited, tapped her index finger against her thigh.

The two men climbed down and rounded the front grille. They glanced her way. Bundled as she was in her ragged, oversized parka, her hood pulled up, her face and form obscured, she offered nothing that might appeal to them. Their eyes skimmed over her as though she weren't there.

They were dressed in dark anoraks with plasguns slung across their backs. AT950s. Big guns. Heavy. Powerful. What was it with ice pirates and the size of their weapons?

Both were handsome, rough, brawny. Tatiana thought that made it worse, what they were, killing machines masked by a pretty shell.

Monsters ought to be ugly; they ought to *look* like monsters.

As they drew abreast of her and then moved past, Tatiana pulled back her hood. Her hair slid free, a straight black curtain falling halfway down her back. She undid the zip-seam of her coat, let it hang open. Now there was something to see. Her tight polyethylene spectra-fiber vest was resistant to plas-shot and puncture, and it hugged her like a second skin. Practicality combined with beauty. She could heal from almost any wound, but why put herself through unnecessary pain?

"Hey," she called, and then, louder, "Yasha! Viktor!"

They turned, their expressions betraying their surprise, and after a long slack-jawed moment, their gazes hardened with lust.

Yasha was the first to move, and that was fine with her. Get him out of the way quickly. It was Viktor she wanted.

"Do I know you?" Yasha asked, striding forward.

"No." She spun, heel to his jaw, then elbow hard in his gut. He slumped forward to his knees, drooling blood and spit, and she brought her laced fingers sharply against the back of his neck. With a sound that was barely a moan, Yasha dropped like shit in a hole before Viktor even took a step.

"And now we're alone," Tatiana said, snapping her gaze to his.

Wary now, Viktor circled, his mouth curving in an ugly sneer. He wanted to rape her before he killed her. She didn't need any special genetic enhancements to be able to read that.

He went for his plasgun.

"Uh-uh-uh," she said, flipping her small Setti9 from her wrist holster and aiming it dead center between his eyes before he could free the barrel of his Bolinger AT from the sheath on his back. Her hand was steady as a titanium girder. "Take it out, slow."

With a leer, he reached for the zip-seam at his crotch.

She shot the ground at his feet, leaving a crater deep enough for his foot, and he leaped back with a yelp.

"Your *plasgun*. Take out your plasgun, or the next hole I make is in your chest." She enunciated each word with care, then waited a beat as he did her bidding. "Good. Now, put it on the ground and kick it to me."

He did as she ordered, and his plasgun slid across the ice to bump the toe of her boot. She kicked it, hard, sending it sliding in the opposite direction, under the barbed wire of the snowscooter yard, beyond his reach.

"Viktor, you have something that belongs to my client." He was circling again, and she moved, turned, kept him in view as she flipped her Setti9 back into its wrist holster. She'd gotten rid of his plasgun, which meant she didn't need hers anymore. This way, things were nice and even.

She didn't plan to kill him, just rough him up a little. "You murdered his son and daughter-in-law. Stole a ring, a family memento. My client would like the ring returned. It's all he has left of his son."

"Don't know what you're talking about." He shrugged, wet his lips, his eyes darting about.

"Bright as the bottom of the ocean, aren't you?" She blew out a breath as he stared at her blankly. "Here, I'll clear it up for you. The ring on your finger. Give it to me. And if you hand it to me without a fuss, I will let you go unharmed." Her voice hardened. "Take my offer. Trust me. You won't like the alternative."

He laughed, threw back his head and guffawed. In a way, she couldn't blame him. She was a light-boned five foot five to his brawny bulk.

Reaching into her pocket, she drew out an expired plastitech trucking pass for the ICW—the Intercontinental Worldwide—the longest highway ever built. It had Viktor's name and holopic inscribed. "You left this by the bodies. By accident, I suspect. Or perhaps it was pure hubris."

"Hubris?" he repeated blankly.

"Excessive pride or arrogance." The definition just popped out, a throwback to her childhood. She shook her head, flicked the card at him, judged his speed as he lifted a hand to catch it. "Just give me the ring."

"Oh, I'll give it to you. I'll give it to you nice and hard. Make you scream for it." He lunged, a wicked blade in his hand. Guess she wasn't the only one who kept a weapon strapped to her wrist.

Tatiana moved forward without thought, without conscious will. Her earlier foray into his mind had told her he wore the old man's ring on his left hand, second finger. Same hand that held the knife. She reached up, closed her grasp tight around his forearm just above his wrist, barely circling halfway.

He grunted, tried to jerk free, shot her a startled look when he failed. The cloth of his jacket had pulled up when he moved, and Tatiana's thumb and second finger touched his skin.

The contact opened a doorway. Images rushed at her in a nauseating surge. The Maori Talisman. A mountain of ice and jagged rock. And a fleeting image, seen only in passing, of Gavin Ward standing in the golden light of the dying sun, silver haired, neatly groomed.

Viktor didn't know him, but Tatiana did.

Disgust boiled in her gut as the gun trucker's memories rolled through her, and she fixated on the image of the man Ward was speaking with. She could get only a vague impression of height, dark hair, and dark thermal gear. Viktor had seen Ward's companion only from the back, and he'd heard a name spoken in Ward's round, clipped tones. *Dr. Tolliver.*

For six months she'd been trying to stay one step ahead of Gavin Ward, while at the same time trying to figure out where the hell he was testing the plague he'd created using her genetic code. Now, thanks to a chance encounter and a disjointed memory found in the mire of Viktor's mind, she had her first solid lead. A place to start—the Maori Talisman.

It wasn't much, but it was better than the big, fat nothing she'd had a minute past. All she needed to do was find Ward's minion, Tolliver. Find him, stop him, kill him, if it came down to a choice.

It would have been a major help if Viktor had actually seen Tolliver's face.

"Tell me about Tolliver," she said.

"Who the fuck is Tolliver?" Viktor snarled.

Her sneak peek into his thoughts told her that he genuinely had no clue. He'd witnessed the conversation in passing and had forgotten it. But she'd dredged the memory from his thoughts because she was thinking about Ward, about Tolliver. A part of her was always focused on them.

She slammed the heel of her hand against Viktor's chest, shoving him back and releasing her hold.

"Just give me the damned ring."

With a snarl, he lunged at her, his blade catching the light from the lamp outside Abbott's store.

In defense, Tatiana lifted her free hand, fingers extended and pressed tight to each other, her gaze locked on his. Her movements were so powerful and quick they were little more than a blur.

She meant only to disarm him.

There was a slurp of suction as her fingers hit his wrist, like fluid through a straw, then a sharp snap, a sound like tearing cloth, and finally, the clatter of metal and the slap of an open palm against the icy ground.

Liquid warmth spurted over her, drenching her skin and the sleeve of her coat. She glanced down to see the gush of blood and the severed stump.

At her feet was Viktor's hand, and beside it, his knife.

"*Oops.*"

Her head snapped up. Viktor was panting, staring at the ground with shock that matched her own. She'd cut through sinew and bone with just her fingers.

Ooookay. That was new.

Genetic engineering ought to come with a user's manual.

With a moan, Viktor slumped to his knees, his face gone ashen, his remaining hand closed tight about his blood-soaked wrist.

"What the fuck did you do to me, bitch? What the fuck did you do?" he screamed, the tone jagged, frenzied. "You don't even have a goddamned knife. What the fuck?"

Yeah, she was wondering about that herself.

"You, uh, might want to elevate the arm." When he stared at her blankly, eyes wild and glassy, she held her own arm up, waggled it a little. "Up. You know, hold it up."

From somewhere to her right, Tatiana heard the hum of a snowscooter, then the hum went dead as the rider killed the engine.

Just perfect. Company. And she hadn't dressed up.

She shot a glance at the scooter. It was the settler she'd seen earlier. He'd ridden out, but now he was back, drawn closer for a ringside seat.

Keeping her attention locked on a sobbing Viktor, she bent and retrieved his hand and his knife. It was a good one. A honed steel blade, nicely weighted. She shoved the knife in her belt, then peeled the glove off the severed hand and freed the ring.

From the corner of her eye, she tracked the guy on the scooter, aware of his movements as he dismounted. As long as he stayed on the periphery and didn't interfere, she had no business with him.

After tucking the ring in her pocket, she tossed the hand to the ground. It lay, fingers outstretched, the tips just touching Viktor's leg. He stared at it, his entire body trembling, a desperate keening sound escaping him.

"Tie off your wrist," Tatiana advised flatly. "And keep the hand on ice." She paused, allowed herself a morbid smile. As if he'd have any trouble keeping the limb cold. "If you stay alive and conscious, you might make it to the doctor in Liskeard in time to get it reattached." She shrugged. "Or maybe not."

Shutting down the instinct to spin and get the hell out

of there, Tatiana slowly scanned the perimeter, checking every nook, every shadow, then turned her attention back toward the settler. He leaned against his scooter, long legs stretched before him, his head and body draped in layers of dark thermal cloth. He should have looked ridiculous, swathed in rags.

Instead, he looked . . . dangerous.

His arms were crossed over his chest. And he watched her.

Tatiana shivered. The wind howled and swirled about her, carrying the metallic scent of Viktor's blood and the smell of ozone and snow.

She couldn't tell anything about this guy. Not his build or age or how many weapons he concealed. And she couldn't read him. Nothing.

Annoyance and unease merged and curdled. Not a nice mix.

"You planning on doing anything here?" she asked, jerking her head toward Viktor and Yasha.

His gaze flicked to Viktor, then back to her. "Doesn't look like you need my help."

She laughed, startled. "No."

"Didn't think so. So, no, I'm not planning on doing anything here."

Poor Vik. He hadn't lucked into a good Samaritan.

Tatiana stepped back, glanced at her sleeve. Viktor's blood was hot and sticky on her skin. Revulsion slithered through her. Off. She wanted it off.

Bending down, she wiped her hands clean on Yasha's coat, then studied the blood on her sleeve. Not much she could do about that.

"Your friend's taking a little nap, Vik." She smiled darkly, straightened. "You might want to try and rouse him before he freezes." She glanced down. "Or you could just leave him here."

"Bitch! I'm gonna fucking kill you." Viktor snarled as she turned away and headed for her snowscooter, but the trembling in his voice detracted from the impact.

Spinning back, she kept moving, walking backwards as she watched him struggle to his feet. He stood weaving unsteadily, his form a dark silhouette against the back-drop of the dancing crimson lights of the aurora.

The guy on the snowscooter didn't even twitch. He just watched and kept his place. That was common in the Waste. Not his business. Not his fight.

She was abreast of him now, and she dragged her atten-tion from Viktor's swaying form, shot the guy on the scooter another glance. The paltry glow of the single over-head light fell across him, making his eyes glitter in the darkness.

"*I'm gonna fucking kill you,*" Viktor screamed, his voice choking on a sob. "*I'm gonna fucking kill you.*"

Tatiana threw a leg over the saddle of her snowscooter and laughed grimly as she hit the ignition. The engine purred, then roared. She raised her head, looked first to the guy on the scooter—he hadn't moved an inch—then over at where Viktor swayed on his feet, clutching his bleeding wrist.

"*Fucking kill you, bitch.*"

How sick was it that she actually found his threats amusing?

"Yeah, well . . . Get in line, Viktor." She shook her head. "Get in fucking line."

•

CHAPTER THREE

Tristan bent his head against the driving wind that howled across the barren, hard-edged terrain to swirl about him and whip at the edges of his thermal gear. He stood by Viktor's rig and watched the Morgat disappear into the distance.

Interesting girl.

Abbott hadn't been able to offer a name. Not even for a price. All he knew was that she'd been in a time or two before, looking for supplies or information, or both.

That in itself made her all the more fascinating.

In the Northern Waste, women were either wives or whores. They were rarely allowed to be anything else.

Unless they were rebels.

But he sensed that the spooky-eyed girl who'd just taken down two gun truckers without breaking a sweat wasn't any of those things. He'd bet his life on it.

She held herself like a trained soldier, cool and calm.

But the New Government Order didn't usually draft women.

Which meant she was an enigma.

The fact that she'd been hunting the same truckers he'd been waiting for made the hairs on his nape prickle and rise.

And he'd overheard her ask Abbott about Tolliver. That was beyond any weird twist that fate could offer, and possibly more than a little dangerous.

He didn't believe in coincidences.

Every night for two weeks, he'd been at Abbott's. Every night for two weeks he'd waited for the damned gun truckers who'd promised him the bootleg supplies he needed.

He hadn't much cared when he walked out of the general store to find one unconscious and the other injured, spurting blood and spewing invective at a slip of a girl who had them both down on the ground.

That was their problem, not his. All he wanted was their cargo.

Picking up a length of discarded pipe, he slipped it under the lock-mech and jimmied the whole thing off with little effort. Cheap equipment.

He shook his head.

Yanking wide the back doors of the rig, he put his palm flat on the trailer bed, vaulted up, and froze.

"Fuck." He punched the side of the trailer, moving on instinct fueled by frustration, paying for it when pain slammed through his hand and up his wrist. Not his smartest move.

He stood staring into the empty trailer, fury eating at him. His right hand rested on the edge of the open door at the rear of the trailer, his fingers curled painfully tight. His left hand throbbed from the punch he hadn't been able to hold back.

Best he spend a little more time meditating for an illuminated state of mind, because right now, he was having a hard time remembering that there was no such thing as good and evil, only enlightenment and the universe as one.

Yeah, right now he wasn't doing so well with reaching

his own version of Kinhin—walking meditation. He was doing a piss-poor job of mastering his rage.

The damned rig was as empty as a Waste orphan's belly.

No differential interference contrast microscope, no atomic force microscope, no carbon nanotubes. And worst of all, no viral cultures and no tissue samples.

Nothing.

So he had seventy million interdollars burning a hole in his pocket and nowhere to spend it. And he was out of time. It had taken him three months to track down that equipment and find two assholes willing to steal it.

In his current reality, three months was an incredibly long time.

The job had been done. He knew the equipment had been stolen because he'd heard the report on the broadband, cheerfully described in the announcer's dulcet tones. Something about declining safety and increased thievery in the Waste.

So where in the frozen fucking Waste were his samples and his microscopes?

He sucked in a breath of frigid air, cold enough that he felt like his lungs were scored by dozens of tiny blades. With effort, he mastered himself, mastered his emotions and thoughts.

One can live only in the present moment.

Fine. He could do that. He took another slow, slow breath, focusing wholly on the stretch of lungs and chest wall.

But thoughts of the girl intruded. She'd taken down Viktor and Yasha. Done the job for him. Lucky ice pirates, because in his present mood he was likely to hack off more than just one hand.

He turned his head and stared out at the flat stretch of ice that went on and on to forever. Unusual girl. Delicate, lovely, strangely ethereal, with her enormous eyes the color of liquid mercury and that silky fall of black hair framing her features. She was at once both exotic and strangely familiar.

Did he know her? Had he seen her before? He thought he had, even though he was certain he hadn't, and that made no sense. It made even less sense that she kept intruding on his thoughts.

Of course, nothing in his life made sense, and he had long ago come to accept that. Vengeance and anger were bitter things. He forgave. He had taught himself to forgive. Everyone but himself. Because he'd failed to save his parents, his brothers, his friends. And he'd brought their deaths to them. Not wittingly. But dead was dead, and it didn't matter if he'd intended it or not.

His lips curved in a grim smile. Some days it was harder than others to rise above the anger, the hate, to reach the meditative state that allowed him to face life. Today was one of those days.

He turned as a whimpering sob carried to him on the wind.

"Yasha, wake up," Viktor cried. "You bastard, wake up."

One can live only in the present moment.

Tristan gritted his teeth. His present moment was not one populated by the gorgeous girl who had sped off into the night, but instead by the sniveling, bleeding Viktor and the unconscious Yasha.

So it'd be *enlightened* of him to live in the present fucking moment, seek them out and offer the deal of a lifetime. Their lives in exchange for information about his missing goods.

Spinning, Tristan yanked the thermal wrap from across his face. He wanted these assholes to see exactly whom they were dealing with. He leaped down from the rig and crossed the distance to where Viktor knelt on the ground trying to rouse Yasha. He scooped up Viktor's severed hand, hefted it, met the gun trucker's bleary gaze.

"Answer my questions, nice and concise, Viktor, and I'll help you get your pal up and in the rig so he can drive you to Liskeard." Tristan tossed the hand in the air, caught it to the sound of Viktor's watery gasp. "Fuck with me, and I'll take your hand with me as a souvenir when I leave"—he leaned in close, slid his blade from its sheath at the small of his back and rested the tip in the soft spot on the underside of Viktor's jaw—"because you've already fucked with me quite enough. Where the hell's the equipment I hired you to steal?"

Tatiana doused her lights, cut a sharp turn to angle her scooter behind a shallow rise, and killed the engine. She wasn't going anywhere until she found out what the hell was in the back of the ice pirates' rig, but she hadn't wanted to pull it open and look while the settler was watching. She figured that she'd drive out a bit, wait for him to leave, then scoot back in and see if the stolen goods were in Viktor's trailer.

And if the guy didn't leave, no problem. She'd follow the truck on its way to Liskeard and check the trailer then. It wasn't out of her way. She was planning to head in that direction anyway to return the ring and collect the second half of her fee.

Crawling to the top of the rise, she lay on her belly, her body flush to the ground, and waited. From this distance, no one at Abbott's would be able to see her. Not unless they were looking for her with a thermal imager or a night scope.

She didn't need either one. She could see as clearly as if the scene were right in front of her face. All she needed to do was focus on the subject, *will* herself to see, and everything became sharp and defined.

She'd figured that out about two months back when she'd spotted a guy in the shadows outside Bob's Truck Stop while she was still a good twenty yuales out. Curious, she'd focused on him, and there you go, he'd hauled out his personal equipment and let loose a steaming yellow stream against the side wall of Bob's. She'd gotten an eyeful, a clear visual, all up close even though she was far, far away. Not the ideal introduction to her newly enhanced telescopic vision.

She'd felt like she needed a wire brush to scrub her eyeballs clean.

Now, her attention locked on the damned settler as he rose from his scooter, ambled over to the rig, and used a length of metal pipe to slam through the cheap lockmech. So that's what he was doing at Abbott's. Not picking up supplies or paying for sex. He was there to steal.

An almost-honorable profession here in the Waste.

Having been in the position a time or two where thievery was her only option, she felt a certain kinship with him. Coupled with that was a grudging admiration, along with a healthy dose of incredulity. What sort of fool stole from ice pirates?

She snorted. A fool with balls of steel and a death wish. Even though Yasha and Viktor didn't rank very high on her personal tough-as-nails scale, they would have deadly friends. And the settler with the pretty, pretty eyes was about to rob them blind.

He threw open the doors and vaulted to the trailer bed, standing with his back to her, tension in every line of his body.

The way he slammed his fist against the side of the rig suggested he didn't like what he'd found.

And neither did she.

She'd hoped to find that the Reavers' goods had some value, planned to steal some for herself, use them to buy an entrée to Tolliver. She needed to find him, use him to find Ward's lab, and destroy the whole slagging mess.

But the rig was empty.

Turning back toward the open doors, the settler yanked the thermal gear off his head and face, a gesture of frustration.

Without the cloth to block it, his breath blew white in the cold arctic air.

Her breath didn't blow at all.

It was gone, stuck, locked in her chest.

Not beautiful. That wasn't a masculine word. But, oh, he *was* . . . beautiful and masculine and dangerous, and she had no business looking at him and feeling like she could lie here forever. Just looking.

The glow from the single bulb at the end of the lot fell across him, highlighting his features in light and shadow. His skin was taut over wonderfully sculpted bone—the straight line of his nose, the chiseled ridges of his cheeks, the stubble-shaded arc of his jaw. There was nothing soft or gently curved about him. He was all angles and planes and shadows.

His hair was brown, hanging almost to his shoulders, dark and thick and raggedly cut, as though someone had taken a knife to the ends with an impatient hand. He reminded her of the imaginary guys the New Government Order used in their holo-vids to entice people to settle the Waste. Rugged. Competent. Ready for anything.

He leaped to the ground, crossed to where Viktor and Yasha lay. There was an exchange of sorts, leashed anger in every line of the settler's body.

After a moment, he turned away, and then everything spun into ten shades of crazy.

Viktor lunged for the plasgun still in the holster between Yasha's shoulder blades, swung it up, aimed the barrel dead center at the settler's back.

On instinct, she tore her own AT450 free, sighted, breathed halfway out. Squeezed.

In the same millisecond, the settler spun, his foot flying out in a snap kick.

And it all happened so fast that she honestly couldn't say if it was his boot or her plas-shot that sent Viktor's gun spinning up and away through the air. It landed some five meters away and slid wildly across the ice.

The settler reached down, caught the front edge of Viktor's parka in his fist, and landed a quick blow to his face. He rose, turned, and stared out into the night, directly toward her. Then he lifted his hand in a gesture of salute.

Her heart slammed hard in her chest, and she was swamped by a wave of relief. He was safe. Unhurt. And she was inexplicably euphoric to know it.

Sliding down the low rise, she let the hill provide visual cover, even though she knew she was too far out for him to see. Then she popped her head up, watched as he slung first Viktor, then Yasha, over his shoulder and into the cab of the rig.

He moved with lethal grace, and she liked just watching him.

Slag. That was not good.

She forced herself to breathe slow and easy, appalled by the pitter-patter of her pulse. What was she doing lying on her belly outside Abbott's hellhole, mooning over a Waste settler with a handsome face and a sexy-as-all-get-out walk?

This job had gone to hell in a heartbeat.

And the fluttering in her belly was ridiculous enough to make her laugh.

That's what she got for spending puberty locked all alone in a dungeon.

Delayed maturity.

CHAPTER FOUR

After the episode outside Abbott's General Store, it had taken Tatiana a week to find the old man, give him his ring, get paid and find her way to the Maori Talisman.

Her client had been incredibly appreciative. He'd taken the ring, cried, hugged her. That had been the worst part. She had stood there, frozen in place, feeling the swell of his gratitude and grief roll over her like the surf, uncertain what to do, wishing he'd stop touching her.

But the part of her that had learned emotion by being buffeted by the thoughts of others hadn't been able to push him away.

She sighed. Add *practice normal human interactions* to her to-do list.

The thought made her queasy.

She slid her scooter out from the shadow of the Maori Talisman and plopped her butt on the seat, wondering how a tribe originally from New Zealand had ended up building a stone sculpture in the middle of nowhere, clear across the world in the slagging Waste.

After leaving the old man and his ring, she'd followed the images she'd stolen from Viktor's thoughts straight to the place he'd remembered seeing Ward and Tolliver. And so here she was, revved and ready to hunt down her quarry, with no idea where they'd gone to ground. There was a certain grim humor in that.

What had she imagined? That she'd get to the Talisman and there would be a plastitech road sign waiting for her? THIS WAY TO WARD'S LAB AND TOLLIVER?

She gnawed on a strip of dehydrated protein supplement as she scanned the horizon. All she saw was white, white and more white.

Man, she hated wide-open spaces. There was just too much . . . space.

Not that she preferred close confines. That didn't do it for her any more than the great outdoors did. Someday, she'd have to figure out a viable option. Maybe a really big room with a really big window.

Or, yeah, she could just do what she'd been doing for the past six months: try to bury the memories and fears so deep that they had little chance to escape. Problem was, they kept finding the cracks in her armor, the route to the surface.

Guess she needed a little work on her psychological repression skills.

Unbidden, an image of deep blue eyes and dark, dark lashes flickered through her thoughts. Frustrated, she tried to divert her mind to a different track, but only succeeded in recalling the sound of a rich masculine voice laced with humor.

Why was the memory of him still following her around?

In the past week, she'd wasted more than a few seconds thinking about the settler she'd met at Abbott's, and she couldn't pinpoint why. She didn't even know his name. But at the oddest times she'd remember the way his eyes had creased at the corners in the suggestion of a smile or how he'd stretched his long legs before him as he watched her finish her business with Viktor. And her favorite recollection? The way he'd let her go about her business without interfering.

Doesn't look like you need my help.

It took a special kind of a guy to sit back and let a girl go about her business.

Stupid romantic infatuation. She had read about such things. Young girls often fixated on an object of affection with no direct knowledge of the personality of said object. She had seen holo-vids about societal custom in the early part of the century where musicians of popular songs were followed by legions of screaming and sobbing girls.

But she wasn't that young, and she'd never been like other girls.

She tore off another bite of the leathery strip in her hand, chewed it, swallowed, not tasting anything, just going through the motions because she needed fuel. She glanced at the sun. After weeks of utter darkness, the sun had started to rise again. At first, it had been for only forty minutes or so, then longer and longer each day. She squinted at the sky and figured she had an hour before it would be dark again, not that she had a problem with that. She could see as well in the dark as she did in the light, but she *liked* the sun. Liked the warmth on her skin and the bright glitter that rebounded off the ice.

There had been no sun in her prison.

It was interesting, and more than a little frightening, to discover her likes and dislikes, to have the freedom to eat when she wanted, sleep when she wanted. Go where she willed.

She still kept a fairly regimented schedule, eating at the same time, exercising at the same time. That schedule was the only thing that had kept her sane during her captivity; she had learned to control what she could and to not waste regret on things she couldn't.

Regimentation wasn't an easy thing to give up now that she was free.

"So, where to now?" she asked. There was no one there to answer her, but once in a while she needed to hear the sound of a voice, even if it was just her own. It was a habit she'd developed in the years that she had been held in solitude, when human contact was wielded as a means of reward and punishment.

There had been times she was so desperate to hear another voice that she'd actually been glad to see Bane walk into her cell. How sick and twisted was that? Then, a couple of years into her imprisonment, he'd started bringing Gavin Ward with him and she'd come to understand the gradations of evil.

Bane had been a horror, but he had never claimed to be anything other than he was, a man who enjoyed the suffering of others.

Ward had been worse, had pretended that what he did was good, that anything was justified in the name of scientific research.

No. Not pretended. He'd actually *believed* that he could justify whatever aberrations he perpetrated by claiming it was in the name of science.

The faint sound of an engine carried to her from a distance. Small engine. Small vehicle. No, *vehicles*. More than one?

She froze. The hairs at her nape prickled and rose. A tingle of awareness tickled her consciousness, kicking her senses into high alert.

Straightening, she lifted her head, scenting the air. People, closing in fast. Dozens of them. She could feel their emotions even from this distance, rage and hate and unsheathed brutality.

Scanning the horizon, Tatiana saw them, one scooter far

to the front and a larger group of riders running it to ground, the gap between them rapidly growing smaller. They weren't after her, didn't even appear to have noticed her yet, but they *were* on a collision course with her. She mounted her own scooter, judged her options.

There was nowhere to hide.

Instinct kicked in and her genetic enhancements took over, her brain spitting out information like a computer. *Thirty-three pursuers approaching at a speed of sixty yuales per hour.*

Her Morgat snowscooter was lightning fast, but she was low on hydrogen. She likely couldn't outrun them.

Besides, she might be able to question them, touch their minds, find some whisper of Ward's or Tolliver's whereabouts, or at least a hint of the research lab's location. That in itself was a good enough reason to stay exactly where she was.

One against thirty-three . . . if it came to a fight, statistical probability was in favor of her success. The thought brought a mordant smile to her lips.

Reaching back, she pulled free her Bolinger AT450. A nice plasgun. Lightweight. Powerful. She settled it across her thighs and waited, opting for the least threatening posture. Maybe they'd figure she had no part in whatever was going on here, and they'd ride on by, consider her merely a spectator.

Yeah, and an orange tree was about to sprout at her feet. Sarcasm was becoming her steady companion.

Her body hummed with a new energy, as though a switch had been flipped and she was all lit up. Her vision sharpened, working like a telephoto lens. She studied the lead rider's features, read the abject terror on his face, heard the rasping breaths he took.

He wore no headgear, no gloves, no goggles, so he was

driving almost blind, the wind freezing his tears as quickly as they formed. That had to hurt. His flight was obviously desperate and unplanned.

Involuntary reflex took over. A part of her mind had been programmed in childhood, and she calculated trajectories and plas-shot speed, how many people she could take out before they took her.

Closer, closer.

The snowscooter blades flew over hard-packed snow, sending a fine spray of tiny glittering crystals arcing out the back.

Her heart beat a slow, steady rhythm, and her breath was even in cadence and depth. She had been bred for this, genetically engineered for it, as had her siblings.

Siblings. Wizard. Yuriko. Dead. They were dead. The rumors that Wizard was looking for her had to be a trap, a lie designed to lure her into lowering her defenses.

Don't think about that now.

The lead scooter drew abreast of her. She felt the electrical rebound of the man's emotion and the emotions of his pursuers. Hate. Rage. Pain. Fear.

Too many of them slapping at her to differentiate individual thought or intent.

Suddenly, clear intent flashed in her thoughts like a magnesium flare, bright and blinding. They meant to kill him. Brutally. Slowly. A punishment.

Disgust clogged her throat.

Who *were* these people? Not rebels. Not truckers. Reavers? They didn't look it, but their thoughts were brutal enough to suggest they might be.

The lead snowscooter hit a deep rut, and the front rose like a sea lion heaving from the ocean, and then slammed down, throwing the rider free. He rolled and tumbled across the frozen ground. Tatiana stood, moving so she was partially obscured by the massive ice-kissed rocks of the Talisman, automatically shifting her plasgun to firing position.

They were on him now, like a pack of starving dogs, kicking his torso, tearing at his clothes, his hair. He rolled tight and whimpered. A boot slammed into the side of his jaw and with a tortured cry he spewed blood and teeth across the snow.

Grabbing his arms, they dragged him to his feet. He was sobbing, struggling. No one even glanced her way, so intent were they on their prey. Or perhaps they simply thought she was insignificant as a threat, a lone rider in the middle of the Waste, come to stand in the shadow of the Maori Talisman.

She could see nothing of their faces. They wore thick, dark material wrapped to protect their heads and bodies, antiglare goggles and thermal gear. Their clothing, their scooters . . . old, but in excellent repair. Everything about them looked as though it had been dragged from a time decades past.

Something about them was vaguely familiar.

Her senses were full of them, the rough sound of their breathing, the sobs of their prisoner, the guttural curses—but not their rational thoughts. She could read only frenzied emotions. Their anger and hate and aggression obscured all else.

She wondered about the man's crime, if anything he had done could truly justify brutality. Was he an innocent, tormented by those who were stronger, whose numbers were greater, who wielded their power with unchecked brutality?

Like Ward.

Slag, that single thought sealed her fate. She couldn't just walk away.

One of the pursuers glanced up. A woman. The man beside her whispered her name. "Gemma."

"What is this man's crime?" Tatiana asked, stepping forward into a fight that was not her own, the smell of fresh blood slapping her. "You pissed at him or just bored?"

Gemma twisted to face her, mouth open, chest heaving.

The rest of the group gave no indication they had even heard her.

A tall man—thin to the point of emaciation, even with the voluminous layers of thermal gear draped over him—stepped forward and thrust the hilt of a long, gleaming blade into Gemma's hand. "It's your right. Kill him."

Lovely. Nice group of friends she'd stumbled upon.

The captive surged forward, no longer meek and mewling, struggling now against those who held him, snapping his teeth and growling like a dog. He jerked and snarled, then let out a high whimper and sagged between his captors.

Gemma raised the blade while the men holding the fugitive ripped open his coat, baring his bruised torso.

Tatiana blinked. He bore the branded mark of a Reaver on his chest.

There was something off here. Not just the fact that a guy—a Siberian ice pirate—was about to be shredded by a pack of rabid pursuers. Something else. The air smelled wrong. Like disease. Like death.

The prisoner was pale, his skin grayish, his eyes darting as he snarled and hissed. And he was foaming. Not drooling. Actually *frothing* at the mouth.

So maybe the rabies analogy wasn't really off base.

"I can't—" Gemma's voice caught on a sob. "We could leave him out here without supplies, without shelter. Leave him to die alone. Better that way. Better for me. I don't want to be near him."

The crowd murmured their disapproval, leaving Tatiana with the ugly suspicion that they would settle for nothing less than blood.

Aiming her AT450, she set it on low and sent a short blast to tear up the snow and ice at Gemma's feet. Everyone froze. Wary, she looked around, realized they had knives, but there wasn't a plasma weapon in sight. Well, that was good.

Weird, but good.

Statistical probability for her success in a fight had just increased considerably.

"Please," Gemma whispered, her head down. She was shaking so hard she could barely hold the knife. "Don't interfere. You don't know—" She broke off, shook her head.

"What is his crime?" Tatiana asked again, forceful.

Gemma turned to her, and Tatiana read it, the ghosting of electrical charge that shadowed Gemma's thoughts hitting her with brutal clarity, releasing her nervous system's neurotransmitters as though the memories were her own. *A little girl, Gemma's daughter, raped by this man, her throat slit and her body tossed into an infinite crevice, but falling only as far as a narrow ledge. Left there and found by her mother.*

Tatiana shuddered, the ache at the base of her skull exploding. What the hell had she stepped into? Vigilante justice? It was common in the Waste.

She shifted to face the prisoner. He mewled and thrashed against those who held him. There were half a dozen men pinning him in place, but still he almost tore free. He was stronger than he ought to have been, even for a Reaver. Again, she had the sensation that something here was very, very wrong.

Testing the knowledge in the man's memories, Tatiana opened herself to his thoughts and found far more horrific images than Gemma even imagined. He had done all she suspected, and worse. A wave of disgust rolled through her, but she pushed deeper, searching out answers.

She found memories of what he had done and something more, there, just beneath the surface of his thoughts, obscured by his terror. Roiling pain. Anger. Hate. A frenzied clamoring of emotion that whipped her with knotted cords. Tatiana reached for it, but she couldn't grasp his deepest thoughts. It was as if the man's emotions weren't rational, weren't human. They were primitive, feral, and— She jerked away, slamming the portal as she felt darkness crawl through her.

With a shake of her head, she stepped back and pressed her fingers to her eyes, the surge of her headache flaring, then fading.

No answers there, but perhaps Gemma . . .

Taking a step forward, she reached out to grasp Gemma's arm. They both moved, an unwittingly synchronized push and pull, and Gemma's blade grazed the skin of Tatiana's unprotected hand.

For an instant their gazes met, held. Gemma jerked away, eyes wide, obviously horrified by the sight of Tatiana's blood.

"You aren't wearing gloves." Gemma reached out as though to touch her, then dropped her hand.

Frowning, Tatiana took a step back. Gemma stared at her in undisguised distress, and then she shook her head from side to side, fast, desperate.

"I'm sorry." The words exploded an anguished cry. "I'm sorry!"

Her gaze locked on Tatiana's, Gemma stood trembling as the wind whipped about them, bitterly cold. Her emotions were too convoluted for Tatiana to read clearly, like a ball of tightly tangled wire, but the overwhelming impression was one of danger and horror.

"Nothing to be sorry for. It's only a scratch." One that would heal in a matter of hours. Enhanced healing capacity was just another recent acquisition to her growing arsenal of unusual talents.

Gemma made a low, choked sound, her gaze shifting to something in the distance.

Turning her head, Tatiana caught a fleeting impression of another snowscooter coming in fast.

"We must be quick," Gemma said, frantic. "He'll stop us."

A sudden shift in the air warned her, and Tatiana spun back—a millisecond too late—as Gemma lunged.

With a terrible cry, filled with pain, rage, hate, Gemma sank the knife into the rapist's belly, low, close to the pubic bone.

Tatiana surged forward, too late, too late.

Her hands closed around Gemma's as she tried to yank the blade free, but the Reaver moved to grab his attacker, and the combined actions of the three of them only served to drag the blade up to his breastbone, gutting him like a fish.

His blood, hot and wet, sprayed them all.

"Slag." Tatiana jerked her hands away.

Gemma dragged the knife free and stood, arms wide, chest heaving, her breath coming in short, gasping sobs.

The Reaver slumped to his knees, clutching the edges of his wound together. Blood dripped from between his fingers to land on the ice in a dark, glistening puddle.

Gemma's knife slid from her fingers and hit the ground with a harsh clatter.

She backed away, her gaze flicking between the Reaver and Tatiana's blood-soaked hands, her expression frozen in a mask of horror.

No one moved. No one spoke.

Finally, Tatiana bent and retrieved Gemma's knife, hefted it, testing for weight and balance.

She was building quite the collection of other people's blades.

CHAPTER FIVE

Abbott's Inn and Pub, Northern Waste

Ammonia sharp, the stink of urine stained the air. The sound of rapid, panting breaths.

"Please," Boyd Abbott moaned. "I don't know nothing else. I don't know nothing. I swear it. I swear it." He was sobbing now, dreadful, slurping sobs.

The man was a veritable fountain. Piss. Tears. Snot.

The only thing missing was blood.

Gavin Ward unrolled his portable tool kit all the way, laid it flat on the desk. Scalpels. Sutures. Saws. Everything perfectly clean and sterile, lined up in neat rows.

He was nothing if not tidy.

"Two gun truckers. Yasha and Viktor. Did you speak with them?"

Abbott shook his head frantically from side to side. "They were supposed to come. Maybe a week back. Said they had an Old Dominion ring that needed selling, and they wanted first run at my shipment of fresh meat. But they never showed. I heard"—he snorted a deep breath, sucking snot up his nose—"I heard Viktor almost lost a hand. That he barely made it to Liskeard in time to get it sewn back on. He was jumped by a dozen Reavers."

Taking up a gauze-wrapped bundle from the cooling container he'd stored it in, Gavin slowly began to unwind the filmy cloth. Around and around. He kept his gaze on Abbott, watched with analytical interest as the man sank deeper and deeper into terror, until finally he recognized exactly what it was that Gavin held.

"*Almost* lost a hand?" Gavin asked in genuine amusement. "No almost about it, and it wasn't just one." He laid both severed hands palm down on the scarred Formica counter. "You see, Boyd, he made it to Liskeard. Got his hand sewn on. But when I arrived a day later, he didn't know the answers to my questions. Just like you."

With meticulous care, Gavin lined up the two severed hands side by side.

"I've been working on an antirejection drug," he said. "One that allows limb and organ transplantation without dampening the immune response to pathogens. There have been so few strides in that field since the early part of the century. With the emergence of antibiotic-resistant pathogens, all monies were diverted in that direction. But I have taken up the torch, so to speak, revived the antirejection work. I just need human test subjects to"—he paused and let his gaze linger on Abbott's hands—"work with."

He lifted a scalpel from his kit. Glancing at a shadowed corner of the room, he nodded at a hulking man, who strode forward on command. "If you would be so kind, Thom," Gavin said calmly, flicking a glance at Abbott's left hand.

Abbott's words ran together in a panicked slurry. "Oh, God, no. Oh, please Mr. Ward—"

"That's *Dr.* Ward," Gavin corrected softly.

Trembling so hard that the chair shook and rattled, Abbott cried out as Thom grasped his forearm and held it tight against the arm of the chair. His hand hung over the edge, the tendons popping at the wrist as he struggled to break free.

"Please Dr. Ward . . . please . . . please . . . I swear I don't know nothing. They were supposed to come. They never came. That's all. I swear it. That's all. I told you all I know. I swear it. I swear it."

"I *do* believe that you have told me all you know . . . at least, all you *think* you know," Gavin said. "But I suspect there is more. Something you have forgotten to mention, or deemed too unimportant to recall. So think carefully, Boyd, and let us try this again."

He drew the edge of the scalpel lightly across Abbott's exposed wrist. A thin line of red appeared at the crease. Abbott's eyes bugged out and he pissed himself. Again.

"The right enticement can ferret out even the most deeply buried thoughts." Gavin leaned in and spoke close to Abbott's ear. "Whatever rumors you heard, we both know there were no Reavers here other than Viktor and Yasha. There was only a girl. Dark haired. Pretty. Strange, silver eyes."

"Yes, yes," Abbott sobbed, nodding frantically. "She bought a hydrogen fill. Supplies. Protein supplement. Vitobars. She paid for it with a vial of sucrose. I told you about her already."

"Yes, you did. But I want more," Gavin murmured. He drew a second thin line across Abbott's wrist. "What did she say? Where was she heading?"

"I don't know. I swear I don't know."

"Oh, I believe you do. Search hard for the memory. Perhaps a little enticement . . ." A third line appeared, precisely aligned with the other two, a tad deeper.

Abbott shook his head wildly, and his body bucked and jerked.

"North," he screamed. "I think I saw her head north. Couldn't have gone far. She was only on a scooter. And . . . and she asked about something . . . a name or a place"—his head jerked up and his expression changed to one of eager relief—"*Tolliver*. She asked about Tolliver."

Well, that was a surprisingly useful tidbit. The unpleasant jaunt to Abbott's General Store had not been a waste of time after all.

Tatiana knew about Tolliver. Which begged the question, what else did she know?

It also meant that Abbott knew Tolliver's name, which meant he needed to die. Gavin sighed. So much for his usefulness as a test subject. Dead animals were of little use in his experiments.

Gavin gave a sharp nod, and his associate released his hold. Blubbering and sniveling and trembling, Abbott sagged in his seat, not stirring as Gavin set his scalpel on the table and circled around behind the chair.

With detached precision, Gavin leaned down and slid the knife from the scabbard on the inside of his boot. In a practiced move, he grasped Abbott's hair, shifted his head into perfect alignment and sank the blade deep between the occiput and the first cervical vertebra, slicing through the posterior atlanto-occipital membrane and, finally, the brain stem where it met the spinal cord.

As Gavin loosed his hold, Abbott's corpse slid from the chair to land on the cracked and blackened tiles with a dull thud.

Gavin turned and stepped over the pool of blood that had sprayed from the incised throat of the second body— Boyd Abbott Jr.—and returned to the small table, where he carefully began to roll up the carrying case that held his surgical instruments. As he worked, he spoke over his shoulder to the three men leaning against the far wall.

"Set a cytoplast charge. I want this place razed to the ground." He smiled. "We'll spin it as my clean-up campaign for the Waste."

"What about the whores?" Thom asked.

Gavin paused, tapped his index finger against his lower lip. He doubted they knew anything, but one could never be too careful. He had absolutely no intention of leaving any sort of trail for Tatiana's brother to follow. Wizard was searching for her, had been for six months. He had put the word out through the Waste, subtle feelers, nothing blatant. Gavin meant to leave no one behind who might point the man in the right direction, because it was completely unacceptable for Wizard to get to Tatiana first.

She was *his*. Bought and paid for, and of use to him still. The ideal test subject. One who could be experimented upon indefinitely, who could heal from almost anything.

The whores would make less perfect subjects, but still, they had some promise. He couldn't take the chance that they had been privy to any secrets. Which meant he either killed them or brought them along.

Killing them seemed so wasteful. He hated to let perfectly good test subjects go to waste.

And they had the additional benefit of being lost souls. They were humans who had either given up their basic rights long ago or who had had them stolen. Either way, no one would miss them. No one would search for them. No one would care.

Even if they did, the whores would never be found.

"Round them up and bring them."

CHAPTER SIX

Tatiana stared down at the spreading pool of blood lapping at the white snow like a lazy tide. Shock and guilt bit deep. She should have prevented this, should have stopped it. That would have been the right thing to do.

Or was it right for Gemma to kill this monster, to take his life as payment for that of her daughter?

Logic argued for the latter—an even trade. But Tatiana was quickly learning that human interactions were far more convoluted than the dictates of logic.

"OhGodOhGodOhGod," Gemma whispered, reaching out to brush frantically at Tatiana's blood-splattered hands.

It was bizarre that this woman could gut a man, but lose it at the sight of blood.

No, not the sight of blood. It was the sight of his blood on her hands, Tatiana realized. Gemma was regretting the spray of blood that stained Tatiana's skin.

"What is it?" she asked, but Gemma just stared at her and trembled.

The man she'd stabbed was on the ground, his mouth opening and closing without breath, without sound, his hands stained red. Tatiana suspected he was beyond help.

Turning in a slow circle, she looked to each of Gemma's

companions in turn. She could see almost nothing of their faces, but their garb, their body language, even the mixed emotions that emanated from them didn't brand them as murderers or monsters. They were distressed, unhappy people. Some crying. Some shuddering. None appeared to have enjoyed the horror they had just witnessed.

As she scanned them one by one, no one spoke.

Then, slowly, each turned away, leaving the dying man on the frozen ground surrounded by the flowering crimson of his blood. They meant for him to die a slow death. An agonizing death. And they meant to leave his remains here for the scavengers and the weather.

Tatiana lifted her plasgun. The crimes she knew this man had committed made her sick, but the thought of leaving him to die like this was equally hideous. It could take him hours. In the frigid temperatures, parts of him would freeze. . . .

She should kill him. Shoot him. Let him die quickly. It was mercy.

A dark humor took her. Guess she needed to add empathy to her growing repertoire of sentiments.

"Don't," Gemma said, and Tatiana's determination wavered. The dead little girl's face—Gemma's daughter—and the knowledge of what she had suffered swam through the shadowy depths of her thoughts.

With a meaningful look at the plasgun, Gemma continued in a rough whisper. "I cannot stop you. I can only ask. Let it be. Let his death be my vengeance. It is all I have left before it takes me."

"Before what takes you?" A shiver crawled along Tatiana's spine, an ugly premonition.

Gemma glanced up, her eyes bright and wild, windows to the suffering in her soul. Then she looked away. "After what I've done, you may wish to turn your weapon on me."

"After what you've done . . . ," Tatiana echoed, able to read nothing more from Gemma's thoughts, finding barbed tangles of emotion when she tried. Did she mean stabbing her daughter's killer?

Tatiana didn't think so; she couldn't imagine remorse had hit Gemma quite that quickly. Which meant that her comment referred to something else she felt bad about. . . .

Opening the portal a little wider, she tried to touch Gemma's mind, to seek answers, but found only a turbid slurry of pain and horror.

Again, eerie premonition crawled up Tatiana's spine.

Gemma wasn't sorry about the guy dying on the snow, she was sorry for something else entirely, and Tatiana had the ugly little gut instinct that whatever it was, it was something that didn't bode well for *her*.

With a shake of her head, Gemma looked to the approaching snowscooter.

"I'm sorry." Her whisper carried on the wind. "I don't know what to do now. But he'll know what to do. He always knows."

Tatiana followed her gaze.

Gemma turned and walked away, the scrape of her footsteps on the ice slow, defeated, suggesting that she had found no solace in this act.

The rapist moaned, drawing Tatiana's gaze. Could she help him? Heal him?

Should she?

She had no guide to help choose her direction. What she knew of morals and ethics, right and wrong—what she knew of life—she had learned from a computer, from Bane or Ward, from the stolen thoughts of prisoners held in cells like her own. Which meant she knew pretty much nothing.

Squatting by the guy's side, she did a cursory evaluation. He appeared to be in shock, his eyes glassy, his mouth slack, his skin the dull gray color of a block of sim-protein. She assessed his injuries, pushing aside his hands so she could see the extent of the damage, a little surprised that he let her.

The knife had cut through skin and muscle, slicing deep, through large and small bowel. Even so, the amount of blood was profuse, far too massive to be explained by those injuries.

Using the dull side of Gemma's blade, she eased aside the loops of glistening intestine, careful not to do additional damage as she bared his aorta. Gemma's strike had slit the peritoneum and partially transected the thick artery. Each pulse wave sent a surge of blood spurting free.

Without rapid surgical intervention, the man would die.

So she had her answer. No, she could not save him. Still, the cloud of ambivalence hung over her. Had she found a different set of injuries, would she have made the attempt? Should she have?

There was absolutely no doubt this man had committed the crime he was accused of. And worse. Who the hell was she to be his savior or his mercy killer, to intrude on whatever laws and customs these people had?

Raising her head, she saw they had all left, all but one man. The latecomer, Tatiana thought, recognizing the scooter she'd glimpsed over her shoulder. This was the man that Gemma believed had all the answers.

Must be nice to be omniscient.

He dismounted and walked toward her, the dark cloth that draped him dancing in the wind. Each step that brought him nearer made her think that the vast Waste had somehow grown smaller. He took up space and air and light.

She switched her grip on the hilt of Gemma's knife. Underhand would do from this angle.

When he reached her, he paced a tight circle, defined purpose in his every step, in every subtle shift of his body.

Familiarity tugged at her.

She rose and turned with him, wary, unwilling to offer her back.

With her own height as a point of reference, she saw now that he was tall, over six feet. The layers of thermal cloth obscured his features, his build, but she could see the way he moved. Confidence and masculine grace.

Hazard and threat.

Why did she think that?

Because she knew him. The thought whispered through her, too unlikely to be given credence.

She swallowed and turned . . . turned . . . watching him move.

Abruptly, he stopped and raised his head, his gaze meeting hers.

She gasped.

Blue eyes, like the cobalt used in corrosion-resistant metal alloys. She had seen those eyes in her dreams almost every night for a week, had been unable to chase away the memory of them.

The settler from Abbott's General Store. *Her* settler.

Only now, faced with the bizarre scene she had just witnessed, she wasn't so certain that he was anything as benign as a Northern Waste colonist out to steal a little cargo from Yasha and Viktor.

His pupils dilated, betraying both his recognition of her and his surprise. Then his gaze dropped to her hands, gloveless, stained with the dying man's blood mixed with a little of her own blood, from where Gemma had accidentally cut her.

He reared back slightly, his head jerking up so his eyes met hers once more in brief connection. Like Gemma, he found the sight of blood on her hands troubling.

Which made her suspect that *she* ought to find it troubling, too.

Feeling strangely self-conscious, she dragged her balaclava out of her pocket and used it to wipe her hands. She never wore the thing anyway. It wasn't like any part of her could freeze.

She paused, stared at the stained cloth, and glanced about. With a sigh, she rolled it into a tight ball—keeping the bloody section on the inside—and shoved it back in her pocket.

The rapist's cries had weakened to mewling sounds of terror, and then, suddenly, he reared up and lunged forward, snarling and hissing like a trapped beast.

Startled, Tatiana swung the plasgun toward him. He showed far more strength than he ought to, given that his blood was leaking out to pool beneath him. Even so, she couldn't view him as a threat.

Uncertainty needled her. She didn't want to kill again. She wanted to uphold her vow not to. But in this situation, what was right?

"It is not your right to end his life," her newly arrived companion said, his voice low, devoid of inflection.

No, it was neither her right nor her responsibility, but a part of her insisted it was both.

Opening herself just a little, she tried to read the electrical shadow of his thoughts and emotions. She gasped as she felt the same infinite black vortex she had experienced a week past when she had tried to read him in Abbott's store, the same dizzying sense of endless space and darkness.

"Is it *your* right to end his life?" she asked, slamming

closed the portal. That particular enhanced sense would be of no help to her here.

"No." His gaze was locked on hers, deep-ocean dark, and so very cold. "But some things are not about rights." He dipped his head, looking at the wounded rapist once more. Dropping to one knee, he studied him with apparent detachment. "The sun that shines on me shines on my enemy. The breath he exhales, I inhale." His exhalation came in a harsh rush. "His pain is my own."

"O-kaaay," she said, for lack of a better reply. The guy was either a genius or, more likely, a few carrots short of a sim-steak stew. She had no clue what he'd just said.

"Yeah, sometimes it doesn't make much sense to me, either," he offered without looking up. "The whole meditation and enlightenment thing can be a bitch."

Right.

He grasped the man's neck and gave a sharp twist. With an ugly crack and a sound like tearing cloth, the rapist's head lurched to an unnatural angle.

Which made the whole ethical argument she'd been having with herself moot. In the end, she hadn't had to choose. She wasn't certain how she felt about that.

"Your plasgun," he said as he rose. "Would you please set it to maximum and incinerate him?"

She blinked. Such a polite request, but the hard undercurrent to his tone made it something else entirely. The complete oddity of the situation struck her, and she only stared at him, wondering if perhaps she had fallen asleep and was dreaming. Vivid dreams. She used to have them in her cell. Dreams of her siblings, and of the lab that had spawned them.

"I could light a hydrogen fire, but it will take longer." He sounded bored . . . no . . . *weary*. Or not. She couldn't tell.

She hesitated, searching for hidden pitfalls, acutely aware

that she could read nothing from this man. The anomaly was distinctly disconcerting. She was used to having the edge, the advantage, having knowledge others lacked. With him, she had only questions and a bizarre fascination that made absolutely no sense.

She'd just watched him kill a dying man, one with no hope of survival, and she found that somehow honorable. She was slagging losing it.

Finally, seeing no harm in obliging, she did as he asked, adjusting her Bolinger to the highest setting. The plasshot hit the body and flared bright, then died. She shot a second blast for insurance. The stink of charred flesh burned her nostrils as the body rapidly turned to ash, the heat so bright that it melted even the metal fastening of his belt.

The wind swirled down, and then even the ash was gone, leaving behind nothing but a blackened groove in the tundra.

No remnant of the life that had been.

Perhaps not a bad thing, given that the life had not been well spent.

"If you would be so kind"—her settler inclined his head toward the spray of blood and teeth that marked a dark trail across the snow—"that as well."

Tatiana turned, paused, studied the spray of teeth and blood and . . . "Is that an ear?"

"Yes."

Okay . . . actually not the answer she'd anticipated. She waited a heartbeat and when he said nothing more, she asked, "So that guy was losing sundry body parts because . . . ?"

Another beat of silence.

"Poor organizational skills."

Yeah, that'd explain it.

Discharging another blast, she watched as the crimson splatter disappeared. Then she shot a glance at her companion.

"So why eradicate every trace?" she asked. It wasn't as though he would get hauled in by the authorities for killing a man. There was no real law this far north. What passed for a police force in the Waste was a loose assemblage of corrupt men who rarely ventured north of Bob's Truck Stop, a bastion of hospitality and goodwill that rivaled Abbott's.

"Good housekeeping." His features were obscured by the layers of thermal gear, but his tone held the definite bite of dry amusement.

"You ever offer a straight answer?"

"Rarely." He was smiling as he said it. She could hear it in his voice. And why, oh why, did she *like* the sound of his voice, low and rich?

"I can understand getting rid of the body," she mused. "A cursory cleanup. But this seems more like a complete purging."

"It is."

There you go. A straight answer.

What was he afraid of?

Tipping her head to one side, she instantly realized her mistake. Not afraid. She couldn't read his thoughts, but she could read his cool gaze and in-control body language, and she was completely certain that he was afraid of very little.

So it was something else that prompted him to erase all evidence of what had occurred here, and that something else was definitely not good.

"Thank you for taking care of the cleanup." His gaze met hers, sparked and flared, and she wondered how she'd thought those midnight eyes cold. "I hadn't thought to see you again."

Just that. Simple words with little inflection, but they made her pulse jump. He recognized her.

Of course he recognized her.

Women alone in the Waste were an oddity. That in itself was enough to make her memorable. But despite her logic, she was secretly pleased.

"Yeah . . . um . . . likewise." Oh, eloquent. She winced.

"What is your name?" Again words so softly, so politely spoken, but underneath was a current of expectation. She recognized that he never considered that she would do other than as he instructed, never imagined she would not answer him now.

"What's yours?" she fired back.

He laughed—low and rich and dark—and his blue, blue eyes danced. They weren't friendly or benign. They were hotter than plas-shot.

"Tristan," he said.

"Tristan. The sorrowful one." She wondered if the meaning of his name held true for him. "Have you known sorrow?"

His eyes narrowed. "Am I alive?" he countered.

Silence hung between them, broken only by the howl of the wind. After a moment, he asked, "And you are . . . ?"

She almost chose not to answer, then weighed the possibility that this man might have information about Ward's lab. Her name wasn't so much to offer. No sense pissing him off. "Tatiana."

"No surname?" His tone carried only the barest shade of interest.

TTN081. The registration number was inked into the

skin on the outside of her upper arm, in breach of the Blood-borne Pathogen Act of 2087.

Was a registration number a surname?

"Just Tatiana is fine."

For an instant she thought he might press her, and she held his gaze, wondering what it was about him that both appealed to her and made her wary.

"You didn't share your surname." She shrugged. "No reason for me to share mine." That was logic he would understand.

"Fair enough." He studied her for a moment, his gaze dropping to her hands. A frown marked two shallow, vertical lines between his brows. "I saw you speaking with Gemma."

There was an undercurrent to the words, almost a question, casually implied, a hint of tension.

How had he seen that? He'd been far off when the brief connection had occurred. She assessed him with a rapid glance, then shot her gaze to his scooter. A set of goggles hung on the handgrip.

"Those goggles are telescopic." She didn't ask.

"Must be."

"Must be," she agreed, wondering what the big deal was about giving a direct answer. The guy talked in circles. It ought to have been irritating, and to some extent, it was. But she also found it interesting.

With a slight nod that she read as sardonic, he turned and strode to his scooter, climbed on and hit the ignition.

"Please, join me, Ana," he said cordially, casting her a sidelong glance.

Ana. He called her Ana.

She'd once had a friend who called her that, a girl long dead. Raina Bowen. The only real friend she'd ever had. There was an Old Dominion adage that misery loved company. Wasn't that the truth. She and Raina had met under the direst of miserable circumstances. And Raina had ended up dead.

It seemed to be a pattern with her. Everyone who mattered ended up dead.

Tristan made a small gesture toward her snowscooter.

"Please, Ana" he said again, the request engraved and tied with a fancy bow.

The thread of steel in his tone said it wasn't a take-a-rain-check sort of invitation.

But it was the possibility of information that made her decide to accept.

She was going to die.

Not all at once. Not clean. Not easy. Bits and pieces of her at a time.

Is that an ear?

Yeah, it was a goddamned ear.

Tristan could hear the hum of her snowscooter close on his tail. Tatiana. Ana.

Have you known sorrow?

She had no idea. But he wasn't inclined to dwell on the memories of his family, his culpability in their deaths and his desperate race to save them, so he pondered the riddle she presented instead.

Pretty voice. Pretty girl, traveling alone across the remnants of the I-pole, a long forgotten highway that had linked continents in a time before the Second Noble War.

No, she was more than pretty. She was tough and smart and brave. He'd thought about her more than he ought to ever since the night he'd watched her take down Yasha and Viktor. Crazy thoughts about meeting her again in a different time and place.

In a different reality, he would have asked her out on a date. The thought almost made him laugh. Dates belonged to a different lifetime, a different world.

In this world, it would have been far better for her if he never saw her again. Especially not with her hand cut open and covered in blood—both her own and the infected Reaver's.

He wanted her as far away from here as possible, living her life, never knowing any of them, and he was not pleased that he wasn't going to get what he wanted. Because any hope she had of getting out of here alive had disappeared the second her hand got cut open and sprayed with infected blood. A little nick. It was enough.

Just Tatiana is fine.

Who the hell was she?

And what was she doing at the Maori Talisman, wearing only the most basic of thermal gear, no shelter, no protection, alone on a snowscooter?

A mystery. One he would unravel as they got to know each other better.

And, yeah, they were definitely going to become well acquainted, because Ana wasn't going anywhere except deep into the ground. With him.

Light from the fading sun bounced and sparkled off the ice, blindingly bright.

The light that shines upon me shines upon my enemy. In this we are one.

He'd offered the bastard mercy, a quick death. At the moment, he wasn't certain if that meant he'd risen above the hate and fury and disgust, or sunk to the lowest rung of the ladder.

The Morgat's engine hummed with a deep pulse as Ana drew alongside him. He wanted to glance at her, look at her, enjoy the curve of her cheek and the poetry of her features. In his mind's eye, he could see the round, high curve of her ass. A damned fine ass, sitting pretty on the sleek saddle of the snowscooter.

He stopped himself halfway to the point of turning his head toward her.

Do not think about her ass.

Get her where he needed her to be. He'd be smart to focus on that and nothing else. Not her lush, sexy mouth, or her incredible, spooky eyes, or the way she moved. . . .

She was a dichotomy, giving both the impression of fragility and improbable strength. He thought she might be hard as tungsten carbide, tougher than the permafrost.

He hoped she was. She'd need it, that toughness.

Wrong place. Wrong time. If she'd been at the Talisman an hour earlier, an hour later, she'd be on her way right now to wherever she had planned to go.

Instead, she had been exposed. She had an open cut on her hand, and she'd been splattered by the spray of the dead man's blood. Which meant she wasn't going anywhere but to an early grave.

He gave a mordant grunt. *Grave.* Actually, he'd have to incinerate her, burn away any trace of her, as she had done with the dead Reaver. Anything else was too risky.

She was the first outsider to be infected. He intended to make damned sure she was the last.

How the hell was he supposed to tell her?

He did look at her, then. She leaned forward on her sleek scooter, her posture at ease. She knew how to ride, looked like she enjoyed it.

Wanting to give her this, one very tiny thing in the face of all she was about to lose, he gunned the engine, increasing his speed until they flew across the ice and snow, the wind biting and howling, stinging his cheeks. She kept pace with him, shot him a glance, her eyes sparkling, her lips curved in the whisper of a smile.

That smile hit him hard.

This would be her last ride, her last taste of freedom. Once they were inside, he was locking down the facility. It was too dangerous to risk the lives of any more outsiders. He should have locked the whole thing down as soon as he'd arrived, but he hadn't realized how far things had progressed, how bad it had gotten.

A long-buried piece of himself shifted and twitched. Not a comfortable awakening.

Abruptly, he closed his emotions down, searching for the calm place he had trained himself to find.

If he allowed himself to feel regret, it would shred his insides and leave him bleeding out nice and slow. Better to shut that door and keep it locked and focus on getting her contained.

So she could die nice and tidy.

Well, as tidy as losing her sanity while her body rotted a centimeter at a time could be.

CHAPTER SEVEN

The dying sun refracted off the ice, bright, glittering beams that danced and flared. Tristan had put his goggles back on, but Tatiana hadn't bothered. She didn't need them. Not for the wind. Not for the sharp glare.

Wariness coiled through her like smoke. She didn't trust Tristan. Why would she? She didn't know him, couldn't sense his thoughts, and she had just watched him kill a man with unquestionable efficiency.

Although . . . that might be considered a recommendation of sorts, given that she'd been considering doing the same thing herself.

She had chosen to accompany him because it was the logical course. She needed a hydrogen fill, and given the fact that these people had scooters, it was a viable assumption that they had fuel. Moreover, they might have information about Ward's lab. It was reasonably logical to think they might. How many buried facilities could there be in the vicinity of the Maori Talisman?

And if it wasn't logical, well, she'd resort to hope. She wasn't much given to wishes, but exhausting her very short list of other options had made her more open-minded.

Besides, she wondered who these people were and what the hell they were up to. Even without her ability to read thoughts, she would have known there was something off balance here.

Her first clue was the guy they'd gutted and left for dead. Her second was the fact that Tristan had asked her to destroy all evidence he had ever existed.

Why?

Slag, she didn't need more questions in her life. And she didn't need a taciturn, rag-draped dictator whose voice made her insides sing when he oh-so-politely ordered her to follow him whether she wished to or not.

It rankled that she *did* wish to because she needed a hydrogen fill, wanted a hot meal, and wouldn't mind a shower. And because her other options were pretty sparse. But mostly because she was curious.

No, mostly because she was just tickled that he'd remembered her. And because her heart did that same stupid little flip that it had done the night she'd first seen him at Abbott's.

What the hell was it with her and this bizarre fascination with a rag-draped, autocratic Waste-rat who had the most amazing eyes she'd ever seen?

Maybe it was his quirky streak of humor that made her like him.

And how crazy was that? She didn't even know him. How could she like him?

She cut him a sidelong glance, catching a glimpse of muscled thigh wrapped in thermal leggings. Well, she liked *looking* at him, anyway.

A moment later, a faint vibration rippled across the terrain. Instinct made her slow her scooter, check the horizon. Something felt . . . wrong.

The ground felt different. She could sense a building throb, carrying through the earth, through her scooter. Something coming. Something big.

Tristan must have felt it too, because he slowed as she slowed, then drew to a halt beside her as she skidded her scooter to a stop.

Or perhaps he did so *because* she did, mirroring her actions rather than sensing anything amiss on his own.

Then she saw them, closing in fast. Two enormous vehicles barreled toward them, monstrous piles of twisted metal, crowned with gun turrets, plated with armored scales. Reavers. Slagging Reavers. They usually traveled in larger packs, so these two must be scouts.

Massive caterpillar tires chewed up the ground, sending a glittering fan of mulched ice and snow arcing out behind them.

She shot a glance at Tristan. Logic told her she ought to gun her engine and get out of there. Her Morgat might make it, even though it was almost on empty . . . if they didn't choose to chase her too far.

But Tristan's ride just wasn't built for speed. He didn't stand a chance. Not her problem. She couldn't save the whole slagging world.

Only she couldn't make herself leave him behind.

Guess she needed to add *bleeding heart* to the list of new discoveries about herself.

Grabbing her lip-com, she held up fingers in a rapid sequence, signaling Tristan the frequency she wanted to use, hoping to hell he had a lip-com, too.

The wind swirled around them, churning up snow in a dizzying cloud. As it settled, she saw that Tristan did, indeed, have a lip-com. He eased it into position, his gaze tracking the movement of the ice pirate rigs.

"Go after your friends," Tatiana ordered. "I'll ride out in the opposite direction and draw them off."

"Negative. We stay together." His gaze slid to hers, crystal cold, night dark and blue as a clear midnight sky.

A high-pitched whine sliced the air, and some thirty meters away the ground exploded, shifting in a massive, undulating wave. Hunks of ice rained down on them like hail. With a stunning collision of sound, a chunk of glassy white ice the size of her Morgat landed maybe three meters away, exploding into shards the size of daggers.

"We move. Now," Tristan ordered. Though she wasn't in love with his tone, she wasn't inclined to argue.

Gunning the engine, Tatiana made her Morgat sing as she leaned forward and set a course across the flat terrain. She shot a look over her shoulder. Tristan was at her flank, the wind and speed combining to fan his thermal gear out behind him like a ragged black flag.

Well, didn't he make just the perfect target.

Plas-shot followed them, peppering the ground with blasts of heat and blue flame. The ground shook as the Reavers' rigs roared in pursuit, gaining on them by meters with each passing moment.

And all around was a frigid, frozen plain, without a dip or bump or place to hide.

"This wasn't the way I planned my exit." She raised her voice to carry through the com and overcome the cacophony that battered them from all sides. "And honestly, Tristan, right now I can't say it was nice to have met you."

A high-pitched whine followed her—a warning—and she skidded her scooter hard left. The ground behind her, slightly to the right, burst into a horrific wall of heat energy and jagged shards of ice that shot up and out with terrifying strength and speed.

"Left," she roared at Tristan, another whine screaming its warning.

He didn't argue, but veered as she ordered.

"We need to split up," she said again.

"Negative."

What was with this guy and his dictatorial manner?

She shot a glance at him. He was holding the scooter only with his knees, his hands nowhere near the handgrips. Instead, they were in his lap, working at the lid of a metal tin. His head was bowed, and he was riding blind. What the slagging hell was he doing?

He slowed, leaned far right, dropped something in the snow.

"Go," he snarled as she slowed along with him.

He cut his scooter in a sharp arc, doubling back the way he had come, leaning far left to drop something in the snow yet again.

And then she saw it. Cytoplast. He was setting mini-bombs in their wake. She had to admire his ingenuity. And had to wonder what he was doing riding around with a supply of explosive. He had no plasgun, but he had bombs. Interesting guy.

"Go," he said again, and this time she listened, sending her Morgat tearing across the ice, wondering if perhaps they might come out of this alive. A cheery possibility.

She glanced over her shoulder. *"What the slagging hell?"*

Tristan was off his scooter, down on one knee. The shadows of the Reaver rigs fell across him, dark and ominous. Her gut twisted as she understood exactly what he was doing, exactly the danger he was putting himself in to save her life.

Cytoplast needed trip wires to make it blow.

So he was setting them.

Crazy. He was crazy.

He surged to his feet and sprinted to the next cytoplast bomb. There, he dropped to his knees, working with fevered speed.

The Reaver rigs barreled down on him, mountainous, deadly, and she had no doubt that he was too far from his scooter to get back to it in time.

He was going to die. He was going to be dragged under one of those monster tires and crushed.

Not an image she found particularly pleasant.

A bead of sweat trickled between her breasts, and a hard burst of adrenaline pushed her to move.

With a groan, she yanked her scooter round, tipping hard up on one blade as she nearly overturned. For a frozen second, she and the machine hung in delicate balance, and then the airborne side slammed down with jarring force.

She found herself zipping toward the ice pirate rigs and the titanic battering rams that jutted out the front. They filled her vision, massive and terrifying, draped with the yellow-white skulls of previous victims.

Perfect. "Nice way to leave this mortal coil," she muttered. "Served on a skewer."

Swerving side to side to avoid the hail of plas-shot that rained down on her from the Reaver gun turrets, she sped toward Tristan as he bounded to his feet and set out at a dead run.

A bright flare of light, violent blue, exploded like a geyser reaching toward the sky a millisecond before the noise and heat hit her. Tristan's scooter was incinerated, the metal twisting and writhing in the flame like a living thing.

Slag. Slag.

Leaning low, she tore toward him, holding out her hand as she drew abreast and cut the snowscooter in a tight 180. Beneath the scrape of the blades, the ice screamed.

Tristan reached out, his fingers closing around her wrist, and hers closing around his. He used her body as a counterweight as he swung up behind her, the Morgat bouncing a little beneath the added weight, the engine revving up a notch to work a little harder.

He slid tight against her, his thighs pressed to her own, his chest to her back. She froze, hating the contact, waiting for the flash flood of thoughts and emotions that usually accompanied human touch. But there was nothing. Nothing. And she felt a little off-kilter because of it.

The Reaver rigs bore down on them. They were almost on her now, two massive beasts chasing down an arctic hare.

She gunned the engine and the Morgat shot forward, flying across the ice. The wind slapped her face, and her heart slammed out a steady, solid beat.

The boom of the first explosion was followed so closely by the second, she barely differentiated one from the next. And she didn't turn to look. Not yet.

She bent low, with Tristan plastered against her like mud on a boot, his chest pressed tight to her back. She rode as she had never ridden before.

A wave of heat and power followed them, and a terrible noise, the metal of the demolished Reaver rigs shrieking in the flames as it twisted and bent. Debris spewed in all directions, showering down on the hard-packed ground. Another explosion and another and another, one piggybacking the next, booming and echoing all around.

Slowing the Morgat, she eased it into a turn. Behind them, the air shimmered and writhed, a column of smoke rising as a cloud. A massive blaze, twice as tall as Abbott's Inn, threw tongues of red and gold in all directions.

"Guess that went fairly well," she said, tipping her head back to watch as a curved bit of metal sailed through the air, spit forth by the force of the blaze. It slammed against the ground with a discordant clatter.

"Guess it did."

And didn't he just sound pleased as punch about that?

"Head north," he said, his voice sounding strange, coming at her both from close by her ear and through the lip-com.

Glancing down, she checked her hydrogen gauge. Her tank was almost empty.

"How far north?"

"Three . . . maybe four hours."

She looked at the tank again. With only her weight, the Morgat could make it easily. With the two of them . . . barely.

Tristan shifted behind her, his thighs moving against hers, his arms tightening about her waist. Very deliberately, she twisted at the waist to look at him.

"See . . . I have this thing about being touched. . . ." About having his arms around her, confining her. About being this close to any other person. "I don't like it. But unless I beat my conscience into submission and leave you here in the middle of nowhere, I'm stuck with you. So . . . grab the seat and hold on to that."

He froze, then took his hands from her waist as she turned forward once more. She figured she ought to be grateful for small favors.

Behind her, he shifted around, his thighs rubbing hers, his crotch sliding up against her butt. She exhaled a sharp puff of air, watched it blow white in front of her face. He moved back, slid forward, his efforts only making it worse.

She stared at the nearly empty hydrogen gauge.

Three . . . maybe four hours.

The Morgat would make it, but would she?

They crested a rise, and Tatiana was surprised to see a neon orange, dome-shaped tent standing out in stark contrast against the snow. The wind caught the material and made it billow and flap like a great balloon, bright as a cleaned carrot. Then the current changed and the material collapsed on itself, all the air sucked out. The flapping sound had a tempo of its own, almost musical.

There was no sign of Gemma and the others. Of course, they hadn't stopped for tea with the Reavers, so likely they'd made much better time.

As they zoomed closer to the tent, Tatiana realized that it was far larger than it had originally appeared. With no point of reference, she hadn't been able to judge its size from a distance, but as they drew near, she had to look up to see the top of it.

The front flaps were tied back, and she slowed her scooter to slide inside to a roomy space, tall enough to accommodate a rig and wide enough to park six of them side by side with space to spare. The interior was lit by a bulb caged behind a metal grate mounted on a pole near the entry.

And—surprise—there was an ugly gray cinder-block building with a large metal door at the far end of the tent. No windows. No markings. Just doors that met in the center and a metal grate that pulled across the front of them.

If they had a building, why did they need a tent? A bright orange tent flaring like a beacon against the brilliant white snow . . . like a warning. . . .

Maybe that was the intent.

A group of scooters was already lined up to the side of the building. Tatiana drew to a halt and paused, waiting to see what Tristan would do next. She'd spent nearly four hours with his hard body pressed against hers, and right now, she was all for leaping off the scooter and dancing away from him, gaining a little breathing room.

But she knew better than to make the first move, so she held her place and waited.

He climbed off and stood beside the scooter to shake out first his right leg, then his left. Turning from her, he went to jerk open the caged, metal door. He had a way of moving that drew her eyes, made her watch him. Fluid grace, but hard, masculine.

She wondered what he looked like without all those layers of draped cloth.

"In here," he said, pulling the grate to one side. Then he hit the release, and the doors slid open with a soft hydraulic shush.

With only the single bulb for illumination, the shadows inside the tent were long and dark.

But the shadows beyond the open doors of the elevator were darker still.

From deep in the ground came the hum of a generator and the clanging reverberation of pipes. Water dripped in a steady patter from the flat edge of the building, the heat within warming and melting a thin layer of ice.

Familiar sounds. Unwelcome sounds. Too similar to the drone she had listened to from her cell for half her life.

Slag.

Tatiana sat rigid on her scooter, her heartbeat measuring time as she eyed the opening warily. It led into darkness, confined space, an elevator that would take her down to the bowels of the earth.

The last place on the whole slagging planet she wanted to go.

Walls all around. Thick, rough stone. Down, down, down . . . no hope, no light.

Her chest grew tight, her palms damp. Her pulse leaped and jerked like a trapped ptarmigan.

How was it that she could face a life-or-death situation

cool as a glacier, but just the thought of stepping inside an elevator reduced her to a pathetic, quivering mass?

She gave Tristan a careful, assessing look. With his face angled away from her, she had no indication of his thoughts.

"You want me to go in there? I don't think so."

His gaze shot to hers. Her refusal seemed to annoy him, but he masked it quickly. Then again, with just his eyes visible, she couldn't be certain.

"If you could just get me a hydrogen fill, I can be on my way," she said. "I can pay."

"A hydrogen fill," he repeated, and the look in his eyes put her on high alert. He definitely had other plans. "Do you deny me the opportunity to offer you a meal? At least accept that. You just saved my life."

A true enough statement, and he looked directly at her, without guile. Still, she didn't quite trust him. No reason she should. She didn't trust anyone.

Would he force the issue if she declined?

Tatiana tensed as the seconds flowed together like water. She didn't want to hurt him. She really didn't want to hurt him. For some bizarre reason, she thought him . . . admirable.

Because he'd broken the neck of the guy she'd intended to shoot. An act of mercy.

And how twisted did all that make her?

He took a step closer, then froze, perhaps alerted by her expression. She *would* hurt him if he left her no option. If it came to it, she'd just try not to kill him.

She flipped her Setti9 from her wrist holster into her palm, but kept it out of sight down by her thigh.

A hum of expectation charged the air. The way he stood told her he was holding back, waiting, watching, just as she was.

Check, but not mate.

Tatiana rose, climbed off the scooter, staring him down.

After a long moment, he raised his hands to the cloth that covered his face. Taking deliberate care, he began to unwind the material, his eyes locked on hers. He dragged away the covering, his movements slow and easy, as though he took pains not to startle her. Finally, the swaths slid away, down his arm, through his gloved fingers, the free end pooling on the ground with a whisper of sound.

A sharp, electric pulse shot through her veins and hit her low in the gut. The same sort of feeling she'd had the night she watched him outside Abbott's.

Up close, the deep blue of his eyes bright against dark lashes, the shadow of his beard accentuating the harsh line of his jaw, his features sculpted and hard, he was everything she remembered. He was more than she remembered.

Her gaze dropped to his mouth.

His lips looked soft. Smooth and soft. The only soft thing about him. They were drawn in a hard, unsmiling line. The incongruity of that was fascinating. And then he did smile, just a little, closed mouthed and tight. Not a reassuring sight, but attractive somehow.

Attractive. No, not the right description. *Arousing*.

"I won't bite," he said.

Maybe not, but she might.

She realized she was clenching her jaw, and with a slow breath, she forced herself to relax. He watched her all the while, his night-sky eyes glittering, seeing far too much.

With or without a hydrogen fill, it was time for her to go.

She took a shuffling step back, bumped up against her snowscooter. "I just need a hydrogen fill. If you can't accommodate me, fine. I'll find it somewhere else."

His dark brows rose, a challenge. "Really? Where?"

Where, indeed. She wasn't about to tell him that she'd leave her scooter—her beautiful, perfect Morgat—behind and walk the Waste if she had to. He wouldn't believe she could, and she had absolutely no inclination to debate the matter.

She shrugged.

He raised both hands, palms forward. "The hydrogen stores are below, as is the pump." He shook his head, looked around at the orange-tinged enclosure, drawing attention to the fact that there was definitely no hydrogen pump here. "I'm happy to provide what you require, but I have no way to fill your scooter unless we go below."

Choices. Choices. Or rather, a lack thereof.

She needed hydrogen and information. And she needed to know exactly what was below. She doubted she could have been fortunate enough to have stumbled on the exact place she was searching for—Ward's hidden research facility—but she couldn't discount the possibility without checking it out.

Perfect. Just perfect. Her one burst of good luck, and it had to dump her here, staring at a dark pit that would take her to places she never wanted to be again. Deep into the earth, possibly into Ward's domain. She wasn't ready for that. Not yet.

The simplest thing would be to just ask, but if Tristan did work for Ward, the odds were he wouldn't tell her the truth. And then she would have given away her advantage for nothing.

Snapping his gloved fingers, Tristan flashed a smile, revealing a deep crease on one side of his mouth and truly lovely teeth, animal white, the front two overlapping ever so slightly. And, yes, she'd been right. His eyes crinkled up in the corners when he smiled.

Cold eyes, like the ocean fathoms beneath the surface. But when he looked at her, they were warm.

Again, that high-voltage jolt hit her gut. Attraction. Lust. *Slag.*

"I have an idea," he offered. "You wait here, and I'll take your scooter below, fill it, and bring it topside again. How's that?"

"Why do you think I'd let my scooter out of my sight?"

His brows rose. She thought she might have insulted him. Or foiled some diabolical plot. Or hit on the truth—that he knew she wouldn't let him take the Morgat, that she'd sooner get in the elevator with him than do that.

Or, perhaps, none of the above. She'd relied on reading thoughts for so long, been alone for so long, she'd never learned the art of reading faces.

Normal human interactions . . . they escaped her. Invariably, she misstepped, chose the wrong words, did the wrong thing. Was this such an instance? Was she being overly wary of an offer that had no ill intent?

Perhaps yes, perhaps no. After all, she'd just watched him kill a man.

Then again, she'd considered doing the same thing herself, so she could hardly fault him.

Plus, he'd risked his life for her own when he stopped to set the cytoplast charges that had stopped the Reavers.

She heaved a sigh. In all likelihood, yes, she was being overly wary.

She was off balance, thrown because she couldn't catch even the faintest hint of Tristan's thoughts or emotions—an uncommon, but not completely unique, circumstance. It had happened to her a few times over the past months when she'd encountered people with what she assumed were unusually strong shielding mechanisms.

Again, he smiled. A little less open. A little less charming. They were facing off here, gazes locked.

"It's cold up here and warm below, and I am finished standing about while the day fades away." He bent, scooped the discarded cloth from the ground, and straightened. "Decide."

Yeah, definitely a dictator.

"My apologies," she said, not even trying to mask her sarcasm as she eyed the shadowed elevator.

In addition to hydrogen, there was probably food below—something other than dehydrated protein supplement. And information. Perhaps even her ultimate destination: Ward's lab.

It was just an elevator. Just a short ride. A few seconds in an enclosed space. She could do this. She *would* do this.

"I can tell you about Tolliver," he said casually.

Her gaze snapped to his.

If she hadn't already decided to get in the elevator, that innocuous little sentence would have been all the enticement she needed.

Bait.

Hook.

Only she wasn't foolish enough to lunge at it. Not in any obvious way. He had obviously heard her ask Abbott about Tolliver, and the truth was he might know something or he might not. She intended to find out, in her own time.

No sense handing him the advantage by appearing too eager.

She smiled a little. Amazing how early-century business manuals—read along with countless other tomes in the years she and her siblings had been in the Old Dominion lab they'd been raised in—had application to all sorts of situations.

"A hot meal sounds just grand." She flipped her Setti9 back into its wrist holster.

Tristan's brows rose, and she wasn't certain if it was because he saw through her ruse, or because he didn't.

Grabbing hold of the bars of her Morgat, she dragged her scooter forward, the runners shushing across the frozen ground. "Are there . . . um . . . a shower and min-dry I could use down there?"

He laughed, a short, low huff of air.

The sound touched her, made her warm, made her wonder if he would offer to get under the pounding stream with her.

Seconds ticked past. He didn't offer.

Faint disappointment wriggled in her thoughts, because she almost *wanted* him to.

What the hell was wrong with her?

An instant of hesitation and she shoved her scooter forward, stepped into the elevator, took a slow, slow breath.

Her hand dropped to her side, and with her index finger she tapped a steady rhythm on her thigh, focusing on that, only on that, on the movement, the tempo, just the way Wizard had taught her all those years ago.

"Shower, yes—"

On instinct, she spun, her body taut and vibrating, her Setti9 flipping free of her wrist holster to fill her palm.

Tristan was right beside her, his voice low and husky. Her movement brought her face to face with him. The scent of his skin, warm and clean and male, enticed her. He watched her, his eyes blue as the heart of a flame, filling her vision, everything else fading away.

"Min-dry, no," he said. "I'm afraid you'll have to wash and dry your clothes the old-fashioned way."

"You shouldn't sneak up on a girl." Tension laced her words.

"I'll remember that." His gaze flicked to her hand, and he smiled again, oblivious to the danger.

Or maybe not.

Reaching to the side, so close that his arm brushed hers as he moved, he punched a code into the security pad, then leaned in to allow a retinal scan. He stepped back, gestured for her to take his place.

"Everyone in or out needs to be scanned," he said. "The system is set not to move until every person in the elevator is accounted for."

His gaze met hers, open, guileless. She leaned in, let the system scan her, and saw the word *guest* flash and fade on the digital display.

"Painless," Tristan said.

Not from her perspective.

He gave a sharp yank, sending the outer cage door to the elevator clanging shut, followed by the inner solid panels that met in the center, sealing them in with the quiet and the darkness.

And the familiar bitter taste of her fear.

CHAPTER EIGHT

Wherever they were going, it was a long way down, and it was a fast trip, one that made Tatiana's gut dip with a sickening twinge. She fought the urge to claw at the walls as the elevator dropped into the depths of the earth.

Slag, she hated feeling this way—uneasy, afraid, out of control—and hated the fact that the influence of her past seeped through the heavy barriers she had erected. Hated the knowledge that if Ward got his hands on her before she had things worked out, the horror of her past would become her present.

Worse, he'd cut away parts of her—in the most literal sense—a tiny bit at a time, and her cells would be responsible for hundreds of thousands of deaths.

How was that for taking the weight of the world on her shoulders?

She willed herself not to think about that now. Not to think about Gavin Ward . . . other than to wonder if coincidence hadn't brought her to exactly the place she sought.

How many underground facilities were there in the Waste? Was it possible that she had actually stumbled on Ward's lab? And if she had, was it truly happenstance?

She had a hard time trusting anything that came quite that easy.

Cutting a glance at Tristan, she found him staring ahead, his expression unreadable. She could ask him straight out. But that would only give her away, and until she got a better read on the situation, she wasn't inclined to share more information than was absolutely necessary.

Something here just didn't feel right. It was unlikely that Ward would house his lab in a rundown facility with out-of-date technology like the snowscooters she'd seen above and staff it with people who rivaled the ice pirates in their brutality, who rode out en masse to gut some guy and leave him on the ice to die.

Those actions were more suited to Reavers than researchers.

Then again, there was limited probability that some other facility was located underground in the vicinity of the Maori Talisman.

Her wisest course was to stay silent, stay alert, and let the situation play out as it would.

With a jolt, the elevator stopped. Tatiana's tension eased as Tristan shifted forward to yank open the cage.

"Ladies first." He stepped back and gestured for her to proceed.

Baffled, she stared at him. "Ladies first? Why?"

Oh. It hit her then. Courtly manners—rooted in an antiquated belief system that women were to be coddled—had been a part of societal structure up until the First Noble War. It had been commonplace at the time to open doors for women and allow them to pass through. Odd, the notion that women were physically inferior, too weak to open a door.

Then she recalled . . . no, it was not that. It was *polite* to offer this. He meant to be polite.

"Oh," she murmured. "You attempt to show me a

courtesy. But it will be easier for me to push free my scooter if I follow you."

He gave a short laugh, and she wondered if it was directed at her or himself.

"Fair enough." With a shrug he stepped through the open door and turned to the right.

Tatiana followed, setting the scooter to hydroplane mode to lift the runners from the cracked concrete floor on a cushion of air as she pushed the Morgat from the confined space. Oddly, her heart rate escalated now that she was free.

Or maybe it raced because she was in the bowels of the earth, and the only way out was an ancient elevator with the dual security of a keypad and retinal recognition.

She gave a mental shrug. She could always climb the elevator cables hand over hand to get out of here if it came to it.

A quick assessment of her surroundings revealed a massive empty area with exposed gun-gray pipes running along the ceiling and a gridded metal rail along the gallery on one side to protect the unwary from dropping over the edge.

Striding forward, she rested her hip against the rail and looked down. Generators. Rows of dead, silent fossil-fuel generators. A throwback to the time before the Second Noble War.

But she'd heard the hum of a generator up above, could still hear it now carrying from a distance. So there was something alive and running down here.

Nuclear? They'd be taking a huge risk to run that as a power source. The New Government Order had outlawed any form of nuclear energy a decade past, unless it was their own facility running it. Getting caught powering a non-government nuclear microreactor would land the perpetrator a one-way trip to work the stone pits of Africa.

Wind driven? She hadn't noted any wind turbines on the surface. Not a surprise. Frigid temperatures made that technology ill suited to the Waste.

Backing away from the rail, she turned and found Tristan watching her.

"What is this place?" she asked.

He exhaled a short huff of air through his nose. "Home sweet home."

How incredibly uninformative. She tapped her fingertips lightly on her thigh.

"Okay. What *was* it? A power station for some Old Dominion city that doesn't exist anymore?"

His head tipped a bit to the side. "If you understand, things are just as they are. If you do not understand, things are just as they are."

She stared at him, taken aback. "That is either the smartest or the dumbest thing I've ever heard." She was leaning toward dumbest. "And it's a non sequitur."

"Is it?" He smiled, blatantly amused. It was a pleasant smile, like she was in on a joke and he was in on a joke, and no one else was there with them. Awareness flickered in her belly, and she slapped at it as she'd slap at a gnat.

Why did he have to smile at her like that?

"Your comment had no relation to the comment it followed," she pointed out.

His straight, dark brows rose. "I wouldn't have pegged you for the analytical sort."

If he only knew.

"So where's the hydrogen?" She was done with this conversation.

With a jerk of his chin, he indicated a spot behind her and she turned, blinked.

Lined up against the wall—just as he'd promised—were massive tanks for the hydrogen fill. Only, they weren't like any tanks she'd ever seen. They were positively ancient, and she was stunned by their sheer size.

"Quite the sight, aren't they?" he asked, ironic.

For a moment, she was speechless, and she stepped closer to study the tanks.

"The oldest storage method I've seen is organic polymer. It stores three percent hydrogen by weight." She shook her head. "But I postulate that this is even older. What is the method of storage?"

"Postulate?" He laughed outright. "You do have a way with smooth conversation, Ana."

The way he said her name, low and . . . sexy, made the little hairs on her arms stand up.

She shot a glance at him. He stood off to one side, arms crossed over his chest, the position dragging up his sleeves to bare inches of his skin. She stared, startled by the powerful appeal of the sight of his naked forearms, corded with muscle.

Seconds ticked past and when he spoke, she was relieved, the sound jerking her thoughts from the places they were starting to wander, places where she stepped closer and laid her hand against his skin, tested the strength and the heat of him.

Such an inappropriate urge.

"These tanks are hydrogen clathrate hydrate," he said. "Stored at atmospheric pressure and minus 320 degrees Fahrenheit."

She studied the massive containers for a moment. They were so old that the one at the far end had actually corroded and sat empty, a useless husk. Disappointment touched her. "My Morgat can't convert that. This hydrogen is useless to me."

He shook his head. "We've rigged a modified pump that heats the clathrate to release the hydrogen."

"Ah." Tatiana nodded. "Innovative." She wondered if he was the one who had done that, if he was a tech or a scientist or just some amazing looking guy who killed people. "Okay if I take the fill now?"

"Please." He took a single step forward, his hands uncrossing, and she had the odd notion that he meant to fill the scooter for her.

"I can—" *I can do it.* No one worked on her scooter but her.

He froze. Their eyes locked.

She'd offended him. He had meant it as a kindness, she realized. It wasn't that he doubted she could do for herself; it was that he viewed his assistance as an act of consideration. Confusion touched her.

He gestured at the middle canister, and his lips made a tight smile, almost mocking.

Feeling strangely discomfited, she turned away and took hold of the handgrips of her scooter. She didn't understand him, not his thoughts or his ways. Strange man.

That made her smile. She was an equally strange woman. So it seemed they had something in common. The thought left her feeling like she was hanging over a gaping hole. One handed. Without a net.

It shouldn't matter to her that she had anything in common with this man, and she was at a loss to explain why it did.

Cutting him a glance through her lashes, she found him watching her, a faintly bemused expression on his gorgeous face, as though he, too, found their interaction multifaceted and confusing.

She wanted to stroke her fingers along the frown lines between his brows, make them disappear, and that wanting made her very uneasy. Finding connections with anyone was not something she was looking for in her life.

She needed to get her hydrogen and a meal and a shower, and get the hell out of here before she did something very foolish.

She dropped her head and pushed the Morgat over to the massive hydrogen tank. With only a brief hesitation to examine the unfamiliar pump, she made short work of filling her scooter.

Undoing the zip-seam on her parka, she slid her hand into her money belt and pulled out a stack of whisper-thin plastitech interdollars.

"Three hundred enough?" she asked, counting them off, then raising her head to look at him.

His gaze slid past her to the openings of three corridors that led off the main space, then to the shadows that hung about the massive hydrogen tanks. The way he did that, slow, methodical—exactly the way she'd do it—made her hackles rise. He was looking for something, and it made her wonder what the threat was here in the place he had called *home sweet home*.

This situation, this man, were not quite what they appeared.

"Hey," she said, flexing her wrist to draw his attention to the interdollars. "This enough?"

He just looked at her, making no move either to accept the money or decline it, but his expression suggested he was leaning toward declining. And that made her wary.

Perhaps the amount was short.

She thumbed off a few more interdollars. Her last fill had been less than three hundred, but that had been almost six thousand yuales to the south, at the Line Sixty-four Fill Station. The prices could be higher here, so deep in the Waste. Hydrogen fills here, so far off the main path of the ICW, must be at a premium, and the Waste was nothing if not capitalistic.

"More?"

"No, three hundred's fine," he said, and strode forward to accept the payment, his expression inscrutable.

She sensed a strange hesitancy in him as the currency changed hands, as though he was loath to take it from her. She was glad that he did. She always paid her own way. Free rides made her wary, because, somewhere down the road, you invariably found out that nothing was ever free.

Ward had taught her that the first time she met him, only she hadn't known it.

Let me take you out in the daylight, Tatiana. Would you like that? A walk in the daylight? No, I ask nothing in return. Nothing at all.

Not then, he hadn't.

Not until much, much later.

Finishing up with the hydrogen fill, Tatiana set the pump back in place. The hairs at her nape prickled and rose, and the sensation of being watched crawled across her skin. She turned and scanned the perimeter, her gaze traveling along the rail of the gallery to the three main tunnels, then to where her snowscooter rested in the shadow of the hydrogen tanks.

She glanced at Tristan and caught him watching her with those amazing ocean-deep eyes, assessing her. So maybe he trusted her about as much as she trusted him. Not unusual. Living in the Waste bred a certain kind of watchfulness.

The setup in this place left her feeling caged. No wonder, given that there were no other elevators, only the one behind her, which was protected by a keypad and a retinal scan.

"So what's with the security?" she asked. "Can anyone get in and out as long as they're scanned, or is that just a way of keeping tabs on visitors?"

His chest expanded on a breath. The length of time he took to respond gave her a pretty good idea what the answer would be. And she didn't like it.

"So I'm locked in down here?" She had a few tricks up her sleeve, but he didn't need to know that. She narrowed her eyes. "How'd that guy get out, then? Climbed the elevator cable?"

"That would be a feat. We're fifty yuales under the ground."

She decided against mentioning that she could make that climb. No sense offering her secrets for free.

Just when she'd about given up expecting any further reply, he continued, "His escape is the reason I'm locking down."

Ah. "So my only way out is if you clear the retinal scan?" Just for clarity. Clarity was always welcome.

"Yes." He made no effort to hide the fact. Did that mean he'd do the scan and let her ride to the surface anytime she wanted, or was he planning to keep her down here?

This was the sort of situation that could go either way.

She kept her gaze on his and thought that it would be a shame to have anything happen to his pretty eyes, but if her only choice was between being trapped down here or using one of his retinas to get past the elevator's security system, she'd choose the latter and worry about feeling sorry about it later.

Because she was not going to be trapped yuales under the earth again. Not ever.

"Food?" Tristan offered, his mellow voice breaking into her thoughts.

"Food sounds great."

He crossed the wide, empty space and paused at the far end near the start of a corridor, waiting. For her to precede him? Was it that ladies first thing again? Or was he watching for something in particular?

He stood very still, his posture easy, no sign of impatience or edginess. But at the same time, he appeared alert, like his sharp gaze missed nothing.

Interesting guy.

She snagged her AT450 plasgun off the side of the Morgat and shoved it in the holster that lay between her shoulder blades. Then she pulled the knife from the sheath on the dash and pushed it into the sheath on the inside of her boot, a backup to the blade nestled at the small of her back.

Tristan watched her, his gaze intent, blatantly interested, nothing subtle or camouflaged.

She froze, stared at him for a single heartbeat, then forced herself to look away.

Flipping the laser lock on the dash, she leaned in to double secure the system with voice activation and set the trip wire with a subtle shift of her hand. If anyone tried to steal her ride, they'd set up a pulsed arc of fifty thousand volts of electricity, fifteen hundred of which would blast through their system. Not enough to kill. Definitely enough to cause a whole world of pain.

She wasn't one to take chances.

She snagged the small travel pack that she kept always at the ready, slung it over her shoulder, and strode along the rail to the far end toward Tristan.

He eyed her bag and his fingers twitched. For a second she had the bizarre suspicion that he was going to offer to carry it for her. But in the end, he said nothing.

"You lead. You know the way," she said.

"And you'll have my back with your miniarsenal."

No, she wouldn't. "I watch no one's back but my own."

His brows rose, and one side of his mouth curled up,

slow and sexy, drawing out the deep crease in his cheek. "Well, honesty's a virtue."

"Nice to know I have at least one."

He laughed. "But you've already broken your own rule. You watched my back against the Reavers."

So she had. She couldn't explain why, other than the fact that he'd been putting his life on the line to save her ass. "If I were smart, I wouldn't have."

"Oh, I suspect you're very smart, Ana. No doubt about it." The way he said that, soft and lazy, like he was tasting the words on his tongue, made her feel as though he were standing far closer than he was, as though the words were a caress running across her skin.

His gaze slid over her. She felt suddenly breathless.

He turned away and strode through a shallow, brackish puddle that spanned almost the entire width of the dim, gray hallway, his boots sending dual sprays of water up on either side. "Watch the water."

Like she could miss it.

CHAPTER NINE

Tristan moved at a brisk pace. Skirting the first puddle and the second, Tatiana followed, only to encounter another and another as they made their way along the bleak passage. They were accompanied by the steady sound of dripping water hitting the floor and the distinctive musty scent of rot.

"You could fix the plumbing," she said, following Tristan straight through the middle of the next puddle, giving up on edging around them.

"I could," he replied, and his tone left her no doubt that he chose not to.

They walked on, and she could hear the hum of the distant generator growing slightly louder with each step.

"So what's your power source?" she asked.

"Hydro. An underground hot spring is a geothermal energy source, and we supplement it with solar panels at the top of the rise outside."

She thought about that for a moment. "Microhydro power. Water pulled into the system under its own current and released in the same condition it left. The energy from the water is drawn from the current itself. Efficient and impressive."

"Thank you."

The way he said that made her think that he'd had a hand in the creation of the system. Definitely a scientist or a tech and not just a guy who killed people.

Something scurried in the blackness of a corridor that branched off the main one, and she spun, stared. Glittering eyes glared back at her.

She blinked, her vision instantly acclimating to the minimal light, and the visual she got—dozens of chunky, fur-covered bodies—flipped a switch, sending a torrent of computer-gleaned facts skimming across the surface of her thoughts.

"*Rattus norvegicus,*" she muttered.

About three feet ahead of her, Tristan paused and turned. His brows rose and he shook his head. "What?"

"The, uh"—she gestured to the shadows that faded to black—"the rats. Straight temporal ridges, rather than curved. They're brown rats."

"Right." A pause. "Because they're brown."

The expression on his face was priceless. For the longest moment, he just stared at her as the sounds of scrabbling little rat feet and dripping water echoed off the walls.

"What are you, a vermin specialist?" he asked slowly.

Now wasn't that the question.

"Yeah, something like that," she said, thinking of Ward and his minions. "It's a calling."

Emotion flickered in Tristan's gaze. Not incredulity or humor . . . something dark, quickly hidden.

Turning away, he spoke over his shoulder. "I had a pet rat as a kid. It was white."

A short, huffing laugh escaped her at that bizarre comment and what it revealed. From the tone of his voice, it was clear that he had felt affection for that pet.

"Weren't rats . . . hamsters . . . even gerbils outlawed as

pets after the rodent-borne bubonic plague outbreak of 2037?"

Silence, then, "Uh, yeah, I guess they were."

"Weren't you the consummate bad boy, breaking rules even as a kid?"

"There were no—"

Whatever he'd been about to say, he obviously decided against it, because he cut himself off, fell silent, and walked on, his boots slogging through the inch-deep water that covered the floor.

She thought the subject dropped, and then he spoke again. "It was the fleas that caused the plague. My rat had nothing to do with it."

Obviously. He was two-thirds of a century too young to have lived through the plague.

His mention of his childhood pet made her think of her own childhood, the days that blended into months and then years, just her and Wizard and Yuriko, and the computer that had raised them. They definitely had not kept pets, rats or otherwise. The only living things in that lab had been her and her siblings. Facts had been their life, their world . . . just the lab and each other and facts. They learned languages, math, literature, science. Anything the computer could offer.

But not emotion. That wasn't in the lesson plan. They'd been designed—engineered—to have none.

The only reason she knew about emotion was because she'd spent the last half of her life picking up and feeling everyone else's, snippets that came at her like satellite channels flipped very fast. Fear. Hate. Love. The emotions of fellow prisoners that flowed to her in snatches, until she'd learned to control the current and let them in only when she willed it.

"You know, the Waste used to be one of the world's few rat-free zones," Tristan said, his tone casual, his body language on high alert as he checked each dip in the wall, every shadow, every branching corridor.

He was back to the rats. It appeared that once he latched on to a topic, he didn't let go so easily. A man of dogged intent.

"Uh-huh."

"Just before the Second Noble War a soybean freighter ran aground in the Bering Sea. The oil spill was cleaned up in a matter of days, but the rat spill couldn't be contained." He glanced at her over his shoulder. "And like magic, no more rat-free zone."

He didn't tell her anything she didn't already know, but it did strike her as odd that *he* knew it. She was a little stunted in the people-skills department, but even she knew that the history of rats wasn't usually number one on the recommended reading lists.

She frowned, wondering at the point of his story.

"You sound like the tour guide at the arboretum in New Edmonton," she said.

"Yeah, I guess I do." He glanced back at her, kept walking. "But my point"—ah, so there *was* a point—"is that there is no action that does not elicit a reaction. Everything links in an unbroken chain."

Great. So he was a philosophical killer. "You mean like twisting a guy's neck elicits his death?"

"Kind of." He didn't pause, didn't look back, but somehow she got the impression he hadn't liked to be reminded of that. "So when did you visit the arboretum?"

"Two months ago." The memory of that teased her senses. She remembered the lush scent of greenery, such a wonderful thing. "I wanted to see a real orange tree. It was an amazing experience. I was so enthralled that I snuck back a second time, bypassed the one-visit-per-year rule. I just needed to smell that scent again, you know?"

His shoulders tensed and he picked up the pace.

"What?" she asked.

"The New Government Order razed the arboretum last week. The new guy in charge said the trees carried the potential threat of disease. That they harbored viroids."

Razed the arboretum. The horror of that hit her, a brutal blow. She swallowed, forced words past the tightness in her throat.

"The trees . . . all of them? *Razed* it? You mean there's nothing left?"

"Yeah."

"You said the new guy in charge. Who?" But she already knew. The new guy was the snake who'd slithered fastest from under a rock after Duncan Bane was killed.

"Guy by the name of Gavin Ward." His tone had a hard edge as he said it.

Bastard. Slagging bastard. Ward had burned down that arboretum because he'd found out she'd been there.

It wasn't imagination or paranoia that made her so certain. She knew it, gut deep.

She must have been flagged by the feature-recognition security when she'd snuck in that second time. And he must have been notified because he'd put out a bulletin on her. If she'd stopped to think about it, she would have anticipated something like that, and she was angry at herself that she hadn't figured on it.

Ward had annihilated all those trees—something so perfect, so beautiful, so rare—as a message to her.

The message was the same one he'd conveyed when he had made her watch while he vivisected a man riddled with strange tumors. He'd offered his prey no anesthetic, and with her ability to feel others' emotions, sense their thoughts, Tatiana had lived every nuance of that horror right along with the guy strapped to the table.

Ward had wanted her to hurt then. He wanted her to hurt now.

And he wanted her to know he could exert control over her, even from a distance.

She blew out a breath and quickened her pace to catch up to Tristan as he turned right. The walls of the tunnel had a greenish hue, cast by lumilights placed every dozen paces or so. Old-style lumilights. Just like the old-style scooters and clothes. This whole place was at least a decade out of date, as though it had been buried and forgotten.

Just as she'd been buried and forgotten.

Hidden away and forgotten. By the world. But not by Ward. He hadn't forgotten her.

Slag. She had to stop letting her thoughts run in that direction.

Focusing on Tristan's broad back, she followed him, looking only at him, not the narrow walls or the dark passages that branched out in an intricate maze. She'd be glad to be done with her business here and get the hell out. She couldn't bear to be underground, to be confined.

And she couldn't bear to be out in the endless stretch of the Waste.

Which kind of left her between an ice floe and a cold place.

Ahead of her, Tristan paused, held up a hand, cocked his head a little to one side as though searching for a particular sound. She froze, listening, and heard nothing but a distant scrabbling that she figured must be the rats.

After a moment, he tipped his index finger forward, indicating they should move on, but said nothing.

A pet rat. A white one.

He was a conundrum.

Curious, she studied his back. They were moving faster now, and she liked watching him, the way he moved, not a bit of wasted energy. Tight. Fluid.

She sucked in a breath as realization kicked her. She wanted to solve the riddle, unravel each thread of the tangled mass. Figure out who Tristan was.

Why? Because he was handsome?

She'd seen handsome men before and hadn't been particularly drawn, other than to appreciate the view.

Because she couldn't read him, not his thoughts or his emotions?

She didn't think that was it either. She'd encountered people whose minds had been closed to her—not many, but a few—and she had never wasted a thought on them one way or the other.

No, it was because Tristan smiled at her sarcasm. He got her humor. Because his cold, cold eyes warmed just for her when she made a quip or caught his gaze.

And because he was interesting.

There was something controlled and distant about him, something dark and buried. She'd seen it flicker in his gaze, then die away. At the same time, he was charming and easy and open.

He was a puzzle that the logical, analytical part of her wanted to solve.

The scrabbling sound came at her again, louder, closer. Something was out there, and it wasn't just rats. Something bigger.

Again, she scanned left to right, a slow sweep. Nothing.

Ahead of her, Tristan kept moving, but the set of his jaw when he glanced back at her made her uneasy. He felt it too, and his pace picked up even more until they both moved at an easy jog.

Her senses on high alert, she looked left to right, a set pattern, pausing for a second as her gaze passed over the opening to a cutoff.

Again, the scraping sound jumped out at her, something dragging along the floor or the wall, something not quite right. She spun to the left, heard heartbeats—not Tristan's, not her own—too fast, too loud. The heartbeats of whatever was out there.

The scent of excitement—*hunger*—carried on the air, sharp and biting. Her senses switched into high gear, preternatural calm mixing with heightened awareness. This was what she had been bred for, what she had been designed and trained to do. Fight. Kill if she must. Win at all costs.

Something was hunting them, and she was slagging sick of being treated like prey.

"Tristan," she said. But he already knew. Whatever he'd been watching for the entire trip along this dank, dim corridor had been watching for them, as well.

"We have a problem, Ana. You might wanna haul out that pretty little shooter."

She'd already flipped her Setti9 out of its wrist holster. *Ana.* The only other person who had called her Ana was Raina, a girl who'd been dead for years and years. She wondered that Tristan had chosen to call her that.

"Keep moving," he said, reaching around to the small of his back to tunnel beneath the loose layers of his robes and drag free a combat knife. Steel combo-edge blade. Black. Plastitech handle with traditional Japanese cord wrap. Resin impregnated.

"Nice," she said.

"Necessary," he corrected, darkly soft, and something in his tone made her think that he would prefer not to carry a weapon at all.

There was a dichotomy here, because from the way he held the knife—like it was an extension of himself—he had practiced and trained with it. He knew his way around that weapon, and she wondered why he disliked it so.

Questions for another time.

"So what am I watching for?" she asked, her gaze passing over walls and shadows.

"Big rats"—he pushed her ahead of him through the tunnel—"and monsters in the dark."

Not exactly the clear and concise explanation she might have hoped for. Monsters in the dark. Right. She huffed out a quick breath.

Her feet pounded along the cracked concrete floor, spraying water as she went. Behind her, she could hear the hammering of Tristan's boots, but no other footsteps. Either they weren't being followed, or whatever followed them didn't have feet.

What the hell was it with her and the way she attracted trouble, like a carcass calling to a starving wolf pack? She couldn't even get a damned hydrogen fill and a hot meal without getting attacked.

"Left," Tristan ordered. Then, "Right."

Tatiana followed his instructions, turning where he bid, running straight when he said nothing, and every step of the way, he was right behind her.

Not that she trusted him. That would be a leap. If he was doing this to try to confuse her, to ensure that she would be so muddled by their circuitous route she'd never find her way clear, he had a surprise in store. Having run it once, she could run it again, blindfolded, right back to her scooter. Her sense of direction was pure, and her ability to memorize a route complete.

She breathed deep. The scent that hovered in the damp tunnels was strong, heavy. Nasty. Like dead fish that had been out in the sun too long. The smell of putrefaction.

"Hold up." Tristan's deep voice came from behind her as they passed through a narrow oval opening framed in steel.

Pausing, she turned and watched as he rammed home the metal door, spun the lock-mech and leaned in to allow for the retinal scan. Like the one in the elevator, the locking system was old technology, produced decades past.

There were flaws in these old systems. They were vulnerable. Retinal and iris pattern scanners could be tricked by fabricated lenses. Old-style voice recognition was susceptible to ambient noise. Biometric identifiers could be hijacked. All these issues had been overcome with current lock-mech technology, but what she'd seen here didn't qualify as current.

She noted the code, different from the one he'd used in the elevator. The man was careful. Of what?

"This way," Tristan ordered, and she allowed him to push her ahead of him. "There's an access tunnel that links with this one. We're not clear yet."

"Clear of what? And if you tell me rats again, I'll shoot you."

"Things from your nightmares," he said, and he wasn't smiling. "Move."

"Well, don't you have the whole enigmatic thing down to a fine art?" she muttered, and took off down the corridor.

The lumilights here were in poor repair, most of them dead, a few flickering weakly against the darkness, casting sickly green shadows to dance along the walls.

Tristan hadn't been particularly forthcoming on what the hell they were running from, but Tatiana could hear their pursuers pounding through the tunnels behind them. Guess they'd found that access route he'd mentioned.

Falling in at her back, Tristan used his body as a human shield.

What was it with this guy and his old-fashioned chivalry?

She was the one who was genetically enhanced, the one who would heal within hours of injury. But she wasn't about to share that information with him right now as an explanation of why it ought to be her bringing up the rear.

Her gut instinct was to stop and fight. She had her AT450, her Setti9, and a couple of lovely little knives if it came down to close confines. Failing all that, she could just use her hands.

Setting her heels, she stopped dead. Tristan slammed against her back, his breath rushing out in a rapid whoosh.

"What the hell?" he muttered, his hand coming forward to splay across her back and shove her forward. When she held her own, not moving a centimeter, he pushed harder and repeated, "What the hell?"

"I have this thing about running away," she said, spinning to face him. "I don't do it unless I know for certain that I have to. Actually, I've only ever done it once in my life. I figure it's better to face down the threat and kill it fast, because otherwise, whatever you're running from just might catch you when you least want it to."

"*What?*" He shook his head, his eyes glittering in the darkness, his tone hiding nothing of his incredulity and disgust. "Are you out of your mind? You don't even know what we're up against."

She shrugged, dropped to one knee, freeing her AT450 as she moved, hauling it into firing position in a fluid sweep.

"So enlighten me. What are we up against?" She shot him a glance. "Or you can just keep running, if you want."

His lip curled as he stared down at her, and he looked as though he was struggling for control. She thought he might be battling the urge to haul her to her feet and drag her off. Like a Neanderthal.

Good luck.

"The air I exhale is inhaled by my insane companion. The darkness that wreaths me, wreaths my insane companion," he muttered, clearly talking to himself rather than to her. "The danger that stalks me, stalks my insane companion."

It was a fair assumption that he considered her to be the insane companion.

CHAPTER TEN

"Is your aim good enough to keep us both alive?" Tristan asked, bending over her, his words low and hard against her ear.

In that instant, Tatiana realized that he didn't have a plasgun. None of the people she'd seen outside had plasguns. Which explained his question. He was standing at her back, hoping she could hit what she pointed at.

Given the reverse situation—him with a plasgun, her with none—she doubted she'd be as trusting.

What *was* he thinking? Her aim was more than good enough—but he had no way of knowing that.

With a hiss of frustration, she flipped her Setti9 through the air, heard the satisfying slap of metal against his palm as he caught it.

"Aim for the head," he said, straightening. With him upright and her on one knee, they made an efficient two-tiered defensive wall. "And don't be surprised if they keep moving for a bit. Only way to stop them dead"—he paused—"so to speak, is to sever the brain stem."

Nice. She shot him a glance. "Thanks for the advice."

He hefted the Setti9. "Thanks for sharing."

"You're—" She never had a chance to finish her reply because a dark mass came at them out of the blackness, crowding down the narrow corridor like some sort of huge, multilimbed spider.

Inhuman cries and snarls surrounded them, echoing off the walls, crashing down on them. No weapons. They had no weapons.

"Don't fire," she yelled. "They have no—"

She broke off as her skin prickled and stung, and she realized that they were being pelted by a hail of jagged metal shards, blown through primitive tubes.

From behind her, she thought she heard Tristan mutter, "You were saying . . ."

Tatiana fired. Fired again. She hit what she aimed at, but the thing just kept coming, breaking away from the group to lurch forward on its own.

She saw now that they had knives, pipes, even crude axes. Primitive weapons, but weapons nonetheless.

They were still meters down the corridor, but the stink was so strong it nearly made her gag. She'd smelled rank and rotting things before. But not like this. Never like this. They smelled like they were dead—for quite some time.

"Whoa . . ." She aimed, fired again, took off the top of the lead . . . um . . . *guy's* head.

With *guy* being a relative term. Overgrown frontal eminences on either side of the forehead, like horns. Pronounced glabella and supercilliary arches. The combined effect was feral facial features. Add to the mix significant muscular hypertrophy, the overpowering smell, and the white foam that collected around its mouth, and it was a recipe for a very bad thing.

Brains and blood splattered against the wall at its back and it kept coming, kept moving, feet shuffling forward, arms reaching.

"Say hello to my little friends," Tristan muttered.

"Human?"

He peeled off a shot, took out another one in front, slowing down the mass of them. The pack snarled and surged.

"Depends on your definition."

That was definitely not an answer she liked. "Explain."

"They were Reavers, which made them barely human."

Were. Past tense. *Slag.*

She surged to her feet and blew a hole the size of her fist in the middle of the next one's chest. Didn't stop him. Barely even slowed him down. Again, the pack snarled.

Tatiana narrowed her eyes, shot again. Same result. The flare of plas-shot seemed to drive them into a frenzy.

"They don't like the light," she said, calm, controlled. Her thoughts spun with horror, but her enhanced physiology was in soldier mode. Focus on the task, the mission. Complete the mission. "It makes them attack all the more aggressively."

"Photophobia. Fuck." Tristan leaped forward, grabbed a creature by its hair, rammed his knife deep in the back of its neck, then heaved the flailing body at the others, using it as a weapon of sorts.

"Retreat," he snarled, breathing heavily.

One of the creatures threw itself forward, caught at Tatiana's foot, tried to drag her down, tearing at her like a beast. She kicked at it. Shot it.

It sank its teeth into her boot.

She fired her Bolinger one-handed at the encroaching mass, used her free hand to snag her blade from the small of her back. With a grunt, she slammed it down into the back of the thing's neck at the base of its skull.

It twitched, flopped. Lay still.

She rolled it with a forceful shove of her boot and turned her attention to the next attacker and the next.

"Don't say I didn't warn you." Tristan's voice carried to her through the melee.

Warn her? He called that warning her? Slagging hell.

They couldn't stay here much longer. The group was slowly gaining the advantage, their success grounded in sheer numbers, and the fact that plasguns didn't stop them dead. In these close confines, they couldn't risk a higher setting; the resulting blast might incinerate *them* along with their attackers.

As she or Tristan took one down, the others simply climbed over it and moved forward along the passage, their advance accompanied by odd sounds. Suction. Crunching.

Stealing a second to glance at Tristan, she opened her mouth to ask, then decided that maybe she didn't want to know.

The Setti9 sat easy in his hand, his movements smooth and confident as he aimed and hit the next creature in line dead center of its chest. It kept coming.

"Autorhythmic, self-excitatory action of skeletal muscle fibers," Tristan explained, his breath coming in harsh rasps. Tatiana peeled off another shot and they backed up together along the passage, her own lungs working a little harder than usual. "Their muscles keep contracting even though the brain's gone and there's no higher thought process generating the action."

Well, that answered her earlier ponderings over whether he was a tech or a scientist. Definitely a scientist. One who knew how to kill both with his bare hands and a plas-gun.

A multifaceted kinda guy.

Problem was, he was talking about self-excitation of muscle, and skeletal muscle just didn't possess that capacity. It had to be the result of some sort of modification.

The situation reeked of Ward's handiwork.

"We need to fall back. And we've got a good opportunity while they . . . snack," Tristan said, his voice low and firm. It wasn't a request. "We'll take twenty paces, switch positions. On my word . . . go."

Tatiana turned and retreated while Tristan offered cover, then whirled and shot to cover Tristan as he took his turn sprinting down the hallway. He dropped to one knee in front of her to form again their two-tiered defense.

A momentary disorientation touched her. She was used to working alone. Always alone. Trusting a stranger to offer cover was way outside her comfort zone. But she did. Trust him. Sort of.

"Another twenty paces," Tristan said. "Go."

His world down here. His rules.

She went. He followed. Again, they fell easily into formation. The odd slurping and crunching sounds she'd heard earlier echoed along the corridor.

"Slag," she breathed, getting a clear visual as bodies shifted and jockeyed for position. "*Slag.*"

Their pursuers weren't exactly hot on their tail. They were busy ripping their downed comrades to shreds.

"They need a large amount of protein, and ions—sodium, potassium, calcium—for the channels of their muscle fibers to function at optimum capacity." He rose, nudged her back a few steps. "Bone is an excellent source of dietary calcium."

"Yeah . . . so is sim-steak. And it's a whole lot less vile." She'd heard that Reavers ate their foes, but she could have done without the up-close-and-personal, front-row seat. And she'd kind of thought they'd cook 'em, first.

Tristan rose, turned to face her. "I suggest we beat a hasty retreat while they are occupied and discuss this at a more convenient time. Let's move."

Closing his hand around her upper arm, he hauled her farther along the corridor. His manhandling didn't sit well with her, but she'd choose her time for battle. A moment later, he thrust her through another oval portal, following close behind. Slamming the metal hatch shut, he keyed in a lock-mech code and leaned in for a retinal scan.

Then he . . . *relaxed*. Visibly and completely, as though tension were a cloak he could drop at will. He rolled his shoulders, shifted his feet, his breath coming slow and deep and even through his nose.

Only, he wasn't just standing there, she realized. There was something very specific about his posture: shoulders loose, arms loose, eyes closed, knees slightly bent and pushed a little outward.

And for a second, she felt like he wasn't there, like she was standing alone next to the sealed hatch, and he was somewhere else entirely.

The fine hairs at her nape prickled and rose.

On a deep inhalation, he opened his eyes, night blue, and she smiled, a little relieved. For an instant, she'd thought she might have to heave him over her shoulder and cart him out of here.

The whole odd episode had lasted maybe twenty seconds.

"Hey," she said. "Welcome back."

"How did you know I was gone?"

"I just"—she shrugged—"did." Reaching over, she took her Setti9 from his hand, eased it back into her wrist holster. Then she slid the AT450 between her shoulder blades, gave a little wriggle to make it sit more comfortably.

She cocked her thumb over her shoulder toward the hatch. "So . . . the flare of light from the plasguns incites them. Photophobia. That's why you and your friends seem to be lacking in equipment."

"Light is a torment for them, yes." Tristan shot her an enigmatic look and arched a dark brow. "And I assure you, I am lacking nothing. My equipment is right where it ought to be."

She blinked, smiled despite herself. "Jerk."

He grinned back, but then his smile slowly faded and he reached out and brushed his thumb along her cheek. It came away smeared in blood.

"Are you hurt anywhere else?"

That made her laugh. He called a scratch on her cheek hurt? He had no idea.

But the way he was looking at her, like he'd wade back out there into the fray to avenge her, made something inside her do a strange little dance.

Whoa, slap that back and stomp it into dust.

"What the hell is going on here?" she asked, a tad sharper than she'd intended. "Maybe start with an explanation of what that was out there on the ice?"

"Murder. Justice." Tristan's mouth curved. Not a nice smile. "Mercy."

"How incredibly informative. At least tell me what the hell was going on in that corridor, with those . . . What exactly were we just running from?"

He shrugged. "You saw them. You tell me."

"Do you ever offer a direct answer, Tristan?"

"Some questions have no direct answers."

She drummed her fingertips along her thigh. "Fine, let's make this simple. Who are *you*?"

"Don't you know the rules?" he asked, whisper soft,

taking a step toward her. "This is the Waste. You don't ask about people's names or where they're from or who they once were. Don't ask. Don't offer."

"Yeah, I know, but you can't blame a girl for trying."

"Can't I?"

His gaze locked on hers, blue and hot as the heart of a flame, direct, and for some reason unnerving. Because when he looked at her like that, so intent, so focused, she felt like the world was doing a sideways tilt and she was tilting with it.

"Christ, you're beautiful," he murmured and took another step toward her, close, so close, the edges of cloth that draped him brushing against her hand.

She had his full attention, his focused attention, and he had hers. Demanded hers, with just a look.

In that instant, nothing else mattered, not even a cytoplast blast.

The urge to touch him made her hand twitch. High cheekbones, straight shot of jaw shaded by a day's stubble, lean angles, gorgeous, sexy mouth. This close to him, she could see the fine scar that bisected his right eyebrow. She wanted to smooth the tip of her finger over it.

Beautiful. She wanted to repeat his words, say to him what he had said to her. Because it was the truth. The pure and simple truth. He was beautiful.

Enigmatic.

Dangerous.

He dipped his head, his face close to her hair. The soft sound of his inhalation made her shiver.

She was already on an adrenaline high, and the heat of his body, the scent of his skin, only pushed her higher. The awareness of him she'd been feeling since she'd first seen him at Abbott's store swamped her now, a hot tide.

Fast, too fast. A freak storm bearing down on her.

It dawned on her then that even though his thoughts had been closed to her thus far, in *this* she could read him, feel him, his attraction and her own, blending and melding. She didn't know which emotion was hers and which was his.

He caught the ends of her hair, twined the strands through his strong, blunt fingers, her hair dark against his skin.

Too fast, she thought again, stunned. But she didn't move. She just stared at his hand and waited, wondering how they'd gone from battling monsters to battling lust in the span of a heartbeat.

Her gaze shot to his as she drew a sharp breath. He smelled like fresh air. Like the arctic wind and the midday sun. Like snow. She remembered her first taste of freedom, the first time she'd been allowed out by her jailers, a bright, cold day, the air hitting her, leaving her dizzy after the dank confines of her underground cell.

Tristan smelled like that, like freedom.

She made an awkward little laugh, averted her face, tried to get herself back on even ground. A compliment. He had called her beautiful.

He moved fast, his hand coming up to plant flat against the wall just above her left shoulder.

A flash of almost-perfect white teeth, the front two overlapping ever so slightly. So sexy. She wanted to run her tongue along the ridge those two teeth made, wanted to know the feel of his mouth, his lips.

Why? Why him?

"I'm sorry," he said, and kissed her. Just like that. Lowered his mouth to hers, his body held away from her, his weight resting on his outstretched arm and flattened palm.

He brushed her mouth with his, lightly, then harder, a

press of his lips and then the swipe of his tongue, so sure of himself, as though he knew she would open to him.

She did. She opened her mouth, took him inside her, and she couldn't say why, didn't care why. She only knew that she wanted to, wanted his kiss on a level so primal she hadn't even known it was there. Not until this second, this frozen second.

I'm sorry, he'd said. It didn't feel like he was sorry for a damned thing. It felt hot and deep, electric pleasure, his tongue in her mouth and hers in his, twining, tasting.

There was an edge of desperation mixed with the white-hot flare of desire.

Then it was done. Over.

He pulled away, his breathing a little ragged, leaving her lips wet, her nerves humming, her heart hammering hard against her ribs.

Tristan turned down a dim corridor, aware of the sound of Ana's footsteps close at his heels. He was glad he didn't need to face her or make idle conversation right now, glad he could drag his sorry ass down the narrow tunnels and pretend to focus wholly on the task at hand rather than on her sweet mouth and her smooth curves and that gorgeous ass.

With *pretend* being the key concept.

Damn. He'd tossed aside every pretense of sanity and control, and he'd kissed her. Worse, he wanted to turn around right now, haul her hard against him, and do it again.

Everything about her drew him like the electrostatic attraction of an ionic bond.

He exhaled sharply and took a quick right. He had already locked down three doors—keying in codes and doing retinal scans—while she guarded his back. Posture rigid, gaze alert, she kept a close eye on their surroundings, her AT450 in her hand.

She was trained. Every graceful, athletic line of her body screamed it. So had the way she'd fallen in—no argument, no discussion, putting aside the kiss and its implications—to do what he said needed to be done. No doubt in his mind. Someone had put a lot of time and effort into turning her into a soldier.

"Who did you fight for?" he asked, pausing to slam shut another metal hatch and key in the code for the lockmech. "New Government Order? The rebels?" She definitely was not an ice pirate.

For a second, she said nothing, leaving him to wonder if she had heard him.

"Myself," she said at length. "I fight for myself."

Her choice of tense didn't escape him. She was still engaged in some sort of battle.

Leaning in, he waited for the retinal scan. It felt like it took ten minutes rather than ten seconds. Damn, this technology was antiquated.

"Who'd you train under?"

Again that hesitation. Then she said, "My brother."

His gut dropped. She had a brother. Someone who would miss her, wonder what had happened to her, mourn her. More ruined lives to add to the tally.

"So who trained *you*?" Guess she figured turnabout was fair play.

United States Army Special Forces. Not an answer he'd offer. Not an answer she'd believe. The United States had dissolved more than fifty years before, along with every other country in the world, replaced by the Northern Waste, the Equatorial Band, Africa and the Southern

Hemisphere. Four chunks of land. Four corrupt branches of government. And a whole lot of human suffering.

"I just picked up stuff here and there," he temporized. "You got any other family?"

"No. My sister . . . died."

There was a story there, but now wasn't the time to ask.

"You mentioned a brother . . . ?"

"I don't even know if he's still alive. We haven't seen each other"—she blew out a sharp breath, and he glanced over his shoulder to find her staring straight ahead, her expression flat and cool, at odds with the pain in her tone—"in a very long while." She laughed humorlessly and gave a short gasp. "I have no idea why I told you that."

He rested his hand on the keypad, waiting for lockdown confirmation. "I asked."

A part of him wished he hadn't. Her admission got to him, touched a chord of empathy he wished he could sever. He hadn't seen his family in a very long while either, but unlike her, he had certainty on his side in regard to their fate. Everyone in his family was dead. And buried. A very long time ago.

He'd tried so damned hard to save them, but the plague had come. No, not just come. He'd brought it to them because he hadn't understood that he could. Hadn't understood how his body had been changed, modified. The plague hadn't even touched him, but he'd brought it to them, and he hadn't been able to find a way to save them.

Standing by their graves, four tidy headstones, he'd wondered why he alone lived, why his DNA differed so vastly from theirs.

One more failing to add to his list. He'd signed on for the experiments knowing that they were meant to design a better soldier. He was a scientist, a researcher. He should have recognized the changes in himself. What had he thought the government was injecting into him? Saline?

Now, years later, he understood at least a part of the reason he had survived when his comrades had died.

His telomeres—little stretches of DNA at the ends of his chromosomes—never shortened, no matter how many times his cells divided. His cells didn't break down, which meant he looked as young now as he had in his army days. He was also immune to pathogenic organisms, his defenses honed to a level that far surpassed other humans.

A half century later and he'd crawled only millimeters closer to understanding what had been done and why. A half century later, and this time he hadn't just brought the plague to those he cared about; this time he'd created it.

"This place is like a labyrinth," Tatiana muttered as he finished his task and turned fully to face her.

Mistake. Big mistake. Looking at her made him want to kiss her again. Kiss her, touch her, comfort her. And that was just plain ludicrous, because he'd never met a more contained, self-sufficient woman, one who definitely didn't appear to need comfort.

Maybe that was the attraction. She was this incredible combination of waif and warrior.

What the hell had he been thinking, kissing her like that?

He hadn't been. Thinking. Instead, he'd acted wholly out of character, without thought or reason, because of her amazing eyes, her beautiful mouth, her tougher-than-tungsten-carbide veneer.

He'd wanted a taste. Just one taste.

Looking to a point beyond her right shoulder, he

hesitated, then said, "I thought about you. After that night. At Abbott's."

"Did you?" The question wasn't rhetorical. She sounded . . . surprised . . . and a little anxious.

"Yeah."

"Why?"

Now wasn't that the question.

"Why?" he echoed, stalling over the answer, not certain he even had an answer. The memory of her had strutted in and out of his thoughts, the image of the intriguing girl who'd come out at the top of a bargain with Abbott, then gone outside to take down two gun truckers. He'd thought about her, wondered if his recollections were accurate, thought that maybe he'd try to search her out once he got things here under control. If he got things under control.

And he wasn't about to tell her any of that.

"Yeah . . ." He scraped his palm along the back of his neck. "I thought about your, uh, Morgat. Great machine. Fastest scooter out there. The hydroplane mode is pure genius."

The corners of her mouth curled up in a little smile that wasn't a smile, so self-contained. "My Morgat is indeed a worthy vehicle."

It made him want to kiss her again.

Judging by the way she'd wrapped her arms around him and damned near shoved her tongue down his throat, she wouldn't offer a whisper of protest at a repeat performance.

Exactly when in the hell had he lost his mind? Lost it to a puzzle of a girl with a plasgun strapped to her back, another at her wrist, and a knife in her boot. And damn if that didn't make her all the more attractive, the fact that she could obviously take care of herself just fine.

Only, she couldn't take care of herself against an enemy she couldn't see, a pathogen that had entered her body through a tiny cut on her hand. She'd been splattered with the dead guy's blood. Doomed.

His gut twisted.

One more thing to haunt him in the darkest hours of the night when he strove for peace and found only regret.

He met her gaze, almost got lost in liquid mercury, forced himself to focus on the task at hand. She'd made a comment way back when, before their conversation had taken a slippery slide into things far too personal.

Something about a labyrinth . . .

"So, yeah, these tunnels are like a maze." He turned and started walking again, ducking through a low arch into a utility tunnel. "If you map them out, there's almost seven hundred yuales of twisting, turning passages down here. It was built to be an energy facility with enough housing for the necessary crew. An underground city."

Nicely done. Smooth, suave change of topic, he thought with an edge of cynicism.

She didn't press the issue, and he was glad.

They were silent for a few moments, and then they reached the cutoff he was looking for. There were no mounted lumilights in this section, so he tunneled his hand beneath the loose folds of thermal material that draped him and fished a portable light out of the utility harness that crisscrossed his chest. He kept a sharp eye on his surroundings, his senses attuned for the faintest hint of movement or sound.

"Do what you need to do. I've got your back," she said from very close beside him, her voice low and husky, her breath fanning his cheek. If he turned he could—

Whoa. That was not a place to let his thoughts wander.

"I thought that you watch no one's back but your own."

Silence, then, "Yeah, well, I guess that teaming up back there changed things a little. For now."

Her grudging tone made him laugh, until she leaned forward and slugged him in the shoulder. Then he stopped laughing and went back to battling the urge to kiss her again.

Stepping forward, he laid his hand on the wall and pressed against the brick.

"I can set a charge here." The tunnel was an access route to the newer part of the underground facility that housed the lab built two years ago by Gavin Ward, a man with unlimited resources and no conscience.

Tristan stared down the passage, the glow cast by his lumilight fading to black. Almost everything he needed was just down this corridor, so fucking close.

It might as well have been a million yuales away.

Because Viktor and Yasha hadn't brought the equipment he needed. Worse, they hadn't brought the samples.

Which left him shit out of luck, because he couldn't set up a makeshift laboratory here in the older part of the facility. And he couldn't leave the route open to the deserted lab in the new part of the facility.

Which left his comrades, his friends, as good as dead.

Without a lab, there would be no cure.

"You plan to blow this tunnel to seal out those"—she hesitated, then chose to use his wording, her tone touched by humor—"monsters in the dark?"

"Seal them out. Seal us in." Blasting the access route was a double-edged sword. It would block his route to the lab, but it would buy his people a measure of safety from the diseased Reavers. There were never any perfect answers, only choices that rippled and swelled to touch other choices.

He glanced at Ana, his gaze meeting hers, then sliding away. He could kill her.

Or he could let her die a slow and unbearably painful death.

Either way, he was a bastard. And either way, she was dead. What a choice.

If he left the access route unblocked, the things they were hiding from would kill them.

If he blew this and all the other access routes, he might not be able to get back to the lab. And even if he did make it back, what was the likelihood it hadn't been trashed by the mutated Reavers?

It wouldn't be long before his people began to turn into exactly what they were hiding from.

He glanced at Ana. She was one of his people now. His responsibility.

Eventually, he'd come clean, share most of this information with her. But not until he had her locked down tight, no hope of escape. Because if he let her escape, she'd carry death with her to the whole damned Waste.

Consequences. Drop a pebble. Watch the ripples. And always remember that even when they disappear in the distance, they can still cause effects far, far away.

Hauling his lip-com from where it hung around his neck, he flipped it into position.

"Lamia, you listening?"

"I'm always listening," came her jaunty reply, but under the surface Tristan heard the sadness, the edge of despair. She'd come here to work communications and send money home to her family. What she'd earned was a one-way ticket to an early grave. They all had.

"Keep everyone away from Access 19."

"Loud and clear, Tris." He could hear her fingers flying

over the keypad as she checked the location of every researcher in the facility.

After a minute, the com crackled and she said, "Everyone's accounted for, and the only people near 19 are you and your guest."

His guest. He cut a glance at Ana, wishing it were that simple. *Guest* was such a temporary term, and her stay here had been extended indefinitely. She just didn't know it yet.

"How does she know where everyone is?" Ana asked.

Tristan glanced at her. "How'd you hear that?"

Her lips curved in that sexy little smile that wasn't a smile. "I have hearing like a bat."

He opened his mouth, paused, made a short, huffing laugh. "You can hear ultrasonic frequency?"

"Think of it as a figure of speech."

"Fair enough." He studied her for a moment, intrigued. "How do you know about bats? They've been almost extinct for over fifty years. Just a few species left in the Equatorial Band."

"I'm well-read." She shrugged, glanced away, then back again. "You need to stop looking at me like that."

"Like what?"

"Like you want to back me up against the wall and stick your tongue in my mouth."

Whoa. Yeah. He probably was looking at her just like that. And he was oddly pleased that she'd noticed.

"That obvious?"

"More than." She turned away, studied their surroundings with a careful eye, then faced him once more, apparently satisfied.

"So how do you track everyone's location down here?"

If she was willing to change the subject, so was he. Definitely.

"Microchips." There was a homing microchip embedded in every single one of them, a precaution Ward had insisted upon. Tristan had been appalled at the time, but now he was glad for it. The chips made the task of maintaining an isolated environment that much easier, because he could track the exact location of every single person down here, researchers and Reavers alike. "The chips emit a radio signal received by nodes embedded in the walls throughout the facility"—he gestured at the walls all around them—"and each signal carries individual identifying characteristics."

"Interesting. My reference to bats was apropos, then. Your microchips are like a form of echolocation." Her gaze skimmed over him, cool, impersonal . . . almost. There was a spark there that told him she wasn't as composed as she wanted him to believe.

"Where do you wear your chip?" she asked.

Wear it?

"I, uh, have a utility harness." It wasn't exactly a lie. He *was* wearing the harness. But there was no microchip in it. The chip was under his skin, just like everyone else's.

Sometime soon, he'd have to get one implanted in her.

And sometime soon, he'd have to slice his own out, again. He'd dug it out before he'd gone to Abbott's looking for the two morons who were supposed to deliver his missing goods. He'd put it back in when he returned a week past. He hadn't wanted Ward to know he'd left.

But next time, he'd slice it out for good.

She was staring at him, her liquid-silver eyes bright, almost glowing.

"You know," she mused, "heart rate and respiratory rate are not considered accurate indicators of lying. Horizontal eye movement is a much better predictor in approximately thirty percent of subjects."

"And your point?"

She shrugged. "I have only my instincts that tell me you aren't being completely truthful. No proof. Only my instincts."

Damned good instincts.

CHAPTER ELEVEN

Gavin Ward studied his environment from the cab of his gleaming black rig. Thom was in the driver's seat, and Gavin had three more of his men riding with him. Another three in the back acted as hidden snipers—a precaution he doubted he would need, despite driving into the dubious hospitality of a group of Siberian ice pirates.

He had something they wanted very badly, and killing him wouldn't get it for them.

Unfortunately, they had something he wanted as well.

Which left him in a less-than-ideal situation. He preferred to approach the bargaining table with the scale more heavily weighted in his favor.

He shoved open the door and climbed down from the rig, aware that his every move was watched by the pirates, who sat drinking and laughing. Aware, too, that he was well guarded by the hidden snipers in his trailer, the most highly skilled in the Waste, their plasguns at the ready in concealed openings.

Thom stepped up beside him, Bolinger AT950 in hand, the muzzle pointed at the ground. Enough of a message, so that the Reavers would take note, but not umbrage.

Gavin adjusted his hood, using the action to mask his quick perusal of the camp.

Located in a valley that offered a modicum of shelter from the wind and the weather, the camp was surrounded on all sides by sloping hills. At the crest of each rise were scrap-metal monstrosities, gun turrets set about the perimeter, each manned by two guards.

The Reavers might be brutal and feral, but they were also careful.

Smoke rose from a massive bonfire set at the center of the valley. The flames roared and hissed, painting the snow-covered hills in flickering tongues of red and gold. The smell of charred wood and roasting meat was thick in the air. Given their well-documented dietary proclivities, he couldn't help wondering exactly what they were roasting. His preference was that they not invite him to dine.

Gavin glanced about in distaste. Primitive setting. Primitive people. He would prefer never to leave his pristine laboratories in Port Uranium or Neo-Tokyo.

After the debacle with the secret lab near the Maori Talisman, he tried to avoid the northernmost parts of the Waste.

But a bit of social interaction with this particular little band of sordid humanity was a necessity. They had ended up with stolen equipment that he wanted returned, and he had no intention of leaving without it.

A ring of domed huts—dented sheets of metal, bolted together and covered with animal hides—surrounded the massive fire. To one side, parked beneath towering evergreens whose boughs drooped under the weight of the snow, were the hulking lumps of twisted and plated metal that passed for vehicles in the ice pirate camp.

Plascannon rigs. Three of them. And a dozen or so smaller trucks—with *smaller* being a relative term—that were equally ugly, and only slightly less deadly. They were decorated with bleached skulls and outfitted with plasgun turrets and enough plating to stop a phosphorous mine.

Sandwiched between two plascannon rigs was a filthy black truck, no plating. The letters on the front had been torn off, but the marks left in the dirt clearly spelled out the name JANSON.

Gavin didn't let his gaze linger. No sense warning them that the truck was of any interest to him at all. It would only drive up the price.

Two pirates leaned against a metal cage set close to the bonfire, perhaps six feet high and six feet across. The bars extended only partway up or partway down, alternating side by side, and the exposed ends were sharpened to gleaming points. Inside was a pile of furs in one corner, and before them a dark red blot on the snow.

Blood. He was close enough to smell it.

One of the pirates straightened and sauntered over, his face vaguely familiar.

Thom leaned in and whispered, "His name's Ljubisa. He had a certain loyalty to Duncan Bane. Bane's death saw him demoted." He shrugged. "He might be looking for a new benefactor."

"Ah," Gavin murmured. Such knowledge had value. That sort of loyalty might be easily transferable . . . for a price.

"Ljubisa," he said softly, stepping close enough to pass the small vial he had palmed into the outstretched hand of the Reaver.

He schooled his features to betray none of his distaste for the man. All his research, all his efforts were geared to sowing the seeds of a better world, to eradicating such vermin and finding the road to ultimate purity for the human race. Only the most intelligent, the most attractive, the most intuitive would be chosen, their progeny nurtured. Those who were worthy.

Vermin like Ljubisa had no place in Gavin's perfect world. But he might be a useful pawn. Easily purchased and expendable.

Smiling, Gavin shifted his gaze to the bloodstained snow inside the cage and asked, "What happened in there?"

Ljubisa sent a jaundiced look at Thom and two other men who had stepped up to flank Gavin. He dropped his gaze, examined the vial Gavin had passed to him, and thrust it beneath the stinking, matted furs that draped his brawny frame. Then he turned his face away and spat on the ground.

A disgusting habit.

"The woman we kept there died yesterday," he said. "We made use of her. Maybe one too many. But what's the difference between two dozen or three?" He shrugged. "She pushed herself into the space between the bars. Impaled herself through here"—he thumped his own chest just to the left of center—"and bled out."

He grunted and jutted his chin in the direction of the fur-covered stone bench positioned at the far end of the encampment, for all intents and purposes a throne. On it sat the equivalent of the Siberian ice pirates' idea of royalty. Belek-ool, a stocky man of perhaps forty, though hard weather and an even harder life had put the marks of a much older man on his face. He watched them with ice-pale eyes, his expression twisted by a jagged and raised scar that ran from brow to chin.

Gavin knew him. They'd had dealings in the past. Gavin had slit the throat of Belek-ool's second in command after a rather unpleasant conversation that had circled and circled like crows after carrion. Seeing no end to their disagreement, Gavin had *put* an end to it.

It had been a necessary show of force, one that had garnered him a modicum of respect and trust. Those elements had been essential in enticing volunteers for his research study. And, of course, the monetary bonus had enticed them, as well.

"Belek-ool wasn't too happy about her dying." Ljubisa snorted. "He doesn't like to be without a whore. So, he killed the last guy who used her. Chopped him up. Fed him to the dogs." He sent Gavin a conspiratorial wink. "I'm glad the last guy wasn't me. Or maybe it was, and I just pushed someone else forward when Belek-ool asked."

Gavin's gaze slid to the dogs. Big, heavy heads. Cropped tails. Short glistening coats and very white, very large teeth. They were held by thick lengths of chain, but from the way the beasts lunged and snarled, he was less than convinced the safeguard would adequately constrain them for long.

Making a wordless reply, Gavin turned his attention to the empty cage that had been home to the camp's recently deceased entertainment.

"Convenient luck that we have such wonderful goods to trade," he murmured to Thom. He had intended to transport the women from Abbott's Inn and Pub to Port Uranium, use them in his lab as test subjects, but circumstances presented him with a far better option. He had a strong suspicion that the ice pirates might like the pot sweetened with a little female companionship in addition to the money and drugs he had brought with him.

He leaned to his left, gave a soft order, and watched as two of his men rounded the back of one of his rigs to fetch the cargo.

Belek-ool remained where he was, silent and grim on

his throne, a plasgun clutched in his hand, casually aimed at Gavin's head. Gavin had no doubt that the Reavers had at least a dozen Bolingers aimed at him from various points in the camp, but he was confident that none would be discharged.

Yes, they could kill him and steal his rigs, his money, his live cargo. But he also supplied them with vials of a-methylphenethylamine and dextroamphetamine sulfate. Kill him, kill their supply. The names hadn't changed much in the past century. The drugs known as ice and crystal were still ice and crystal, only now, given the state of the northern hemisphere, there was a certain apropos irony to the monikers.

The Reavers were unlikely to do anything to undermine the river of drugs Gavin ensured flowed their way—both for their personal use and for sales that provided their income—which meant that the likelihood he would leave here with his head intact was extremely high.

Whatever minimal risk there was, was a necessary evil. The truth was, these creatures would never respect a man who hid himself away and sent his underlings to do the deal.

For now, Gavin needed them, which meant he was forced to smile and nod and act as though he didn't wish to detonate a phosphorous mine to blow them and their disgusting camp to oblivion.

No matter. They would all be dead soon.

He needed only one thing to ensure that outcome: Tatiana. His little genetic bomb. His precious girl. She could withstand an incredible amount. She'd already proven that, time and again. And her genetic material would provide answers to all his questions as he poked her and prodded her and sliced bits of her away to study and experiment upon.

She was the key, to both genocide and salvation.

He was most anxious to have her in his care once more. But he was a patient man, as any true scientist should be. Eventually, she would come out of hiding, and he would be there, waiting.

The sound of chains and sobs drew his attention, and he turned to see his men dragging Abbott's whores forward. They had been so quiet, so malleable, the entire trip, but faced with the camp of ice pirates, a few had suddenly found their buried emotions in the form of abject terror.

A young girl threw herself at his feet, sobbing and begging. He stepped back in distaste as her hands grasped his booted foot.

Glancing up, he saw that Belek-ool was on his feet now, his expression no longer impassive. He was smiling, his eyes glittering.

Gavin reached down and grasped the chain that bound the girl's hands. He dragged her to her feet and shoved her forward, half pushing, half carrying until she collapsed at Belek-ool's feet on her hands and knees, her head bowed, her hair falling forward across the toes of the Reaver's boots.

Gavin breathed deep, enjoying the satisfaction that touched him. The stolen microscopes and the store of vaccine were small bonuses, but his true interest lay in the tissue samples labeled TTN081 that had been taken.

They were about to be returned to his possession, all for the price of a few whores that he himself had stolen.

He found a luscious irony in that.

CHAPTER TWELVE

Flipping aside the edge of the thermal cloth that draped him, Tristan drew out a laser distancemeter and measured the parameters of the tunnel.

"What are you looking for?" An innocuous question, but the sound of Ana's voice turned the words into something that was sexy as all hell.

"The section that had the most symmetrical alignment," he replied, turning to look at her.

She didn't so much as blink.

"Why?"

"So I can set cytoplast charges and blow this tunnel. Block it as an entry point."

She tipped her head slightly to the right, studied him for protracted seconds, then gave a sharp nod. "Understood. You want to block the threat we encountered earlier. But won't that also block an exit?"

"There is no exit point beyond this tunnel." With all their senses heightened to a painful degree, the mutated Reavers were photophobic, hating the light, and the bitter cold was agonizing for them. Even the touch of snowflakes on skin drove them mad. They were highly unlikely to venture from their underground domain, but Tristan wasn't inclined to take chances, so he had blown the elevator shaft in that section of the facility weeks ago. "The only way to and from the surface is the route you took with me earlier."

And at some point—probably sooner rather than later—he needed to blow that route, as well. No way in. No way out. No chance of the goddamned virus making its way to the general population of the Waste.

What he'd seen Gemma and the others do out there on the ice today had sealed the deal. They were losing their civilized veneer, becoming more feral and primitive by the day. Not that the rapist's actions hadn't earned him exactly what he got, but the method of his execution had lacked even a whisper of judicial recourse. What had gone down out there was bad, even for the denizens of the Waste.

Definitely outside the norm for a group of analytical scientists whose propensity for violence ought to have measured a zero on the scale.

The infection had entered the prodromal stage.

He wasn't certain how much longer any form of reason would prevail, how much longer before they turned into the same deviant creatures that the test subjects had become.

"Understood," Ana said again, and he thought that she understood a whole hell of a lot. Maybe more than he wanted her to.

He took a small titanium case from his utility harness and pried it open with the tip of his knife. He measured the distances again, used his knife to scrape a mark in the appropriate places, then carefully set five pellet-sized chunks of cytoplast charge around the tunnel.

Arms crossed over her chest, Ana stood beside and slightly behind him as he worked. He was aware of her perusal, the practiced way she scanned their surroundings for threat, like it was second nature to her to watch every shadow.

She had to have questions. About a million of them. But she held them until a more appropriate time, as any trained soldier would. Because right now, her task was guard duty.

Yeah, she was definitely a puzzle.

He set the first three fuses and let the wire dangle before moving on to the next.

"Not quite," she said, and stepped up beside him to carefully loosen the cytoplast he had placed high on the wall, slow and easy. She pressed it back in place, in what looked to him like the exact spot she'd taken it from.

Glancing at him, she shook her head. "The explosives must be set in a symmetrical placement in order to trigger a spherically imploding shock wave. You had it three millimeters too low."

Right. Three millimeters.

Pulling out his distancemeter, he checked the measurement. Well, waddaya know. She was dead on.

"Thanks." He wondered how in the hell she'd managed to note the discrepancy. She moved back, and he stepped up and set the last two fuses, then turned to look at her. "You trained in explosives?"

"Something like that." Her smile was a little edgy, a little mysterious. "I have had the opportunity to study a variety of things."

She didn't sound particularly happy about it.

Together, they backed down the tunnel, rounded the bend, and backed up a little farther, with Tristan unwinding the trip wire as they went.

"Get behind me," he ordered, his head coming up when she made no move to comply.

She was watching him with a faint frown. "Why?" she asked.

Yeah, why . . . ?

Ana definitely didn't need his protection.

But he was a guy who remembered his dad opening doors for his mom, holding her chair, bringing her flowers. Running out in the rain to fetch something so she wouldn't get wet. Wrapping her in his arms to make her feel safe when things got rough. The protector. It was the way he'd been raised, and some habits died hard.

But the truth was, he had been a piss-poor protector of those who needed him most, then and now. So what the hell was he thinking, offering to shield her?

"Uh . . ." He actually felt embarrassed. Hell. "In case there's debris . . ." He made a vague gesture, feeling incredibly ridiculous. "In case the blast sends out debris."

She tipped her head a little to the side and studied him long enough to increase his discomfort tenfold.

"Understood," she said. "You wish to shield me. As you wished to have me precede you out of the elevator. You mean it as a courtesy."

"Something like that. Yeah."

He busied himself with his tools, carefully stowing them back in his utility belt, focusing all his attention on that.

"You are an enigma, Tristan," she offered softly. "You kill a man without compunction, fight like a berserker when attacked, yet you wish to care for and protect those in your charge. Do you think I, too, am in your charge now?"

The words cut through him like a blade to the gut. "Everyone in this facility is in my charge."

His responsibility. And he'd failed them. Every last one of them.

Guilt and remorse were a bitch. He'd spent a very long time training himself to rise above them, to forgive. Tried to rise high enough to forgive himself, only he was so far away from that level of enlightenment, he hadn't even climbed out of the primordial sludge.

Because everyone but him died.

He had brought bubonic plague to his family, and then he'd been unable to save them.

And even if that was forgivable, what he'd done now sure as hell wasn't. He'd collaborated with a monster and created a plague that could kill millions.

So, yeah, self-forgiveness wasn't high on his list.

Tatiana laid her hand on his forearm, the easy gesture demanding his full attention.

"What is it you're afraid of, Tristan?"

There it was. The stinking, ugly, naked truth.

He was afraid of a whole shitload of bad. The plague he'd created. The mutation and permutations it had gone through. The creatures it had spawned.

Not afraid for himself.

He was afraid it would get out and infect the entire Waste. Hell, maybe the entire world.

The scenario was like some Old Dominion doomsday propaganda touting bioterrorism as a constant threat, only it was real, not some distorted, overblown scare developed by a corrupt government.

It was real, and he'd created it. Doomed the whole human race if it got out of here. He meant to make certain it never would, and the only way to do that was to eradicate the pathogen. Or eradicate the host.

So how screwed up was it that he wanted to protect her even though, in the end, he meant to kill her?

Meant to kill each of them in turn: Gemma, Alan, Kalen, Lamia. He would kill thirty-seven people, one by one, as the disease progressed. Thirty-seven people he knew and liked. Because the alternative—letting them live like that—just wasn't an option.

Mercy.

That's what he was calling it.

Just another name for murder.

Ana made the count thirty-eight.

Fuck.

He couldn't risk telling her. Not until he had the place sealed up tight. Not until she was trapped down here, leaving the rest of the world safe.

She wanted to know what he was afraid of? Well, she'd find out soon enough, and then she'd wish she was still unenlightened.

So he didn't answer. He just shoved her behind him and yanked the trip wire to trigger the cytoplast blast.

A hard *whump* hit the air, slamming outward in a circumferential pattern as the hollow tunnel imploded on itself, crumpling inward. The force of the blast shoved him back against her, and she wrapped her arms about his waist, steadying the both of them.

His ears ringing, he turned to face her, their bodies close enough that he could feel the rise and fall of her chest against his own. The sounds of settling gravel, the remains of the blast, filtered to him as though from a great distance. His gaze dropped to her lips.

A heartbeat. Two.

The moment spun out, and then his com crackled.

"Report, Tris?"

"Detonation complete."

Dropping her hands, Ana stepped away and stood only an arm's reach from him, watching him with those amazing eyes—liquid mercury, bright against her dark lashes. The distance between them might as well have been an ocean.

How long did she have left? Weeks?

How long did any of them have?

None of us is alone. As others exhale, we inhale. The universe as one.

He needed to believe that.

They would die, every one of them, people he had come to care about despite his best efforts to stay aloof. He would be alone once more. With his guilt. His remorse.

With only the echo of the memories of those who had once been.

With the memory of Ana's kiss, the question of what might have been if the situation were different.

The virus had mutated from the original strain. He couldn't predict it, couldn't accurately extrapolate its next permutation.

There was no stopping it, no changing the outcome.

In the end, everyone died. Alone. They died alone. As he was alone.

Everyone died. Except him.

He was completely alone in his immunity to the monstrosity he had created.

Tatiana tensed as scent and footfall alerted her to someone's approach. Not the mutated Reavers. The sounds were wrong for that. People.

The shadows shifted, and two men stepped into view along the tunnel. Both were swathed in the same layers of thermal cloth she had seen outside, but they'd uncovered their heads and faces. They stared at her for a moment, their expressions completely devoid of emotion.

If they'd been packing plasguns she might have felt a momentary unease, but there wasn't a weapon in sight. And now she knew why. Knives were more effective against the . . . monsters in the dark.

"Kalen. Shayne." Tristan inclined his head to each of

them as he stepped up beside her, angling his body between her and the approaching men. She had to smile at that. If it came down to a threat, she would take them down as fast, or faster, than he would. "We had some company on the way here. I need a perimeter check. North quadrant."

Company. Interesting word to apply to a bunch of mutated Reavers who'd been reduced to their most primitive killing instincts.

The taller of the two men, Kalen, nodded at Tristan, his gaze flicking to Tatiana, then away.

He was very slim, handsome, with skin the color of well-steeped tea, full lips, dark eyes and short, tightly curled black hair.

"She shouldn't be here."

Friendly guy.

"Too late for should or shouldn't. She's here." Tristan smiled, a confident baring of teeth that brooked no argument. "And I say she should be."

They stared at each other in that oh-so-special way that men do, and then Kalen huffed a short blast of air through his nose and stalked off. Tatiana watched him go.

Someone didn't want her here. The question was, why?

Before she could spend more than a second or two pondering possibilities, a girl came bounding down the corridor. She looked to be about eighteen, tall and slim. Athletic build. Pretty, with a strong jaw and straight brows, dark eyes and thick dark hair that fell to her shoulders in a blunt-cut curtain.

"Hello. I'm Lamia. I'm so glad you're here." She threw herself at Tatiana and hugged her. *Hugged* her.

Tatiana froze, her heart rate kicking up a notch, her arms held out wide at her sides. She didn't like people touching her. There was too strong a possibility of thought transfer, too great a risk of reading far more than she wished.

An electric pulse crackled through her, from Lamia into her, a tangle of thoughts and emotions.

The girl was glad to have someone here close to her own age. She was happy. She was despondent. She was desperate and giddy at once. She knew such depth of fear that it was an endless well, dark and overwhelming. She knew such faith and hope that it shone like a beacon in her thoughts.

Nothing in the twisted nest Tatiana encountered here made a bit of sense. Every thought contradicted every other thought, the tumult of it leaving her dizzy. A dull ache pulsed at the base of her skull, and she slammed shut the portal with all her might.

Lamia jerked away as though she sensed Tatiana's mental rebuff. Or perhaps she merely noted that Tatiana did not return her exuberant embrace.

"I'm sorry." Lamia laughed and reached up to shove her hair behind her right ear. "I'm sorry. I'm just so glad for the company. I want to hear any news you can think of. Any gossip. Where was the last place you visited? What do you like to do? Any hobbies? I like to do satellite jumps and splice the feeds into my own holo-vids. Do you have any microdiscs on you? I'm so sick of mine. Maybe we can trade. . . ."

Tatiana cast a desperate look at Tristan and found him staring at Lamia as though she had a second head.

"She's not usually like this," he said, clearly bemused. "She's usually—"

"Calm and efficient," Lamia cut him off. "But that's because there's no one here to *talk* to."

She stepped forward, reached out as though to link her arm with Tatiana's, then paused, frowned. "You don't like to be touched, do you?"

No, she didn't. Only it hadn't seemed to bother her when Tristan touched her, and she didn't have an explanation for that.

Tatiana opened her mouth, closed it, gathered her thoughts as Lamia withdrew her arm with obvious reluctance. She had read studies on female friendships. Knew that such a thing as bonding existed. But it was far beyond the scope of her experience. She didn't want to hurt this child's feelings, but she did want to set some sort of boundary.

Child. Why did she think of Lamia as a child? She appeared to be only a shade younger than Tatiana herself.

"I, um . . ." She shot a glance at Tristan, who was watching her with an amused expression. "I'm Tatiana. I do not have any microdiscs. I like to—" Fight. Train. No, not *like*. She did those things because she had to. What did she like? Her gaze dropped to Tristan's mouth. "I, um, I . . ." She jerked her gaze away. "The last places I visited were Liskeard and Port Uranium. As to gossip or news"— *I cut off a man's hand outside Abbott's General Store*—"I heard that Reaver attacks are escalating in the Alberta Corridor and that Dorje Station is almost . . . overrun . . ."

Her voice trailed off.

Tristan and Lamia were both staring at her.

"I was thinking more along the lines of gossip about the latest exploits of Acid Tongue, or maybe a hint about their new underground release. . . ." Lamia laughed. "You know . . . something that isn't on the regular broadband news."

Acid Tongue? Tatiana fixed her gaze on Tristan, silently willing him to explain, but he only shrugged and looked away.

"Anyway, it doesn't matter," Lamia said. "Come on.

We have sim-steak potato pie and carrot slaw for dinner.
I bet you're hungry. How long are you staying?"

"I am—"

"As long as she is my guest," Tristan interrupted, his
tone hard, "Ana is to be regarded as one of us."

The words ought to have been reassuring. Welcoming.
But they weren't. Something in his tone, combined with
the shocked look that Lamia shot him, made Tatiana certain there was a dark undercurrent here she had no understanding of.

"When?" Lamia whispered.

"During the . . . outdoor altercation," Tristan replied.

On a sharp inhalation, Lamia reared back, her eyes
wide, her hands jerking up in an instinctive action before
she mastered herself and schooled her features.

Definitely a dark undercurrent, Tatiana thought. One
more tricky twist to the maze she'd stumbled into.

It seemed that whatever had happened during the *outdoor altercation* was not good. Was Tristan referring to the
man's death out on the ice? Most likely.

"Carrot slaw, huh?" Tatiana said, forcing a light tone.
"You trade for your vegetables or grow them?"

The innocuous question had the opposite of the intended effect. Instead of defusing Lamia's tension, it made
her close up tighter than the entry to an arctic fox's burrow.

Lamia's gaze snapped from Tatiana to Tristan, and her
mouth froze in the open position, a little round O of
uncertainty. Her demeanor sent warning sirens clanging
through every cell in Tatiana's body.

"We used to trade for most of what we needed," Tristan
said, answering for her. "But I felt it was . . . more econom-
ical to grow our own. We instituted a hydroponic grow-
tube about six months ago. It's been very successful."

The slight hesitation in Tristan's voice didn't go unnoticed. Tatiana suspected that economic reasons had nothing to do with the decision to grow vegetables instead of trade for them.

"So why don't you just head into Liskeard for news and gossip?" Tatiana turned to Lamia, shifting her body to block Tristan from the conversation.

"Oh, Tris doesn't let—"

"Lamia."

One word, spoken soft and calm, and it was enough to make the girl jerk back in visible distress. In that moment, Tatiana didn't like Tristan very much. Didn't like him at all.

"I have some things to attend to," he said. "Lamia, will you show our guest to her quarters?"

Tatiana glanced up to find him watching her, his expression unreadable. He inclined his head and took his leave, and as much as she wanted to ignore him, she couldn't. She turned and watched him until he disappeared down the corridor.

She couldn't say she was unhappy to see his back. Firstly, she liked watching him walk, even though she was phenomenally annoyed with him right now. He was loose limbed. Confident. Each step long and purposeful. A man with a plan. Secondly, his presence unnerved her, so she was relieved to be quit of it. Not something she liked to admit, even to herself, but the truth was, he fascinated her, and that made her nervous. Very, very nervous. Thirdly, she figured Lamia would be easier to pump for information without his grim interjections. Definitely easier to ditch than him, so she could do a little recon and make a three-step plan.

She liked plans and short lists. Clean. Brief. Straightforward. Anything more than three steps could end up in a real mess.

"Is he always such a dictator?" She turned and found Lamia watching her watching Tristan, and grinning ear to ear.

"Always." Lamia laughed. "He's not so bad. He just feels responsible."

"For what?"

For a frozen moment, Tatiana felt the chill of Lamia's genuine fear, heard the refrain of that question echoing from the girl's thoughts to her own. Tentatively, Tatiana reached out, tested the current, tried to unravel the winding thread of the answer.

But there were only the tangled emotions she'd read when Lamia first came down the corridor.

And overwhelming horror and sadness and dread.

CHAPTER THIRTEEN

"This way," Lamia said.

She led Tatiana down a barrel-ceilinged hallway, bouncing on the balls of her feet as she walked, all energy and good humor, in direct opposition to the ghosting of her emotions and thoughts.

Tatiana shook her head and followed behind. Something about this place, these people, hampered her ability to grab hold of the residue of electric current and plumb their thoughts. Her efforts were not obstructed; they were merely obfuscated. It was a distinctly unusual situation, one she'd not encountered before.

The passage was brighter and wider than the ones she and Tristan had taken on their way here. And the flooring was different. Not concrete. No puddles. No stink of mildew and rot. Just clean white tiles.

Shooting her a glance over her shoulder, Lamia gave a megavoltage smile that lit up her whole face. Tatiana couldn't help smiling back.

"You have brothers and sisters? I have a brother. He's as protective as Tristan, and as bossy. No"—she laughed—"Tristan's bossier. So what about you? You have siblings?"

"Yes." *No*, not *siblings*. She knew that Yuriko was dead. Her fault. And Wizard . . . well, she'd heard a rumor that it was Wizard who'd killed Duncan Bane six months past. If it was true, then her brother was alive, he was out there somewhere in the vast Waste. She'd even heard a rumor that Wizard was looking for his sister. For *her*.

But could she trust the rumors?

She couldn't find anyone who'd actually seen her brother. No one had spoken directly with him. People said the one asking about Tatiana was a blond woman, tough as the tundra, armed to the hilt. Definitely not Wizard.

Which meant that whoever was looking for her just might work for Ward.

Gavin Ward was smart, eerily smart, and he understood human hopes and dreams. He knew she ached to see her siblings once more.

He would lure her with the dangling carrot of her hope.

Just the thought of him made her gut clench and bile crawl up her throat. Slag, she hated it that he had that sort of power over her still.

Guess the only way she'd get past that was to kill him. Not for vengeance, because she wasn't certain whether that would help heal the dark, gaping holes in her soul or just tear new ones. No, she'd kill him because it was the only way to stop him, nice and quick, a dirty job that was best done fast.

She'd kill Ward and Tolliver and anyone else who got their jollies by creating a plague that could decimate the world.

Her lip curled.

A girl was entitled to her dreams.

Lamia cleared her throat, and Tatiana realized that they had come quite a way along the corridor and the silence had stretched too long.

"A brother," she muttered, recalling herself to the moment. "I have a brother."

"Older? Younger?"

"Older."

"Bossy?" Lamia asked.

Tatiana thought of cool, logical Wizard. "You have no idea."

A moment later, they reached a section in the corridor that had a dozen or so metal hatches on each side. Lamia stopped and gestured at a portal.

"You can have a shower here. Wash your clothes. Rest. It's private. Once you're inside, you can code your own password. Not that anyone would bother you. I mean, Kalen isn't happy that you're here, but he wouldn't . . ." Lamia's voice trailed away as she paused and glanced back at Tatiana. "That isn't as bad as it sounded. Really. Kalen has his reasons."

"I'm certain he does." Didn't everyone have their reasons for the choices they made? "So how did you end up here? You seem so . . ."

"Young?" Lamia laughed. "It's okay. Go ahead and say it. I'm not offended. I am young. Twenty come March. As to how I ended up here . . . I answered a holo-ad for a communications officer. Seemed like a good idea at the time. I'm amazing at comm. Guess you could say an inborn gift. The pay was great. Enough to send some home to my family to help out and still save some for"— she broke off, shook her head—"well, that doesn't matter now."

But it did. Tatiana didn't need to trespass into Lamia's thoughts and emotions to know that. She could hear in the girl's tone and in the things she didn't say, and to her amazement, she found that she felt bad for her, empathized with her obvious regret and sadness.

There you go. She was practicing normal human interactions and learning something new along the way.

Lamia released the handle and pushed the door wide. She made a grand, sweeping gesture. "Here you go."

"Thank you." Tatiana stepped inside, turned back. Lamia stood silhouetted against the lumilights of the corridor, her head slightly bowed, the thick curtain of her hair leaving her face in shadow. "What were you saving for, Lamia?"

The girl raised her head, her dark eyes shimmering.

"Tell me, please."

A faint hum colored the air as the generator kicked in somewhere deep in the twisted underground maze.

"School. I was saving for school. I wanted to be a nurse. To study at the Medical Institute in Neo-Tokyo." She shook her head. "A pipe dream. That's what my dad called it. He'd ruffle my hair and say, 'You keep saving for that pipe dream, pet.' I never knew what he meant, but I figure now that it means a dream that will always be just a dream." She made a rueful sound and shoved a hank of her hair behind her ear. "Why did I tell you that?"

Tatiana's heart twisted, and she felt a tickle of surprise. She wondered why she cared about this strange, exuberant girl she barely knew.

"I asked." As the words left her lips, she felt the echo of them deep inside her. Tristan had said the same thing to her. Did that mean he'd cared for her answer as she cared for Lamia's? The possibility was foreign and strange.

"Yeah, you did ask." Lamia smiled. "Thanks. Anyway. . . ." She flicked her hands away from her body as though shooing away an unpleasant smell. "You want to check out your room, have a shower? Or you want to eat first?"

There was a hopeful note in her voice. She obviously wanted Tatiana to choose food and company over a solitary shower.

"Food first," Tatiana said, not inclined to lose the opportunity to pump the girl for information. And, truth be told, she liked Lamia. Liked her youth and her exuberance and her easy, open nature. Liked having the chance to talk with her, hear her voice, make that connection. It was odd . . . she'd had so few opportunities to interact with other people in a positive way, yet because she'd vicariously sensed such things in the thoughts and emotions of others, read about them in studies archived in computers, she craved such experiences for herself. "Just give me a second to take off my gear and set a pass code."

Lamia's face lit up like a full moon on a clear night. "Great. I'll wait in the hall." She stepped back and the door slid shut with a soft whoosh.

Tatiana keyed in a password. Not that she counted on its impenetrability, but there was something to be said for maintaining the illusion. It was wiser to at least go through the motions, go along with expectations, even though she suspected that Lamia could hack her password with her eyes closed. That meant that whatever Tatiana had on her person stayed on her person, unless she could afford to lose it or leave it behind should the need arise.

She quickly examined the small room. Bed, plastitech table, microdisc player, holo-vid player, antiquated plasma screen. The thing had to be three inches thick.

There was a doorway to a bathroom that was about the size of the storage bin on the back of her Morgat. Maybe a shade smaller. She checked out that space as well.

The toilet was vacuum flushed—*flushed!*—rather than using chem-solve to simply disintegrate the contents. *Wow.* Just . . . *wow.* She wouldn't have thought there was a vacuum-flush toilet left anywhere on the planet.

She'd just bet collectors would pay a few interdollars for that. Maybe she ought to disassemble it and take it with her when she left, leave some money to cover a reasonable cost.

She backed out of the bathroom, then took less than three minutes to evaluate every crack and cranny of the room for cameras, comm equipment, anything that might breach her privacy. She ran her fingertips over and under shelves, the mattress, the frame of the bed, even the frame of the door hatch. She found nothing except a living space that was clean, tidy, and at least three decades out of date, but for the microdisc and holo-vid players. They were current.

All of which made this place a bit of an enigma.

She didn't find that particularly reassuring. The only thing she trusted was the certainty that nothing was ever what it seemed on the surface, and nothing was ever free.

Including a meal and a shower.

Tristan wanted something from her, something other than an amazingly torrid kiss in a dim hallway. And it *had* been torrid. Just thinking about it made her skin tingle.

So she wasn't going to think about it.

Why was it that a man she wasn't even certain she liked flipped her switches like no one before?

Don't think about it. Or him.

She folded her parka neatly and set it away on the shelf. Beside it, she placed the small pack she'd grabbed from the Morgat. In it were a hydropic for her teeth, a change of clothes, a hairbrush.

She glanced at the holo-player, hit the button for imaging and checked the three-dimensional visual of her appearance.

Oops. Not so good.

Since when have I cared what I look like? The thought rankled. This had nothing to do with her appearance. Nothing to do with Tristan.

It just wasn't polite to arrive at a meal bristling with weapons.

Keeping an eye on the hologram, she bent down, shoved the knife a little deeper into her boot so the hilt didn't protrude quite so much. Straightening, she hid the scabbard at her lower back underneath her clothing, and pushed the wrist holster for her Setti9 a little higher on her forearm until it lay beneath her sleeve.

The only thing she couldn't camouflage was the massive AT450. She left it hanging between her shoulder blades.

A girl never knew what she might be called upon to shoot.

"You ever think about consequences?" Tristan asked, shooting a glance at Kalen as they turned down yet another access tunnel. "You know, think about how everything has consequences, even when they aren't intended? Like dropping a pebble in the ocean and causing a tsunami clear across the world."

Kalen frowned, shook his head. "I doubt a pebble could cause a tsunami."

They both stopped dead as they came up to a massive pile of rubble and shattered concrete that completely blocked their way.

"Tunnel's blocked," Tristan said, angling his meter to bounce ultrasonic waves at the pile.

"So I see," Kalen replied, sardonic.

Unfazed, Tristan checked the readout. "Rubble's ten meters deep. Too thick to clear."

"What about Access 27? You didn't blow that one. Maybe it's still clear."

Together, they turned and headed back the way they had come, disappointment burning in Tristan's gut. Everything was sinking in the muck, and he was waist deep in the mire. Yasha and Viktor hadn't delivered, and time was melting away faster than the Greenland Glacier in 2023.

He was set with an impossible task. Keep the tunnels blocked so the mutated Reavers couldn't get through, and find an opening large enough so he *could*.

"Yeah, but do you ever think about connections?" he asked, picking up where they'd left off. "Millions of tiny connections. The universe as one."

To hold on to his sanity in the impossible darkness that had become his reality, he'd accepted the millions of tiny connections to everything, anything. He had learned to be calm, to meditate away the rage, the pain, the loneliness. Long ago, he had recognized that was the only way he could survive, the only way he could stave off madness. Accept the thoughts that strayed into his consciousness.

He didn't need to welcome them. He simply needed to let them come—and go—without dwelling on that which he could not change.

Kalen huffed out a breath. "Everything has consequences."

Tristan knew that better than most.

So what were the consequences of kissing Ana, a woman he had tricked into being imprisoned in this stinking hole, a woman who would die here because he could see no other course?

The Reaver's tainted blood had sprayed her, a form of direct contact. Still, there would have been a small chance she could escape without becoming infected if her skin had been intact. But Gemma's blade had sliced her hand, and sliced away any hope. The exposure was blood to blood. Which left no question that she was infected. If he let her go free, anyone who came in contact with her would likely also be infected before she died.

And she *would* die, a horrific death of pain and torment. Just like everyone else down here, unless he got through the access tunnels to the lab and found that the experiments he'd started weeks back had incubated and borne a cure.

In which case, he just might be able to save them. Save her.

Ana.

If he kept her here, locked away fifty yuales beneath the earth's surface, she could infect no one else.

No, not *if*. She was staying.

There was no other option.

Tatiana followed Lamia to a large room, lit by the same old-style lumilights she'd seen elsewhere in the facility. At the far end of the space was a grouping of ancient-looking, battered and torn brown-checked couches and a plasma screen that, like the one in her chamber, looked about fifty years old.

Closer in were a dozen or so long Formica tables lined up in neat rows. Old tables, more modern chairs. Plastitech.

The place was a mishmash of stuff. And the air smelled like . . . food. One cheering thing in a less than cheery place.

Several people were already seated and eating. She recognized Gemma and the other man she'd seen earlier in the afternoon, Shayne. No one spoke. No one even looked up.

Friendly bunch.

Opening herself just a little, she tried to read the situation, tried to catch enough electrical ghosting to help her understand the somber mood.

Like a satellite feed on fast forward, images slapped her, a bone-deep *knowing* of things best left private.

Not just fear. Terror and horror. Self-loathing. They permeated the room. These people hated themselves . . . what they had done . . . what they would become. Ill. They were ill. . . .

So many thoughts, so much emotion, all rushing at her from every side. It was almost . . . not human.

She sucked in a breath, fought the urge to stumble back, feeling as though she'd been battered by ruthless fists. Nausea nagged at her, and she swallowed, collected herself. This was new.

Years past, when the thoughts of others had first begun to invade her mind, she had been shocked, alarmed. Over time, she had trained herself to channel the stream, to control the flow. She rarely opened herself too wide, and rarer still did she butt up against a mind she could not penetrate.

But she had never felt like this, as though she was accessing emotions of some . . . primitive beings. Inhuman. A foreign consciousness.

Which made absolutely no sense, because there were a handful of people sitting here. *People.*

Masking her confusion, she turned and followed Lamia to the open kitchen. She helped herself to a plate of food and used the moment to collect her thoughts and steady her unease, then followed Lamia toward Gemma's table.

After an initial awkward silence, Lamia filled the void with chatter, easing the way into conversation.

Tatiana was just finishing her meal when Tristan turned up, looking a little rough, a lot dangerous. He'd shed his draping thermal gear, and the black shirt and pants he wore were loose and comfortable looking. Somehow, without the layers of tattered, ragged outdoor gear, he seemed bigger, taller.

She cut him a glance through her lashes as he spoke to Kalen and Shayne, his back to her. Her gaze lingered on his broad shoulders, then dropped to his ass. Wow. Nice ass. Well-developed glutes. Long legs. She could see the hint of muscle beneath his pants.

Across from her, Lamia snorted, catching her out. But Tristan didn't spare her a glance.

And why the hell did that piss her off?

Feigning enormous interest in the gray-brown blob on her plate, she speared a chunk of sim-protein and morosely pushed it around with her fork.

A moment later, conversation lulled as Tristan crossed the room. Lamia and Gemma sidled apart to make room for Tristan directly across from her.

Oh, joy. Did she have a neon sign above her head that read *interested*?

"Settling in?" he asked, carefully unfolding a cloth napkin and laying it across his lap. She stared for a moment, startled by his actions.

He looked up, caught her questioning gaze and shrugged. "My mother was a firm believer in fine table manners."

"Okay, but then why put the napkin on your lap instead of on the table?"

"Good question," Lamia chimed in from her place beside him. "Do tell."

"It's so that . . ." He frowned, looked about. Everyone else's napkins were on the table. "In case crumbs fall."

Made sense. Sort of.

Tristan shifted his feet beneath the table, his toes bumping hers, the contact making her edgy. No, not just edgy. His proximity left her feeling all kinds of dangerous things. She wanted him to feel them too, to be as aware of her as she was of him.

She stretched out her leg until her toes batted his and gave him a nice, hard nudge just as he lifted a forkful of food. His gaze shot to hers and, raising one straight, dark brow, he trapped her foot between his own, holding her there as he continued his meal.

She had no idea why she'd done that, baited him, tried to annoy him on purpose. It was just that something about him fascinated her. Enticed her. Made her want to needle him.

"So, I asked if you were settling in?" he repeated.

"Settling in?" She laughed. "That has an awfully permanent sound to it. I'm only going to be here for the night."

Lamia's head jerked up, her dark eyes wide, her expression making Tatiana more than a little wary.

Cutting her a sidelong glance, Tristan finished chewing, swallowed. "Aren't you on cleanup tonight, Lamia?"

"Yeah," she muttered, pushing away from the table and gathering her empty plate and utensils. "Yeah, I am."

"I don't like the way you bully her," Tatiana said softly as Lamia rose. "If she has something to say, let her say it. You keep cutting her off and giving some kind of unspoken warning every time she tries to talk to me. So just stop!"

"Yeah, Tristan, just stop," Lamia echoed. "Looks like I have a champion now." She laughed and cuffed him lightly on the back of the head, leaving Tatiana wondering if she'd read the entire exchange wrong. Suddenly, Lamia didn't appear particularly cowed.

Reaching for Tatiana's empty plate, Lamia asked, "You done?"

"I'll help with cleanup." Tatiana collected her own plate and utensils, then tried to pull her foot free from its place between Tristan's.

He held her tight. A flicker of unease touched her, and she jerked her foot a little harder. It was enough. Her foot slid free, and as his gaze lifted to hers, she saw that he was frowning, as though he regretted holding her in place. Or maybe he regretted letting her go . . . ?

Lamia led her to the open kitchen area and showed her where everything was. From her place behind the counter, Tatiana watched surreptitiously as Tristan tore into his food with both gusto and impeccable table manners. She liked watching him, the way he held his fork and knife, the way he cut his food, even his posture at the table.

Funny thing to find appealing.

But the truth was, in the Waste, a guy who didn't spew crumbs and spittle was quite a catch.

Some catch. He'd cajoled her into the ground with the promise of information—*I can tell you about Tolliver*—only he'd made certain he hadn't put himself in a position where he had to deliver.

An oversight or a well-executed sidestep? Tatiana figured the second option seemed more likely by far.

Funny, she hadn't pegged him for a coward.

Some of it she'd figured out for herself.

Mutated Reavers crawling through a maze of tunnels fifty yuales under the frozen tundra had to mean Gavin Ward had a hand in whatever was going on down here. While this antiquated hole in the ground definitely was not his hidden laboratory, the place had to be close. Very close.

Not that she had proof. Yet. But having spent half her life locked in a cell, training cockroaches to fetch crumbs, she had some familiarity with both patience and dogged intent.

She would find the lab and find Tolliver, and in the end, she would find Ward. Save the slagging Waste from the plague. It was her nice, tidy, three-step plan.

"I'll walk back to your quarters with you," Lamia offered when they were done washing up. "Unless you want me to ask Tristan to take you."

Slag. Was she that obvious? She read the blatant humor dancing in Lamia's eyes and made a huffing, embarrassed little laugh.

"Come on." Only, she couldn't help herself from stealing a last quick look at Tristan as they walked past.

Later, after rechecking for surveillance equipment, Tatiana took a wonderfully hot shower, then settled in to spend the night using the satellite link to the plasma screen to research viruses. She knew Lamia would be able to track her link use and the hours she'd spent awake. Didn't matter. All that would reveal was that she was interested in immunology.

And that she suffered from insomnia.

She, and a lot of other people in the Waste. Weeks of endless night could do that to a person. Make them lose sleep. Make them go mad.

She knew that better than most. Sensory deprivation had been a favorite game of Gavin Ward's.

The memories surged, trying to claw free, and she shoved them back. Not now. Some other day she would face them. But not today.

She paced the confines of her small quarters, willing her thoughts away from deep, cavernous places that would only cause her pain.

She reminded herself that the dark was no longer her enemy. Her night vision had evolved into a thing of beauty.

As to the insomnia, well, lately she'd found that she needed very little sleep. Another genetic engineering bonus. She remembered that about Wizard and Yuriko. Years past, while she'd required seven or eight hours, they'd gotten by on two.

She was becoming more like them every day. The thought was bittersweet. If they were alive, would they even recognize their baby sister now?

Swallowing, she turned back to the linkpad, searching for the latest published research on the application of engineered viruses as nanomachines.

The following morning, Lamia came to fetch her and the first words out of her mouth came as no surprise.

"Not much one for sleep, huh?"

"Not so much, no," she said, with a gesture at the walls. The slagging four walls that had kept her on edge the whole night through. She couldn't bear to be confined. Only, she had to bear it. Talk about a quandary. "Unfamiliar surroundings."

A shadow crept into Lamia's eyes. "They'll become more familiar with time."

"Wasn't planning on moving in permanently." Tatiana slid her AT450 between her shoulder blades and forced a laugh.

The shadow grew darker. "I know, but sometimes life doesn't play out the way we plan." Lamia shook her head, and her smile didn't reach her eyes. "Come on. Breakfast'll get cold."

Keying her pass code behind her, Tatiana locked down her chamber, going through the motions, though she doubted the precaution would keep anyone out if they really wanted in. There was nothing there to find, anyway. Everything of import was stashed on her person.

The breakfast fare wasn't much different than what she would have made for herself: sim-protein simmered with spices, a complex-carb bar and fortified soya milk. Balancing plate and cup, she made her way to where Lamia had taken a seat and eased in beside her.

Conversation was stilted until she caught a trailing thought of Kalen's. He was thinking about his knife collection. Perfectly matched butterfly knives. He kept them mounted on the walls of his chamber.

Tatiana smiled. She'd studied enough about human interactions to know that the best way to encourage any sort of dialogue was to ask questions that pertained to the interests of one's companion. So she fixed her gaze on Kalen until he looked up, his dark eyes narrow and wary, his full lips drawn in a taut line.

"So, uh, what kind of knives do you collect?" she said into the dead silence.

He blinked. Stared at her. And so did everyone else.

Maybe she needed to work on the segue.

"They're ancient butterfly swords," Lamia said, filling the awkward silence.

Then Shayne made a comment, and soon there was a conversation taking place, with Kalen slowly becoming engaged.

"It is a style of sword that was developed as a defensive weapon," Kalen explained, his dark eyes glowing as he warmed to his topic. "Their beliefs prohibited Shaolin monks from killing, so they developed these weapons to disable rather than take life." He looked down, cut a bite of sim-protein, popped it in his mouth and chewed thoughtfully as he watched her with onyx-dark eyes. Then he leaned a little toward her and said, "Tristan shares a measure of such beliefs."

At the mention of his name, Tatiana's heart gave a crazy little lurch in her chest. She wanted to reach inside, grab it and make it be still.

She could feel the attention of the others shift toward her, could sense their interest, like that of wolves scenting a meal.

Turning her attention to her own meal, she ate a bite, and asked with a sideways glance through her lashes, "Does he?"

Kalen slid a look her way, the kind of look that said her attempt at feigned disinterest had been a dismal failure. One more thing to add to her to-be-worked-on list, she thought with a sigh.

"It must be a very small measure he shares, then," she observed. At Kalen's questioning look, she continued, "I've seen him kill. Yesterday."

There was a sharp intake of breath from just about everyone at the table, a concerted synchrony of sound. She had said something wrong, and the weight of it hung in the room like thick smoke.

She found the sudden wave of tension almost comical.

"Choices and consequences," Kalen said at length, sounding too much like Tristan for her liking.

She looked around the table. Everyone was either focused on their plates or staring at her with wide-eyed wariness. Carefully, she set her utensils down, pressed her lips together, chose her words with care.

"Is this the point," she said, fixing her gaze on Kalen, "where you tell me something circuitous and meaningless like"—she deepened her voice—"'if you understand, things are just as they are; if you do not understand, things are just as they are'?"

Kalen blinked, and the corner of his mouth twitched in a whisper of a smile. To her right, someone snorted. She thought it might have been Lamia.

"Not so meaningless, if you understand," he said, at last, his tone slightly choked.

Silence reigned, and their gazes held. They stared at each other for an instant, both speechless, and then they each made a short, chuffing laugh.

And an instant later, the rest of the table joined in.

Tatiana looked around, feeling a momentary disorientation.

Was this the beginnings of friendship, this searching out of common interests, this shared amazement and amusement?

She thought it must be, and she stored the realization away for future reference.

Opening her mouth, she almost asked about Tolliver, almost asked about Ward's hidden lab. Then she looked around at the smiling faces, thought about the morose mood that had permeated the room when she first arrived, and she found she couldn't destroy the moment.

Later. There would be time later to ask her questions. And perhaps the seeds of companionability she had sown now would help ensure that she got her answers.

"So, maybe when we're done with breakfast, you can give me the full tour?" she asked, turning to Lamia.

She frowned, confused, as her question brought about fresh peals of laughter.

"Not till later," Lamia said. "You're on kitchen duty today. I signed you up yesterday. You wanna eat, you have to make yourself useful."

"Kitchen duty?" Tatiana echoed, shooting a desperate look at Kalen. "I can cut sim-protein into strips. Boil water with my plasgun. That about sums up my kitchen skill."

She'd never cooked because she had never had a kitchen to cook in. The lab of her childhood had been designed to provide for their needs, with a synthesizer serving them appropriate portions of all required nutrients.

The next part of her life had been spent in a cell, with all her meals provided.

Or *not* provided, depending on how her captor was feeling that day.

In the six months she'd been free, cooking hadn't been high on her must-learn list. She pretty much stuck to dehydrated fruit-and-veggie bars, sim-protein and veggi-sim. Not particularly tasty or palate stimulating, but nutritious, which was all she needed.

The look on her face must have given her away, because Lamia patted her reassuringly on the arm.

"Kitchen duty?" Tatiana asked again, not even trying to mask her horror.

CHAPTER FOURTEEN

That night, Tatiana stepped from the shower, thinking that a min-dry would have been nice. They'd had one at the quarters she'd rented temporarily in Gladow Station a few months back, and she'd gotten used to the convenience of showering and washing her clothes at the same time, then stepping from the cubicle already dry.

Looking about the tiny bathroom, she found spare towels on a shelf beneath the sink. She had showered with her knife in her hand—a girl could never be too careful—and she took care now to dry it, wiping the soft cloth along the blade and handle.

Moments later, dressed and fully armed, she leaned close to the hatch and listened for sounds of activity in the corridor. All was silent as the grave.

Perfect.

She was restless. Edgy. One night spent in this tiny room had been one night too many. Tonight was for prowling about and poking into things and places she had no business seeing. Because tomorrow she was leaving, whether Tristan shared his information about Tolliver or not. She refused to stay another night buried here beneath the earth.

She keyed in her code and opened the metal hatch.

The only sound was the faint and distant hum of the generator.

She stepped out and paused to look in both directions. The lumilights were set to night mode, glowing faintly green at intervals along the shadowy hallway, the light coloring the clean white tiles, making everything the color of the edge of the ocean in late spring, green and blooming with algae.

Her heart gave a hard thump in her chest as she looked around. The walls of the corridor felt too close.

Fifty slagging yuales beneath the surface of the earth. What the hell was she thinking?

She didn't want to be here, didn't like the way it made her feel. But she'd had a couple of hot meals, showers, a hydrogen fill, and some surprisingly pleasant and informative personal interactions—all of which made her somewhat glad she'd come.

Oh . . . and she'd learned to chop sim-protein and potatoes, peel cucumbers, and cut carrots into impossibly thin strips—something Gemma had described as julienne. Those lessons made her somewhat less glad she'd come.

At the moment, she was glad for the quiet. So many people around her, so much conversation. Add to that the continuous tide of electrical ghosting that buffeted her from the thoughts of those around her, and by the end of the day, her reserves had been taxed.

She found both the experience, and the people here, strange.

Coming from her—a woman who was as far from normal as Gladow Station was from the Equatorial Band—that was quite the observation.

Gentle inquiries about who exactly everyone was and what the slagging hell they were doing down here had been met with stone-faced silence.

Don't ask. Don't tell. The motto of the Waste. But the people nesting down here like Siberian lemmings in a burrow seemed to take the adage to the extreme.

She'd learned all she could from them, which amounted to little enough. So tonight she would try her hand at mazes and puzzles, and a little exploration.

Looking up and down the corridor, she saw nothing of particular interest, nothing that would help her decide which direction to explore. So she chose left, mostly because she'd gone to the right earlier in the day.

She assumed that the other hatches in the immediate vicinity led to living quarters, as her own did, so she moved on, rounding a corner that led to yet another green-glowing corridor. The place was indeed a maze.

A second turn brought her to a passage where the tiles were cracked and broken, a number of the lumilights burnt out. Pausing outside a hatch, she leaned close and listened carefully for sounds of movement within, but she heard nothing.

She pressed the handle, pushed the door open, and found a dark, empty room. Withdrawing, she moved on to the next hatch and the next, each time rewarded with only darkness and echoing, empty spaces.

A step and then she froze, drawing tight to the wall and the shadows. She could hear a heartbeat and the sound of steady breathing, footsteps in the corridor, very quiet.

Moving inside the empty room, she drew the door almost completely closed, leaving a small crack, wide enough for her to catch a narrow view of the hallway.

The footsteps drew closer, gradually growing louder. One person. The gait had a male cadence. His heartbeat and breathing were even and steady.

A shadow fell across the tiles, the shape of a man. And

then she saw him, the pallid light bringing his features into sharp relief for mere seconds.

Tristan.

Without the layers of draping thermal gear hanging on him like seaweed off a rock, he was a sight to see. Broad shoulders, strong chest, taut belly. He wore a black shirt that molded to every plane and ridge. Black pants hugged muscled thighs. A utility harness crossed his torso, metal tools catching and reflecting the paltry glow of the greenish lumilight.

She let her gaze slide over him as she appreciated the view.

He drew abreast of where she stood concealed by the near darkness and the drawn hatch.

Tatiana stopped breathing, her body held in perfect stillness. He didn't even glance her way as he moved on without pausing. She watched him until the broad expanse of his back disappeared, swallowed by the shadows.

The sounds of his footsteps grew faint and fainter still as he walked in the direction she had intended to go. She waited until she could barely hear even the smallest sound of his movement, and then she eased the hatch open and slipped into the corridor, taking care to make her own steps far stealthier than his had been.

She followed the path he had taken, hugging the wall, staying far back and trailing him by auditory clues alone. He quickened his pace as he moved into a shabbier area of the facility, taking less care to ensure silent passage.

Which made perfect sense. Likely, he'd been quiet before so as not to disturb—or perhaps, not to alert—his sleeping comrades. He had no reason to exercise such consideration now because he was far enough from the living quarters that he likely expected no one to be about.

He made her job easy.

Moving at a fast clip, Tristan turned down the branching corridors. Clearly, he knew the way, knew exactly where he headed. He had to, because he was almost jogging down passages that had no lumilights, and he took quick turns as though he could pick them out blindfolded.

Why didn't he use a portable light? Maybe because he didn't want the glow to attract unwanted guests. Or because he was wary of being followed. He was smart and canny, she'd give him that.

And gorgeous. She'd give him that too.

Just ahead, the corridor stopped dead, a pile of rubble blocking the way. Tatiana froze as Tristan drew to a halt ahead of her. He pulled out a portable lumilight and snapped it on, the glow casting eerie shadows all about.

"You might as well join me," he said, his tone flat and cool.

She took a step forward. The toes of her boots just touched the edge of the circle of light.

"How long have you known I was behind you?" she asked, a little surprised that he'd made her.

He laughed, the sound rich and warm, and he cast her a sidelong glance. "I didn't. Not until right now. Maybe five minutes past, I thought I heard a sound, but I wasn't certain."

"Then why did you invite me to join you?"

"A gamble. If you answered, then I would know you were there."

There was nothing to say to that. She'd answered, more the fool, but she supposed it mattered little. He seemed intent on finishing whatever journey he'd started, only now she was along for the ride rather than watching from the sidelines.

"Where are you going?" she asked.

He angled her a look through his lashes. "I suspect you already know."

"There's something on the other side of these access tunnels, isn't there? A newer part of the facility."

"There is," he agreed. "And it has supplies that I want . . . no, *need*." He paused. "I don't suppose that warning you that there are mutated Reavers beyond this point will dissuade you from accompanying me."

She shook her head. "No more than the knowledge dissuades you from going in the first place."

They feinted and parried, she realized, dancing about each other without revealing any truths. Only hinting at what they meant to hide.

"Then we've wasted enough time." The dictator had returned.

Setting the toe of his boot into the pile, he began to climb. She saw it then, a narrow opening at the top of the rubble heap. Big enough for rats, but definitely not big enough for people. As he raised the lumilight, she saw that the rubble heap had some depth, making it more a tunnel than a hole.

"You planning to clear that?" she asked.

"Yeah. Take maybe an hour, I'm thinking."

"I'm thinking far less than an hour. Come down."

He glanced at her over his shoulder, his gaze locked on hers. Then he shrugged and stepped down from the pile.

Squatting, she tapped at the base of the heap, then tipped her head back to stare up to the top. She calculated angles and probabilities to determine the easiest clearance path.

She rose, tapped at a couple of rocks wedged in tight. The third one shifted almost imperceptibly. Digging her fingers in on both sides, she wriggled it back and forth.

Tristan moved up behind her, his hard chest brushing her shoulder as he leaned close.

The smell of his skin teased her senses, clean and fresh, a distinct and wonderful contrast to the faintly rotting, damp scent that clung to the tunnel walls. She turned her face a little toward him and breathed deep, wanting to bury her nose in his neck where it met the bulge of his shoulder, to inhale him. Perhaps to open her mouth and let her tongue trace the salt of his skin.

She let out a sharp exhale. Okay. Okay. Delayed maturity. She had a crush on him. She just needed to remember that, and everything would be fine.

Only, it felt like something else. Something not quite as shallow as a puddle in drought season.

And if she had even the smallest modicum of intelligence, she wouldn't let her thoughts slide any further in that direction.

"Here, let me," he said, reaching forward.

"You put your hands on this rock, and I'll hit you," she warned, using her shoulder to nudge him away and wondering why it mattered to her that she do this herself.

She had nothing to prove. Nothing to gain. It mattered not if he respected her abilities, if he believed her able.

"Ana, I know you can do this yourself," he said. "I've never met a more capable woman"—he made a low sound—"a more capable *person*."

She froze, her hands on the rock, her heart flipping over. She wanted that. Wanted him to see her as an equal. A partner. Not as a woman. And at the same time, she *wanted* him to see her as only that, a woman.

It was a ridiculous thought, given that women in the Waste were more likely to be seen as either possessions or expendable product. Even more ridiculous, given that she intended to leave tomorrow and would likely never see him again.

What did it matter how he thought of her? And yet she held her breath, waiting for him to say more, to touch her, to stroke his hand along her cheek as he had before. She ached for that, the warmth of that contact.

Her blood was a rushing flow, the pulse loud in her ears.

He drew his hands away, and she felt the harsh crush of disappointment.

"I'm sorry," he said, curt. "Old habits. Go ahead. I didn't mean to interfere." He stepped off, not far, but enough.

Wrong. He read her wrong, and she read him wrong, and in that instant, she hated normal human interactions. How did people get by without having a window into each other's thoughts?

She dug her fingers in again and hauled out a large rock about halfway down the heap, then leapt back as a small torrent of debris rolled down the incline. Fine granules of crushed rock and particulate matter rolled up in a cloud.

Tristan's arm—solid, brawny—slung about her waist, taking her weight as he dragged her back.

"You don't want to breathe that in," he said, his voice low.

Something twisted in Tatiana's heart. She didn't want him looking out for her. Didn't want to like the fact that he looked out for her. And she didn't. She *didn't*.

But the feel of his muscled forearm tight across her belly and the hard wall of his chest at her back made her feel things that went against logic and rationality. Primal things.

Frightening things.

She wasn't completely inexperienced. Determined to understand all aspects of her newly won freedom, she had chosen a clean, pleasant-looking settler in a camp outside Gladow Station soon after her escape from her cell.

The encounter had been unremarkable. Not unpleasant, but certainly not anything she was eager to repeat. Which was exactly the reason she had repeated it. From a purely analytical perspective, she needed more than one episode for a statistically relevant study. So she had pursued interaction with that man once more and with two others thereafter, twice each. Every encounter had been exactly like the last. Not unpleasant, but not particularly stimulating, either. Dowel A in hole B.

Based on the data she had gathered, she had concluded that she'd not been designed for physical interactions of that nature. She'd had no reason to further examine her hypothesis. Until now.

She suspected that with Tristan, sex would not be a cool, analytical act of pieces fitting together. It would be hot and feral and unguarded. It would demand emotion, the lowering of shields and fortifications, things she wasn't certain she was capable of . . . wasn't certain she *wanted* to be capable of.

The inescapable vulnerability held no appeal.

Emotion was something that flowed *to* her from others, something she *took*. In a way, it was something she fed upon.

Slowly she turned to face him, pressed full against him. He didn't drop his arm, didn't step away. Their bodies were separated only by thin layers of cloth, and she could feel every hard edge and smooth ridge of him, camouflaged by nothing. She tipped her head back and stared up at him, the sculpted planes of his face, the shadow of stubble along the solid curve of his jaw.

His eyes glittered in the dim light, heavy lidded, focused.

The way he looked at her sent a shiver chasing along her spine.

"Cold?" he asked, a low rasp.

"No." The word slid from her in a whisper. She knew she lacked finesse, lacked subtlety, and she didn't care. "My response is sexual. But you already knew that."

Silence, and then he gave a hushed laugh, the sound rolling from him through her, the vibration shifting his body against her own. It was a wonderful sensation, one that made her ache to press her hips harder to his.

This was what she had searched for and never found in her attempts at experimentation. This ache low in her belly. This racing of her heart.

She liked it very much.

And she liked it not at all.

"You don't dance the dance, do you, Ana?" Even the sound of his voice touched her, made her shiver.

"I never learned," she said. "I find human interactions . . . challenging."

"*Human* interactions . . ." He laughed again. "Because you're not human?"

"Because I am not good at being human."

His smile faded. His mouth opened. She thought he meant to ask questions she had no wish—and no ability—to answer.

Rising on her toes, she followed instinct, cutting short his words by pressing her mouth to his, eager, a little clumsy.

He made a sound low in his throat, a dark groan, and his arm tightened about her waist, dragging her closer still, his mouth moving on hers, opening, his tongue thrusting to meet hers. Heat flared, mingled with anticipation and sparking need. His free hand cupped the base of her skull, his fingers sliding through her hair as he angled his head to kiss her more fully.

She knew only his hard body, soft lips, his tongue

twining with hers. Sensation washed through her, a crashing wave that sank into her lungs, her belly, her limbs, filling her and heating her.

Her hands twisted in his shirt, dragging the material into her fists. She wanted to touch his skin. Taste his skin. She was greedy for taste and experience. Greedy for him.

She froze.

Slag. One kiss.

One inappropriately timed kiss.

One wet, deep kiss that rolled through her and flicked the on switch in every cell of her body, and she was lost to him. Not thinking. Not analyzing. Only reveling in sensation.

It was a path to problems so big she could barely imagine them.

Panting, she drew away, her heart hammering, her thoughts spiraling out of control. He reached for her, meaning to draw her back, and she shook her head, pressed two fingers against his wonderful mouth.

Whatever she had thought the joining of bodies could be . . . this was better. Sweeter. Darker. And they had yet to join anything more that lips and tongues.

She drew a sharp breath.

"Who are you, Tristan?" she asked softly. "Do you have parents? Siblings? What made you who you are? Where do you fit into this world?" She couldn't say why she pursued this, why she asked him for his secrets when just the questions themselves were so revealing of her own.

Perhaps it was because the kisses they had shared were so deeply personal.

He stared down at her, clearly bemused. Then he nipped her fingers, and with a shake of her head, she pulled away.

"Ana, love, you ask the strangest questions." He held out his hands, palms up, and smiled. "You looking for character references?"

Ana, love.

There could be no meaning behind the endearment. She knew that. It was a slip of the tongue.

He brushed her cheek, studying her with careful interest. However odd he thought her queries, he chose to answer.

"Not much to tell. I grew up in a typical family. Nice middle-class parents in a nice middle-class neighborhood with bikes and square patches of front lawn and all the kids out front on Rollerblades playing street hockey."

She stumbled over the concepts, unable to understand what he was saying. He was speaking English, but the words were foreign, the context out of place.

"Middle-class?" she repeated, riffling through the files in her mind, trying to place the term. "Street hockey?"

"Things from my past, long gone." He shrugged, stepped back from her. His tone, his actions, were casual, but beneath them she sensed an intensity that made her pay attention. His shrug suggested that the information he revealed was of little importance, but her senses were at high alert. There *was* something important here, she just hadn't figured out yet what it was. "My parents were just average people. I had two brothers, both older than me."

"And a pet rat."

"Yeah." He laughed, the sound hollow. "A pet rat."

"But you didn't grow up here, in the Waste?"

"No. I lived in a city."

He seemed to be telling the truth. Yet there was something evasive in the way he spoke.

"Which city?"

He smiled, a dark curving of his lips that held no humor. "A big one."

And with that, the connection was gone, the lingering warmth of their kiss thrust aside. Disappointment tarnished the sheen.

"No, you don't," Tristan said, grabbing her wrist to stop her as she made to turn away. "Whatever's between us, Ana, will have a time and a place. We'll find that time and place. But not now. It can't be right now."

Whatever's between us.

Mutual attraction. There could be nothing more.

She wanted to say it to him, to correct his erroneous implication that it was something deeper. But though she opened her mouth, the words refused to come out.

Because there *was* something more here, and they both knew it.

Gavin Ward stared at the cinder-block building, the only visible remnant of an energy-generating facility from a time long past. A time long dead. And buried.

The thought made him smile. Burial was exactly what he intended. Neat and tidy. He was so pleased this answer had come to him.

Before coming here, they had stopped at the hydraulic lifts that led to his now destroyed state-of-the-art laboratory, only to find that the shafts were collapsed, full of rubble. Useless as a means of entry.

Tolliver's work. The bastard was as handy with cytoplast as he was with a microfuge.

Stamping his feet, Gavin turned and watched as his men disassembled the massive orange tent. The thing had been put up for his convenience, as both a warning to interlopers and an easy way to track the back door to his laboratory, should he need it. Now the tent was no longer convenient, nor was the back door.

"Why do we need to destroy this worthless hut? Seems like a waste of perfectly good explosives," Thom muttered as he squatted to set a locked metal box on the ground. On the side was stenciled AMUNITIONS — DANGER — EXPLOSIVES.

Phosphorous mines. While cytoplast was perhaps a more refined method, the phosphorous mines would suffice for this job.

"Actually, this is an excellent use of explosives," Gavin replied, holding on to his temper by a thread. He disliked being questioned, challenged, disobeyed. But his association with Thom went back to boyhood, a fact that allowed the burly man some small latitude. "When I built my lab, I accessed this place because of the underground hot spring. By linking the two, I had both a convenient energy source and a perfect cloak of invisibility. Who would look for a new lab buried beside an old generator facility suspected of nuclear contamination?"

No one had. The orange tent had served as a warning. Anyone familiar with Old Dominion technology would have stayed away for fear of deadly irradiation. Anyone not familiar . . . well . . . even a fool would recognize a giant orange tent in the middle of the fucking frozen Waste as a warning.

"Tolliver did us the courtesy of blowing up the front doors, but he left the back door accessible." And he'd used that back door to bring Tatiana into the ground. Gavin was well pleased with the young comm specialist who had noted her retinal scan processed by the ancient elevator security system and brought the information to Gavin's attention. He would have to remember to reward him.

Perhaps a promotion. "We'll have to take care of this entry ourselves."

"I can do that." Thom frowned. "Is there anyone still alive down there?"

"Maybe. My epidemiological models would suggest that some will not have succumbed quite yet." Gavin stamped his feet again, anxious to finish the task and move into the heated rig, out of the cold. "When I pulled my troops out, there were still some three dozen researchers. And a child . . . though I believe she was a victim of a Reaver attack early in the study. . . ." He shrugged. He couldn't recall, and it really didn't matter. "In all likelihood, by now the researchers will have served as a food source for the escaped test subjects. Alive or dead, it matters not. What I propose is to seal everyone in, let the plague take its course, and then dig out the lone survivor."

"Survivor? Who the hell could survive that? And why dig him out? Won't he be a carrier?"

"No." Gavin smiled. His lovely Tatiana *would* survive. She could survive almost anything. He knew that. He'd done enough to her over the years to make very certain.

She had adapted. He particularly liked that. As a scientist, he was fascinated by adaptation.

And he prided himself on his own adaptability.

He had changed his plans slightly since repossessing his equipment and samples from Belek-ool. Prior to that, he had been eager to retrieve his sweet girl as soon as possible. But now, with both her stolen tissue samples and the viral samples back in his possession, he could afford to wait.

It was a matter of efficiency. Waiting was a far less messy prospect than sending troops into the infected facility to get Tatiana out. That, in turn, would mean sacrificing the troops exposed to the plague, and the entire thing could become quite a labor-intensive proposition.

Best to let the inevitable take its course. The researchers had been—or soon would be—eaten by the mutated Reavers. The Reavers would then be eaten by the plague. All so very neat and tidy. Survival of the fittest.

And Tatiana was the fittest.

She alone would walk away.

All he needed to do was wait for everyone else to die, and then he could send a retrieval team down for Tatiana.

After what she was about to live through down there, he could only imagine she would be very glad to be saved. Perhaps even glad to see him. He closed his eyes and imagined the blade of his scalpel kissing her skin.

He would certainly be very glad to see her.

"The key?" he asked Thom. The big man dragged forth a titanium key hanging on a thick chain about his neck as Gavin drew out its twin.

Together, they strode to the small building that housed the ancient elevator shaft. First Gavin, then Thom, inserted his key. They turned them, cutting all power to the elevator, trapping it at the bottom and arming the laser grid that made the shaft a death trap.

If those trapped did try to escape by this route, they would find that the exit had been blown to an impassable mass of rubble.

The thought made Gavin smile. No one could reach that point. First, they would have to try and climb the cable, and the laser grid would slice them into tiny, bloody bits long before they reached the top.

CHAPTER FIFTEEN

As he stepped up to drag free a large, jagged block near the top of the rubble heap that blocked the tunnel, Tristan noticed that Ana eased away, taking deliberate care not to touch him.

Which made her far wiser than he was.

What the hell had he been thinking kissing her like that? Again.

He was forming some very dangerous habits.

"Wait," he ordered as she dragged a chunk of rubble out of the pile. A heavy, rancid smell wafted up from the debris, hitting him with enough force to make him rear back.

"No reason to wait," she replied. "I know what we'll find."

"Ana—"

She hauled out another chunk of shattered concrete, and they both stared down at what was left of the Reaver. His limbs were torn from his body, gnawed clear to the bone in places. The teeth marks were way too big for rats.

"They ate him. One of their own." No inflection. No dismay. Just a statement of fact.

"You know they do. You saw it yesterday." He glanced at her, wondered how the hell she could be so calm. Most people would be sliding down a slippery slope into hysteria by now.

But Ana wasn't most people.

He wanted to tell her he admired her composure. Admired *her*.

Instead, he said, "We need to move." And he thought, Now that was fucking eloquent.

He sidestepped the corpse and scrambled up the remnants of the debris pile, taking the lead.

Whatever the hell they met along the way, he wasn't putting Ana in the line of fire. He'd take a hit himself before he'd let anything hurt her.

The thought actually made him laugh out loud, low and mordant. Because if she knew what he was thinking, all macho and protective, she'd probably shoot him herself.

"Is laughter an appropriate response?" she asked from close behind him. The sound of rubble shifting and rolling followed their every step.

Odd question. He'd noticed that she did that sometimes . . . asked odd questions. "It's either that or puke."

She was silent for a beat. "In that case, I agree with your choice."

The hole was big enough to squeeze through now. Together, they'd accomplished in fifteen minutes what would have taken him an hour working alone.

"Did you set the charge that blew this tunnel?" she asked.

"No. If I had, we wouldn't have been able to clear a path so easily."

"You sure about that?" She made a low laugh, the sound incredibly sexy. "You might have set the cytoplast . . . oh . . . three millimeters too high . . . too low . . ."

"Aren't you a funny girl?" he sniped, but he knew his

tone lacked conviction because he was actually enjoying her teasing.

"A funny girl . . ." she mused from behind him. "I never considered myself such. But I like that you think so."

And he liked it that she liked it . . . and didn't that just twist them both up in a cozy little knot.

He scooted down to lie flat on his belly, then dragged himself through the opening. Sharp stones gouged him, the roof of the tunnel scraping his skin. It would be easier for Ana—he was too big for the hole; she was smaller—and he was glad for that.

Beyond the hole, the hallway was pitch dark, the lumi-lights there shattered and ruined, most fallen to the ground, some hanging by a single screw. There was no question in his mind as to the who and why of this destruction. Photophobia was one of the early signs that the viral infection had reached the point of no return. Enraged and terrified by the light, the mutated Reavers had hacked the light sources to bits weeks past to escape even the dimmest glow.

Tristan hit the phosphorous pack on his utility harness, creating a faint green light that let him see a few meters in front of him. Because of the army's modifications, he could detect wavelengths above and below normal human visual limits, and he could see better than average in the dark. That, combined with the phosphorous pack, was enough. But he'd have to keep an eye on Ana to make certain she didn't run into any walls.

A cursory inspection revealed no threat, so he drew his knees tight to his chest as he cleared the opening, then twisted his body and skidded sideways down the far side of the rubble heap, landing ankle deep in water.

"Puddle," he warned, too late. Tatiana came down behind him in a controlled slide. Her booted feet slammed down in the water, sending up spray in all directions.

He caught her elbows, steadying her. Only she was already balanced, ready to move, Setti9 in her hand.

"Sorry," she offered, dropping her gaze and pulling free of his grasp with a deliberate movement.

He felt an instant of disorientation.

Why did he keep getting it wrong, offering aid when it wasn't wanted or needed? If he read her right, she was offended by those offers.

"Ana, I mean no disrespect. It's a matter of old habits, deeply ingrained."

She was silent for a moment. "Understood."

From the lack of inflection, he couldn't be certain of the sentiment behind the curtly spoken word, couldn't be certain she *did* understand. Something about the way she said it gave him pause, not only because he couldn't gauge her mood by the word, but because the tone and inflection seemed so strangely familiar.

He'd heard the response before, a short answer spoken with the exact same cool inflection, but he couldn't place the recollection. This wasn't the first time he'd had the odd sensation that Ana reminded him of someone. He just couldn't think who it was.

"Insulting you is the last thing I mean to do." He trusted her to hold her own. She'd already proven she could, time and again. Hell, she'd faced down armored and plated ice pirate rigs without flinching. It wasn't a question of guts. She had that in spades.

It was a question of patterns of behavior he'd learned in his youth, deeply ingrained in who he was.

His father had been both a tough bastard and a gentleman, the two parts of his personality working together in a strange harmony. And he had taught his son to be like him, simply because he knew no other way.

Tristan glanced at Ana, watched her scout the darkness and the shadows for threat.

He wanted her. Which made him want to protect her. Because she was *his*.

Yeah. That was perfect. The epitome of enlightenment and a progressive attitude.

Might as well put a club in his hand and leave him to beat his chest while he gathered her hair in his fist and dragged her off to mate.

Only she wouldn't make it easy on him. She was tough enough that she might end up being the one doing the dragging.

And damn if that thought didn't hold a hell of an appeal.

They were quiet as they walked, moving slowly out of caution and care because there was only the faint glow from Tristan's phosphorous pack.

Tatiana knew that Tristan was moving almost blind, while her vision was unimpaired.

From somewhere to the left came a faint scrabbling sound, tiny claws, tiny feet.

"There's something here," she said, her voice low.

"Yeah." He killed the phosphorous gel, and the darkness came down upon them like a thick blanket, smelling faintly of damp and rot. "Rats. They're in the walls."

Within milliseconds, Tatiana's gaze adjusted to the change in light.

With each step that took them deeper into the darkness, the smell grew stronger. Rot and decay and something else, reminiscent of what she'd smelled when she and Tristan were attacked by the mutated Reavers.

With a dull thud, Tristan's boot hit something as they

rounded a bend. He offered a single word of warning, softly spoken. Skirting the object, he moved on.

A body, Tatiana realized. A mutated Reaver laid out on its back, limbs splayed, what was left of its face set in a death grimace. Parts of it were gnawed away, parts still laced with decaying flesh. A huge metal girder, bent and twisted, pinned the corpse in place.

She squatted, frowning. Something wasn't right. . . . Bits of the body were too neatly arranged, not strewn about as though torn from the whole, but fallen in a bizarre pattern of perfect organization. Fingers, three small bones each, neatly aligned. Eight little wrist bones. All perfectly in place. The remnants of cartilage and skin that had once been an ear aligned with the place it ought to have been if still attached to the head.

Tipping her head back, she studied the area. A large section of wall had caved in, and the girder had been thrust free, pinning the guy in place. From what she could see, parts of him had simply fallen off as he lay here, trapped.

It was a slagging filthy way to die.

And it made no sense to think he had lain here and simply fallen apart.

Suddenly, she had a recollection of the guy Gemma had gutted, the way his ear had torn free when he'd been punched in the head.

She froze, horror churning like a deep ocean current. The perfect alignment was no accident, the idea of him falling to bits no impossibility. She reached out, almost touching the remains of one finger, then jerked her hand back, curled her own fingers into a fist.

These Reavers hadn't just been genetically modified. They'd been *exposed* to something. Purposefully infected.

The plague Ward had created.

It wasn't confined to his hidden lab anymore. It wasn't just plated and incubated and grown in artificial medium or live-cell in vitro culture. It had progressed to live-subject in vivo trials, and these mutated Reavers were the subjects.

She swallowed.

"Ana," Tristan called her name, a sharp bark of sound that demanded her reply.

"Here."

He made a short, huffing sigh that spoke of either irritation or relief. Perhaps a measure of both. "We need to move. I have no desire for unwanted company."

"Aren't I unwanted company? I did follow you, uninvited."

"Uninvited at first, perhaps. But not unwanted." He paused, and his thigh brushed against her shoulder as he stepped closer. She could feel the heat of his body through his clothes and her own, proof of life, a contrast to the horror before her.

"I do want you," he said. His voice, low and rough, tunneled into her heart, made her ache to reach out and touch him. She curled her fingers tight to her palm, thinking that those four simple words had more layers and depths than she wanted to explore right now.

"You say that to me here, in the dark. In a narrow, crumbling corridor. With a dead Reaver at my feet," she murmured. "How am I to answer you?"

"Exactly as you did." He shifted, and she felt his hand on her hair, a fleeting caress. "Wake from a darkened dream and see the beauty that surrounds you."

Her dreams were ever dark, but he had no way to know that. She stared straight ahead at the blank wall, shocked by his words. *Wake from a darkened dream.* How could his nonsense hold such truth?

"There is no beauty to see here," she said, rising.

"There is you," he answered softly.

Her breath rushed from her in a sharp huff. Slowly, she looked up at him, his profile hard and masculine, clear to her, despite the darkness. And she knew she'd lied. There was beauty here. *He* was beautiful. Despite where they were and what surrounded them.

She could no longer hold back the urge to touch him. Tentatively, she reached up and cradled his cheek in her hand. He leaned in and rested his forehead lightly against her own, touching the other side of her face. They breathed together. Completely connected.

After two heartbeats, he abruptly stepped back. "We need to move. Now."

Dizzy with his sudden change in manner, dizzy with the thoughts and emotions that spiraled through her, she stared at him. These were not the emotions of others. They were her own. Her own feelings, set free. Here, in this place.

Tristan did that to her. Had done it since the first moment she met him. He turned everything upside down. Her perceptions. Her ideas. Not by imposing his own upon her, but by making her approach her thoughts from a different direction.

She cast a last glance at the decaying remains of the Reaver and focused on that, on the safe puzzle of what the remains represented, rather than the terrifying question of exactly why Tristan made her feel things, think things she never had before.

She stared at the tiny wrist bones, inhaling sharply as the last bits of the puzzle snapped together.

The Reavers had been infected with something. Something that made them afraid of light. Something that made bits and parts of them fall away.

Ward's slagging plague had gotten free. Or been freed.

Who else had been exposed? Kalen? Lamia? *Tristan?*

The thought swept through her like a brutal northern wind, driving away all warmth and light. Horror and fear rocked her as she mechanically followed Tristan along the corridor.

The guy Gemma had stabbed had been foaming at the mouth. Aggressive. Stronger than he ought to have been, even when injured. Even for a Reaver.

Just what the hell had Ward crossed her DNA with? What the hell had her genetic code created?

She could argue that she had no proof. That there could have been another lab, another experiment, and this was the result. But she knew that for the false hope it was. This plague was hers. Her fault. Her genome.

How many people would die because of her?

She walked faster, her rapid gait matching the racing of her heart.

Ahead of her, Tristan stopped so quickly that she barreled into his back.

She lifted her hands, rested her palms between his shoulder blades for a second, feeling the heat of him through his shirt and the supple play of muscle, the steady movement as he breathed.

"What is it?" she asked. "What's wrong?"

"Nothing. I just needed to know you were there." Reaching back, he closed his fingers on her wrist, gave a light squeeze. "It's dark as sin in here. Stay close enough that I can hear you breathe."

Dark as sin. Aptly put. *Her* sins. Anguish burned in her gut. She should have stopped Ward long ago. But this time, she would stop him. She *would*.

"Yes, sir," she muttered, but he only made a hushed laugh in reply.

The smell she'd noted moments past grew stronger as

they pressed on. Tristan moved as though he was following a path he had taken many times before, relying on the map in his mind for guidance, but he couldn't possibly see the terrain as it was now.

"We could use a light," she suggested.

"It might draw them. I'd prefer to get in and get out without being served up for dinner."

Tatiana battled with herself as she assessed the logic of offering to lead. That would necessitate revealing a measure of her secrets, at least enough to explain how she could see in the dark.

How much was safe to reveal? She trusted no one.

"Then let me watch for debris," she said at last. "I have exceptionally good night vision. I can actually make out a few shapes."

"You're kidding." He gestured for her to precede him, not because he thought less of her, or more. But because he thought her his equal. The thought was a revelation. "Then you take point, Ana."

She figured he'd have a whole lot of questions if she told him she could see in the dark as though she were using night-vision goggles. Questions she had no inclination to answer. So she kept the pace slow as she moved into lead position, deliberately creating the impression that she was feeling her way with care.

"Dead end," she said a moment later as they came to a sealed metal hatch. Surprise touched her as she studied the entry. Laser-locked with voice recognition release. Unlike the other security she'd encountered here so far, this portal was guarded by the most current technology.

And Tristan knew the way in.

Interesting.

"I've got it." He stepped ahead of her, did his voice recognition magic. Only this door was guarded by more than just a retinal scan. He slid his finger in a slot. Fingerprint pattern? she wondered. Then she realized it was equipped to take a blood sample, assess it for genetic markers.

Which meant his genetic markers were stored somewhere for comparison and that the computer running the security system in this part of the facility was on a separate energy feed.

Tristan tipped his face up, and the scanner evaluated his features. Face-recognition software. Finally, he keyed in a code fourteen digits long.

"Talk about overkill," she muttered.

As he finished the code, she pondered the implication of the fact that he could do all this in dead darkness.

Because he'd done it enough times before that he didn't even need to think about it.

Unease skittered through her on little rat feet. This equation was adding up to a sum she didn't like.

The vacuum seal released with a soft shush, and the door slid open. Once they were through, Tristan turned and repeated every step over again, sealing the way. In and out.

He'd grown tense, his body language rigid, his attention focused and funneled solely into his task. Her wariness kicked up another notch.

They continued along a wide, high corridor lined with plastiglass-fronted doors that led into spacious rooms, some ruined, some in pristine condition, looking as though someone had simply killed the lights and walked away a moment before.

Through the doors, she could see long white countertops set beneath nucleoplast screens. There were linkboards, keypads. State-of-the-art technology, a distinct contrast to the antiquated equipment in the other part of the underground facility. Again, wariness crawled through her, amplifying the sensation that there was something very wrong with this scenario.

Pausing before a metal door that was blown clean off its hinges at the top and hanging by twisted metal shards at the bottom, she reached out to lay her hand on Tristan's arm and halt his progress.

"What happened here?" she whispered.

Inside was a small room, completely lined with metal, the walls fitted with shelves and mounts that suggested there had once been weapons here.

"They cleaned out the weapons room when things started to go south," he said. "Took everything with them when they left."

Not much of an answer. It raised a lot more questions than it put to rest.

"They. You mean Ward's troops?"

A pause, then, "Yeah."

"Which is why no one here has plasguns. Why you're fighting mutated Reavers with only knives."

She heard his slow, steady inhalation.

"Yeah."

There you go. Everything tied up nice and neat. Only it wasn't neat. It was a tangled, ruined mess that stank like death and rot.

Why had thirty-eight people been trapped in an underground facility with genetically modified monsters? And why the slagging hell didn't they just leave?

Tristan shifted to one side, moved past her, staying close to the wall. She followed, questions hovering at the tip of her tongue.

A moment later, he paused before a door that was solid

metal. Again, there was a security system in place, with an independent power source. Their presence triggered the keypad, and it glowed with a faint light that seemed incredibly bright in the surrounding darkness.

Tristan worked the lock, opened the door, and stepped forward.

"Thought you said it's ladies first." She tried to keep her tone light, but the words came out taut and brittle. Every instinct she had was screaming the alert, the fine hairs on her arms standing on end.

She couldn't see it. Not yet. Couldn't hear it. But whatever it was, it was here.

Trouble was here, just waiting in the dark.

"Now you want to go first?" He sounded aggrieved.

"Not for some antiquated idea of courtesy." She freed her AT450, shouldered past him, paused in the doorway to do a 270-degree turn, checking every corner of the room for threat. Nothing moved.

Satisfied, she stepped forward.

"It's just that I can see better than you can," she muttered. "And I'm the one with the plasguns."

"Fair enough."

Her gaze swept the interior of the spacious room, registering everything at once.

Beakers. Electron microscope. Centrifuge. Microfuge. Wetting trays. Microtiter plates. Thermal cycling device.

It was a lab. One still in use.

Assaulted by a horrific wave of bleak and terrifying memory, she froze, struggled for control.

The smell. Not like the stink of the mutated Reavers that hung thick in the air of the corridors. Antiseptic sharp, the laboratory smell swirled around her and through her like smoke.

Memories clawed at her, dark and vicious. Gavin

Ward's laboratory in Port Uranium had looked much like this.

No, not much like this. *Exactly* like this.

At her back, Tristan spoke a single word. "Lights."

The lights went on, triggered by voice-rec technology. Whatever this place was, it was on an independent energy supply, because other than the security system, everything else in this part of the facility was dead.

Whatever this place was. She *knew* what it was. Ward's lab.

And the voice-rec was programmed to the inflection and pitch of *Tristan's* voice.

He knew the way here, could walk it blindfolded. And his blood, his voice, his code opened the door.

He'd offered to tell her about Tolliver.

Of course, he could do that. He *was* Tolliver.

And she was a blind fool.

Horror and disbelief held her immobile. Her lungs were blocked, her chest, her throat. She couldn't breathe, couldn't speak.

And then she did. One word. A whisper.

"Tolliver."

Tristan turned toward her, reached out. She jerked back as though burned by a live plasma line.

"No."

A flicker of dismay touched his features.

She turned, looked frantically around the lab, and she saw that not everything here was pristine. Along one wall, cabinets were torn open, the contents broken and shattered. In the corners, the shadows moved and shifted.

"No," she said again, but the sound was lost, buried beneath a cacophony of howls and snarls. From the corners, they came, and she saw then that there were bolt-holes in the walls.

This was their domain, the domain of monsters. They had made it their own.

On instinct, she leaped forward, turned her body so she stood back-to-back with Tristan, and all around them were monsters slinking forward from out of the dark.

With a horrific cry, a massive creature lunged across the counter. It snatched up a metal stool, swung it at the ceiling, smashing all but one of the lumilights.

Jagged bits of plastiglass rained down on them, falling on their heads, their shoulders, tinkling to the floor. She felt the sharp bite of a shard as it scratched her cheek.

She had her AT450 out and firing, flipped her Setti9 clear of its holster.

"Take it," she screamed, shoving the plasgun at Tristan, firing her AT450 as a creature leaped at her from the shadows. With a high shriek that went on and on, the thing fell to the ground, slapping frantically at the hole in its chest.

Tristan was reaching for the plasgun she held out to him, everything moving too slowly. Her heart slammed against her ribs. Her vision narrowed to just his hand, his reaching hand, then burst wide once more as, from across the counter, three of the mutated Reavers seemed to fly through the air, arms and legs extended, the moment frozen.

On instinct, she turned, tried to protect him, both plasguns locked on her targets.

Her heart was beating too fast, too hard. Where was her enhanced physiology now? Where was her preternatural calm?

Tristan. *Tristan.*

She heard him then, his voice, coming at her as though through a long tunnel.

He was shouting for her to get out, to run.

To leave him. Save herself.

Never.

She fired. Fired again.

But the Reavers were on him, snarling and growling, her perception of her surroundings snapping with sickeningly abrupt speed from frozen impossibility to frenzied movement.

"Ana! Get out! Get out now! Run!"

With a cry, he went down in a tangle of legs and arms, bared teeth and flying droplets of blood.

CHAPTER SIXTEEN

Already firing—each burst of plas-shot driving the modified Reavers to a shrieking, snarling frenzy—Tatiana watched Tristan go down, watched his blood splatter in an arc across the floor.

Instinct made her move, crouch, defend.

The sight of his blood made her own heart bleed.

Her mind whispered that he was *Tolliver*. A monster. A murderer. The man who had partnered with Gavin Ward, the man responsible for creating a deadly plague from the tissue samples that had been stolen from her.

But she couldn't quite align those thoughts with what she knew of Tristan. The dictator. The protector.

Then the soldier inside, the thing she was bred to be, took over, freezing her emotions, kicking her into action.

The close confines made her plasma weapons the least valuable of her tools; she might hit Tristan, and the light of each burst only fed the Reavers' killing rage.

She slung her AT450 into its holster, flipped her Setti9 away.

Yanking out both knives, one in each hand, she vaulted onto the high counter, and slid feet first to the end. With a cry, she hurled the knife in her left hand. It flew, a blur, the metal blade catching the glow from the remaining unbroken lumilight.

With a dull thwack the point of her knife smacked dead center between a Reaver's eyes, sinking deep.

The creature howled, reared back, but Tristan was still overwhelmed by a swarm of them. She couldn't tell if he moved, couldn't tell if he yet breathed.

Couldn't tell if the spreading puddle of blood on the floor was his or the Reavers'.

An icy killing rage took her. She'd never felt anything like it before. But Tristan was hers. *Hers.*

And she meant to keep him safe.

"Slag. Slag. *Slag.*"

Her momentum carried her along the length of the workspace, her feet clearing the path, kicking aside beakers and trays as she slid across the smooth surface. With jarring force, she slammed to a dead stop, her feet ramming into the belly of a creature that loomed at the end of the countertop.

The thing doubled over with a howl, and she caught its hair, held it still, sank her second blade into the back of its neck. A sharp, hard thrust. In, then out.

Shoving the mutated Reaver aside, she leaped from the counter, yanked her knife from the forehead of the one she'd stabbed between the eyes. A hot spurt of blood flowed over her hand. But it wasn't dead quite yet. With a snarl, it grabbed her throat, clawed hands digging deep as it slammed her head to the side against the edge of the counter.

With her ears ringing and her vision swimming, she curled her fingers tight around the knife hilt, punched the Reaver hard in the jaw. Its head rocked back, but its grip tightened, clawed nails tearing through her skin and muscle.

With a snarl, she stabbed at the exposed throat. Burbling blood, the thing stumbled back, then lurched at her once more.

From the corner of her eye, she saw Tristan's booted feet moving, heard a grunt of effort and pain. His? She couldn't tell. But he was alive, and that realization jolted through her like an energy boost.

Double fisted, she sank her blades into both sides of the Reaver's neck at the carotid sinuses, then tore them free. Blood poured down on her in a torrent. The thing kept walking, two steps, three, and then it sank to its knees and keeled over.

She could hear someone screaming, loud, rhythmic. The same word. Again and again.

And then she realized that someone was her.

Tristan. She was calling his name.

Snapping her mouth shut, she struggled for control. She couldn't see him. He'd gone down under the three Reavers, and she hadn't seen him come up.

Tolliver. He is Tolliver. He is a killer. A monster.

But he was Tristan. And somehow, in this gore-laden instant, that seemed more important.

Another Reaver came at her, its claws raking her skin, and then it sank its teeth into her shoulder, tearing away a chunk of muscle and fascia and skin.

Pain exploded down her arm, up her neck. She felt like she was on fire.

Nausea burned her gut and clawed up the back of her throat. She moved without thought, all training and speed, knives whistling through the air. When she straightened and sucked in a breath, the Reaver was on the ground in a pool of blood.

There was no time to look at her wound. Blood ran down her back, her arm. A river of blood.

Hauling out her Setti9, she flung herself at the pile in the middle of the floor. She reached down and rolled a Reaver off the top. Dead. Its eyes stared blankly at the ceiling, blood dripping from wounds in its neck and chest.

Gritting her teeth, she reached for the next one, jerked back as Tristan pushed it free and struggled to sit up.

Her heart twisted. His hair was matted with blood.

But he was alive. Alive—

"Ana! Behind you."

She turned, twisted to the side, her injured shoulder slamming against the ground. Pain rocketed through her, bright, hot.

Tristan took the blow for her, the Reaver that had dived for her hitting him instead. The sound of his pain escaped through his gritted teeth.

Rolling, she came to her feet.

With a chilling howl, the creature peeled back its lips and sank pointed teeth into Tristan's forearm.

"Fuck." He snarled, slammed it against the edge of the counter, once, twice, trying to dislodge its vicious hold.

Fury and fear and desperation mixed in her gut, a roiling slurry.

Slagging hell. If anyone was going to kill Tristan Tolliver, it was her. He was *hers*.

Tatiana leaped on the Reaver's back, wrapped her forearm across it neck, caught its chin in her palm and yanked hard.

She meant to snap its spine.

But its whole head tore free with a horrific slopping sound. For an instant she just stared at it, holding the weight of it, her hand tangled in its hair. Then she tossed the head aside, and scrambled back like a crab as it landed on the floor with a squelching plop.

Breathing heavily, she jerked around to find Tristan

shoving his blade into the neck of yet another mutated Reaver, taking his turn at saving *her*. He was on his feet now, standing over the slumped creature, legs wide, lips peeled back in a snarl.

On a harsh exhale, he shoved the Reaver aside, and lifted his head. His gaze locked on hers, feral, wild, his chest heaving as he struggled for breath.

"Any more?" His shoulders rose and fell with each inhalation and exhalation.

Pushing to her feet, she held the edge of the counter for balance, her hands dripping blood, her gaze scanning each corner of the room.

Nothing moved. Nothing.

The single remaining lumilight flickered on and off, sending greenish bursts lurching along the wall as it flared and died in intermittent flashes. The light and color added to the horrific detail, reflecting off the puddles of blood.

"No more." She dragged in a breath. "Not right now. But there might be more on the way."

"We aren't safe here, Ana love."

"Don't call me that," she snapped. Then she repeated, softer, "Don't call me that. *Tolliver*."

He didn't even flinch. He studied her for the span of a heartbeat, his gaze gone cold as liquid hydrogen.

She had no idea what he was thinking. Hell, she had no idea what *she* was thinking.

Tiny shards of the broken lumilights fell from overhead, drifting over them like snow, tinkling against the floor. At last, he looked away.

Stepping to the side, he used his elbow to smash the plastiglass front of a rectangular wall-mounted cabinet. He reached between the jagged edges and dragged out a small case.

"We aren't safe here. But I know a place we will be. Come on." He held out his free hand.

A sense of unreality settled over her.

Tolliver. He hadn't denied it, and until this very second, she hadn't realized how desperately she had wanted him to tell her she was wrong. To tell her she had leaped to a conclusion that bore no resemblance to reality.

But he didn't. He just stood there with his hand outstretched and his cold-as-the-frozen-Waste eyes locked on hers.

He was Tolliver, Ward's minion, the monster who had created a plague from the tissue samples Ward had sliced from her body. She needed to remember that.

But as she stood here looking at him, bruised and torn and painted in blood, she was just so slagging grateful that he was alive.

Because he was *Tristan*.

She shook her head.

"Ana," he said again, and stepped forward, his hand still outstretched.

"I know who you are. I know what you did here. You did this. You created *this*"—her voice broke and she made a desperate little gesture to encompass the carnage—"and if you touch me, I'll kill you, Tristan Tolliver. I will kill you."

He tipped his head to one side, and his eyes crinkled up a little as he smiled. But it was a shadowed smile, laced with pain and torment.

"But you just risked your life to save me."

"So that I could kill you myself, you slagging rat bastard." The words tumbled free. She tried to snatch them back, but they came in a rush, half wail, half snarl, and she was appalled by all they revealed.

He nodded as though she made perfect sense. "There is a sort of twisted logic in that."

But there wasn't. Not a damned bit of logic.

At last, he dropped his hand, as though only now understanding that she wouldn't take it.

She dropped her gaze to the pile of bodies on the floor, and her emotions fell away, just sank into some deep pit in her soul. She was left feeling nothing and everything, her confusion so vast it made her dizzy and sick.

Raising her head, she found him watching her in the flickering light. Watching her with those amazing night-dark eyes, bitter now and cold as a winter storm, his smile faded away to nothing.

There was blood on his face, his arms, his chest. One sleeve was torn away and half his shirt, his flesh gouged and cut. She imagined she looked as battered as he did.

"What the hell was so important that you risked your life to come here?" she demanded, looking around at the ruined lab.

"Hope." Tristan strode to the far side of the lab. There was a containment unit there, destroyed and mangled, the protective plastiglass walls shattered, the warning signs sprayed with blood. He jerked open a metal door. Inside were toppled shelves, broken beakers and petri dishes, the contents left where they lay. He jerked open the next door and the next, and each revealed the same destruction.

His breath hissed from between his teeth.

"This," he said. "*This* was so important. But they must have destroyed it weeks ago. I thought it was safe behind locked doors, incubating and replicating. The cure. The damned cure. And now it's lost. It's all fucking lost."

Sweeping his arm before him, he knocked the shattered contents off the lowest shelf, sending everything flying to the floor, raining bits of plastiglass and agar and tissue. His frustration and despair were palpable.

In her mind's eye, she saw him as he had been that night outside Abbott's, his fist flying to punch the side of Viktor's rig, that outburst and this one all the more revealing because he was so coldly controlled and controlling most of the time.

His open hand slapped the cabinet, leaving a bloody handprint, and he froze, one hand stretched before him, resting on the frame of the door.

He dropped his head, his matted, shaggy hair sliding forward. His back was bowed, every muscle taut and strained.

"Everything was here," he said, his voice shaking with fury. "Fetal calf serum, hydrocortisone, pH-balanced culture medium." He drew back his hand, and she thought he would slam the cabinet door again, but he didn't. He mastered his action at the last second, drawing up short, forcing his hand to his side with obvious effort. He spoke again, his voice now low and controlled. "My tissue samples. Viral samples. Everything's gone. Destroyed. Any hope of a cure, destroyed."

He straightened, but didn't turn. His back rose, fell, a deep slow inhalation.

Then he did turn and his gaze met hers, barren and bleak.

"We need to go." An order.

But he was right.

Because she could hear the distant sounds of monsters gathering in the dark.

The faint smell of sulfur tickled her nostrils.

"Watch your head," Tristan ordered. He'd hit the phosphorous gel on his utility harness to light their way. She was surprised it hadn't been torn loose in the battle.

Still, given that her vision far surpassed his, she almost laughed. Almost. But she had a horrible suspicion that if she started, she wouldn't be able to stop, so she swallowed it and ducked her head and followed him into a narrow, damp crevice. It wasn't an access tunnel, or a man-made passage of any sort. It was a narrow crack in a solid wall of natural rock.

And after the first few steps, she had no wish to go any farther. The walls were close on all sides, the ceiling low, and the floor sloped sharply down, taking them deeper and deeper into the ground. With each step, her heart clutched and her belly rolled with greasy sickness.

She didn't want to be here, didn't want to be buried in the earth, surrounded on all sides by slime-draped stone.

Clenching her fists, she forced herself to put one foot in front of the other, to walk the path Tristan led. Because as little as she wanted to be where she was, she had even less interest in returning to the place they'd just left.

"Watch your step," Tristan warned, his voice taut with pain. "There's a boulder."

He was supporting his left arm with his right, pressing hard against the wound that dripped blood in a macabre trail, like breadcrumbs dropped by characters in an ancient children's tale.

"I see it," she said, and shifted to avoid the rock, her shoulder dragging along the stone wall as she passed.

The walls were too close. A crypt. She gritted her teeth against the rising swell of panic.

Stone walls on all sides.

The tunnel narrowed as they moved on. At first, she could spread her arms wide to touch the sides, then she could touch them by bending at the elbow. Finally, the slick stone drew so tight that her shoulders rubbed on one side or the other with each step she took.

Deep in the earth. Stone walls all around. Trapped. Chained.

Her heart began to pound—too hard, too fast—and

sweat slicked her palms. She stopped dead, the coil of panic so tight she felt as though her chest was collapsing under the weight of it.

"Ana?" Tristan paused to look back at her over his shoulder.

She swallowed, shook her head.

"What is it? Are you hurt?" His tone took on an edge of concern.

Again, she shook her head, the terrible laughter threatening to tear free. Only, she didn't have enough breath to laugh with.

"The walls—" She gasped, a sharp, whooping inhalation.

There was nothing more to say. How to explain a lifetime of being locked away in the bowels of the earth? How to explain what that did to a person?

And even if she could find both the breath and the words, she would not betray herself to Tristan Tolliver, the man who had used her stolen genetic code to create the monsters that hunted them. He didn't know who she was, her connection to all that had passed. And she wasn't about to enlighten him.

Tristan stepped back toward her and took her hand. Warm skin. Strong fingers. His hands—and her own— were still sticky with blood. And she could smell it. Sharp. Metallic. His. Hers. The dead Reavers'. All of it mixing with the smell of sulfur that carried down the tunnel.

"Close your eyes." An order, softly spoken. He offered no choice but to obey. "Close your eyes and let me lead you. Trust me to take you through. Don't think of the walls. Think only of my hand holding yours, and yours holding mine."

She couldn't imagine it. Couldn't imagine trusting this man to lead her anywhere. He worked with Ward. Her enemy.

And he was the man who had shouted for her to run and save herself.

It made no sense, but she had absolutely no doubt that he had been willing to die for her, more than once. The day they had been chased by the armored rigs—it felt like a million years ago—and again today. He would have sacrificed himself for her.

What had he said in the lab when she had asked him what was so important that he risked his life to go there?

A cure. He wanted to find a cure.

That hardly sounded like a criminal.

Or maybe it was that she didn't want the man who had kissed her and made keen emotion blossom inside her to be the same man who had doomed millions of people.

Never in her life had she wished for a portal to someone's thoughts the way she wished for it now.

She was so confused, and so afraid.

"Wake from a darkened dream," he said, his voice calm and soothing.

A darkened dream. A nightmare, her past. She had escaped. She had survived.

"Where does this lead?" she asked, unable to move forward on blind trust. Unable to trust *him*.

"Do you remember that I told you about the underground geothermal spring that feeds the generator?" His voice was low, his fingers twined among her own. "This tunnel will take us to the spring. We need to tend to our wounds, and it's a good place to do that. The Reavers won't follow."

"Why not?" She didn't even try to curb the sarcasm. "Do they have a problem with tight spaces?"

Tristan smiled. "Funny girl."

Oh, she felt anything but funny right now. She felt out of control, wildly terrified, and the horror of it was, she knew that she needed him, needed to let him guide her. Needed to trust a man she had spent months hating because he was working with Ward to create a plague that would kill millions of people. And because he was using her cells and DNA to do it.

So why did she cling to him as though he were a raft in the ocean?

Because he was her only choice if she meant to stay afloat. If she let go of him, she would drown in the dark, greasy tide of her secret terrors.

Turning to face her, his eyes locked on hers, his hand offering solid comfort, he took a step backwards, drawing her forward. They walked like that for a few steps and he nodded his approval.

"The mutated Reavers have a problem with water. Hydrophobia. You're doing great, Ana. Keep moving." Tristan turned now to walk facing forward, but he kept his arm twisted behind him, his fingers twined tight with hers.

Vaguely, she realized that he had stopped supporting his injured arm, that he offered that support to her instead. She thought she ought to protest, to draw away. But she didn't, because right now his hold on her hand was her anchor, the only thing holding her fears at bay.

"Hydrophobia," she murmured, focusing on what he told her rather than the tight walls of the tunnel. "That's why you didn't fix the plumbing. They don't like the passages in the old part of the facility because of the water. So they stay away."

"Exactly."

She shuddered as her shoulder brushed the stone wall on one side. Too close. Her throat clogged and she felt like she couldn't breathe.

"Breathe deeply through your nose, slowly. Feel your

lungs fill with air." His voice reached back to her, guiding her, so sure and certain. She followed the thread of it, dragging in a slow breath, noting that the scent of sulfur had grown stronger now, and the tunnel a little wider.

"Were they in on it? Kalen? Gemma? Lamia? Did they know?"

"They were, as you said, in it with me. But not to create what came out of it." There was bitterness in his tone. Disillusionment.

"What? You thought you were creating a plague to *save* the world? Do you expect me to believe you were that naïve?" Anger flared, slapping down the panic. Good, that was good. She embraced it. Of the two choices, she preferred anger.

She felt his fingers twitch against her own, and when he spoke, his tone was laced with self-derision.

"It was never supposed to be a plague." He ran his thumb back and forth over the back of her hand, a tiny reassurance. "Ward thought I was like him, that I was a protégé. That I shared his beliefs. He lured me with the promise of first-rate facilities and unlimited funds. I thought I was doing something good."

"Do not expect me to believe you were that trusting and blind." Her words were flat, hard. She didn't care. There might be a seed of truth in his explanation, but she was not so gullible as to believe he was ignorant of the implications of his monstrous creation.

"I knew my work had possible military application, of course," he said. "But Ward assured me it would be used to help injured soldiers make it home. Or for Waste settlers lost in storms or hurt in a remote area without access to medical care. This was supposed to be a way of keeping people alive until they could get help. Not that

I absolve myself." He laughed harshly. "I hold myself ulti-
mately responsible for everything that's happened here."

He was silent for a moment, the only sound the scrape
of their boots along the stone ground. Then he spoke
again, whisper soft. "Gavin Ward can make you believe
almost anything. I suspect he could sell ice to the rebels if
he set his mind to it."

She knew the truth of that. She shuddered, memories
of Ward winding through her like a bad smell.

*Let me take you out in the daylight, Tatiana. Would you like
that? A walk in the daylight? No, I ask nothing in return.
Nothing at all.*

Tristan told nothing but the truth. Gavin Ward was a
master at manipulating human frailties and dreams. She
knew that better than anyone alive.

"So what did Ward make you believe?"

"That we shared a common goal. I started with the rabies
virus. There were symptoms that would be beneficial in the
short term for the application I had in mind—excitation, ag-
itation, insomnia. All good things for a Waste settler several days away from the nearest medical facility. Those things
could keep him alive long enough to get there."

The tunnel had widened quite a bit now, and her feeling of being entombed eased. Glancing down, she suddenly felt self-conscious to have her fingers linked with
his, to have him leading her through the stone tunnel as
though she were a child.

Dragging her hand away, she stopped dead, waited for
him to turn and face her. He did, the light of the phosphorous gel on his utility harness bouncing up to highlight his
features in fearsome relief.

"Keep the science short and sweet, and tell me in three
sentences or less exactly what you did."

"I modified the rabies virus, hybridized it with a genome supplied to me by Ward, one that added a level of"—he gestured, his hand palm up, as he searched for words—"enhanced ability. The early tests were promising. I just needed human subjects. Ward brought the Reavers on board, paid them for their participation. And then he took the tests out of my hands. He was in charge of the human subjects."

A genome supplied to me by Ward . . . Her genome. The samples of her tissue that Ward had sliced out of her every time he needed more. Only, Tristan didn't know it. He had no idea who and what she was.

She stared at him, her gut sinking, knowing that the story would only get worse. "That's more than three sentences."

"So it is." His smile was dark. "Ward crossed my work with *Mycobacterium leprae*, the organism responsible for leprosy. By the time I understood what he'd done, understood his vision of 'cleansing' the Waste and creating a fresh palette for his vision of a new world, it was too late. The Reavers had mutated into what they are. And everyone down here had been exposed."

Suddenly everything clicked into place. The suspicion that Tristan had wanted her down here for something other than a hydrogen fill and a meal. The terrible mix of emotions she'd read from Gemma and Kalen and Lamia every time she opened a portal and tried to catch a ghosting of their thoughts. The way Tristan had collapsed the tunnels . . . not only a way to keep the Reavers out, but a way to keep everyone in.

"You trapped everyone down here. To contain it. The plague."

He made a short nod. "I did, yes."

"Including me," she said slowly.

There was pain in his expression, vast and deep. "Ana . . ."

"I'm exposed. Because Gemma cut my hand and that Reaver bled all over me. And that's why you brought me here . . . to keep me from infecting anyone else." She looked down at her hands, covered in blood, and she laughed, a horrible, mirthless sound. "And if I wasn't exposed then, I sure as slagging hell am now, right?"

"Ana." Her name was little more than a breath. Stepping forward, he grabbed her arm, pulled her against him, holding her tight as he wrapped her in a one-armed embrace. She could feel the hard, steady beat of his heart.

She almost told him then. Almost blurted that she was Ward's genetic miracle. Almost told him that no matter how often she was exposed, she could never get sick. Her body's defenses could fight any pathogen.

But the words locked in her throat.

Just because she was attracted to him, liked him, admired the fact that he wanted to save the slagging Waste— or, at least, claimed he wanted to—didn't mean she could trust him.

What had he said earlier? That Ward could sell ice to the rebels if he set his mind to it. That he could make anyone believe anything.

Well, maybe Tristan Tolliver was telling her the truth.

Or, maybe he had learned manipulation from the master.

CHAPTER SEVENTEEN

A quick turn, and the tunnel grew so cramped that Tatiana had to turn sideways to slide through. She held her breath, pushed herself to a place in her mind that was cool and blank, and eased into the tight space . . . because she had to.

Though he was no longer touching her, the knowledge that Tristan was near lent her a measure of strength. Which made no sense because she didn't trust him.

She stepped free of the crevice, and her breath caught in her throat. The narrow space opened to a towering cave, warm and moist, the sound of water amplified as it echoed off the ridged, rocky walls. Outcroppings sent shadows dancing across a rippling pool, and at the far end, a thin waterfall cascaded from a chunk of yellowed limestone.

Amazed, Tatiana stopped dead, admiring the magnificent sight. But the part of her that was ever vigilant scanned the cavern for any potential threat.

Lumilights were set in the walls behind metal cages, and halfway up the cave was a metal walkway guarded by a low railing. She narrowed her eyes and followed it around until it disappeared in a dark, narrow crevice in the wall.

"That route is blocked," Tristan said from close beside her, his breath fanning her cheek.

Nodding, she stepped deeper into the cave. The towering ceiling with its pointed stalactites was far enough away that she felt far less confined than she had in the tunnel. She could breathe here.

The burble of the water drew her gaze, and she turned to study the blue-green pool. Mats of algae grew near the edge, and the distinct smell of sulfur was strong here.

"On the far wall . . . the rocks look pink," she murmured.

"A type of bacteria." Tristan eased past her and shot her a look. "Nonpathogenic."

He walked to a group of large boulders near the edge of the pool. Dragging the small case he'd taken from the lab out of his utility harness, he set it on the rocks.

A med-tech kit, she realized, as he opened the zip-seam and pushed back the lid. He glanced at his hands, turned them palm up then palm down, and grimaced at the dried blood.

"You wash my back, and I'll wash yours," he said with a grim smile, as he cast her a sidelong look. Then, turning away, he reached back to draw what was left of his shirt off over his head.

She froze, the sight of his broad, naked back making her feel things that she didn't want to examine too closely. She noted three deep gouges in his shoulder and another at his waist—broad shoulders, narrow waist—but mostly, she noted smooth skin over layers of lean muscle, supple and strong.

Reaching into the kit, Tristan removed a clear cylinder filled with round discs, each about the size of a thumbnail. He removed one, squatted by the water's edge and dipped his cupped palm. The water streamed down as he raised his hand and dropped the disc into the small amount of water that remained.

In an instant, the disc blossomed and grew, uncoiling to become a large, square towel.

"Biodegradable vegetable fiber," he said, glancing at her over his shoulder.

Moving closer, she helped herself to a disc and followed his actions. From the corner of her eye, she watched him tend his wounds as she tended her own, ever aware of him, the expanse of naked skin over corded muscle, the dark hair that trailed in a neat line down his belly.

She forced herself to look away and sift through the med-tech kit for a biotech sealing agent. The kit was a good one, well stocked, and there were more than enough supplies to treat them both.

Turning slightly away from him, she pulled her over-shirt free, angling her body so the outside of her right arm was hidden from his view. A quick check showed that the synth-skin she always wore to hide the tattoo inked in her flesh was still in place, her call numbers obscured, the artificial skin blending almost seamlessly with her own.

One more thing not to trust him with.

She trusted no one with the knowledge of her tattoo. Partly because it breached the Blood-borne Pathogen Act, a fact that could get her shipped to the stone pits of Africa. And partly because she didn't want anyone to recognize what she was. There were rumors about her and Wizard and Yuriko, about how they'd been raised by a computer in an isolated laboratory buried by the Old Dominion.

Tristan Tolliver would have heard those rumors. Maybe Ward had even shared information with him about the subject he harvested cells from. She wasn't about to take any chances.

Her tattoo—the call numbers TTN081—would mark her for what she was if anyone saw it. So she made certain that no one ever saw it, and she was grateful for the incredible authenticity of sim-skin. Waterproof. Sweatproof. Wiped clean with water. An amazing technical advance, as far as she was concerned.

She'd thought about going under the laser and having the tattoo burned away, but two things had stopped her. She didn't trust whoever wielded the laser not to report her to the New Government Order—which would in turn see her brought to Gavin Ward's attention. And she wasn't certain that she wanted the numbers gone. They were part of who she was. *TTN*. Tatiana. She'd chosen the name herself, a long time ago.

Turning back toward Tristan, she saw that he had sealed the wound in his arm and was reaching around to get at the ones on his back.

"Let me."

His gaze slid over her as she approached, lingering on the bare skin revealed by her snug, sleeveless undershirt. Something deep inside her twitched and writhed, coming alive at the look he cast her. A hard look, one that spoke of wanting and lust. And caring. Slag. There was a flicker of softness there that she could mistake for nothing else.

It unnerved her, that underlay of emotion.

Lust, she could handle. Caring was a whole other thing entirely.

She took the cloth from his hands, dipped it in the water as he turned away, and wrung it out over his back, watching as rivulets sluiced over his skin. Raising her head, she found him watching her over his shoulder, so close, his indigo eyes dark and fathomless.

Swallowing, she reached out and laid the pads of her fingers against his warm skin. He had washed the blood from his face, and she could see there was a bruise starting, high on his cheekbone. Careful not to cause him pain, she made her touch gentle.

She had the oddest urge to lean in, to press her mouth to his hurts.

"You could have left me," he said, his voice like gravel. The sound stirred her.

He was watching her with such focused intent that she felt as though the world had melted away, with only the two of them left behind.

"I ordered you to get the hell out, but you stayed." One dark brow slashed up in question. "Why?"

Why? If only she knew the answer. "Partly because I don't take orders. Not from you. Not from anyone." He made a hushed laugh that both stirred and annoyed her. "But mostly because, as I said, I wanted to kill you myself," she finished, low and fierce.

"Bloodthirsty, aren't you?" With another low laugh, he moved quickly, reaching around and dragging her knife from its sheath. Hilt forward, he offered it to her, his eyes meeting hers, his expression both mocking and serious, as though he knew she wouldn't hurt him, but acknowledging the faintest shadow of doubt.

Because she could, if she chose to.

Dipping her head, she stared at her knife, hating the sight of it, the blood still marking the blade.

With a hiss, she knocked it from his hand. There was a clatter of metal against stone, and the knife spun round and round, sliding away from them, stopping just shy of the edge of the pool.

"Ana—"

"No." She cut him off, not looking at him. "I don't want to talk." Because of his incredible stupidity in choosing to work with Ward. Because of everything that had happened and everything he had said earlier, about the Reavers and all the researchers being infected.

All. That meant him. *He* was infected. The thought made her ill.

She was used to the emotions of others, coming and going like the tide. She had had no personal attachment, no personal sense of loss, since Yuriko had died and Wizard had disappeared. There had been no one in her life for her to care about.

But now she felt the horror of losing people she had only begun to know . . . Kalen, Lamia. Tristan. Oh God, Tristan.

He was infected and he would die.

She was overwhelmed by emotions she didn't understand and had no idea what to do with.

So she stared at the ground and shook her head, and she was grateful when she saw the toes of his boots shift away from her, toward the pool. When she looked up, she was presented with the wide expanse of his muscled back.

Carefully, she closed the gouges with the biotech sealing agent, and then turned and let him do the same for her. The wound where her neck met her shoulder was the worst, and she winced as he touched it.

"This is already scabbing," he observed, his tone confused.

She held very still as his fingers brushed her skin, electrified by even this, his impersonal healing touch.

"I heal fast." Too fast. She'd have to be careful not to let him see how quickly she recovered. By tomorrow, there would be only a shiny mark on her skin to define the places she'd been hurt, and by the day after that, there would be nothing at all. No mark. No scar.

It was the wounds inside that would take far longer, the

heartbreak of knowing what would befall these people she was coming to know and like. The confusion. The ache of betrayal.

Those wounds would scar.

But why did she feel that way . . . betrayed? Because he hadn't told her that he was Tolliver?

The truth was, she hadn't asked. Not outright. Hadn't even thought to ask.

And the greater truth was, the thought of him dying was the greatest betrayal. That he would leave her, become what the Reavers had become, tormented and mad, a ravening beast, parts of him falling away. . . .

Slag.

What did she care if he left her? If he died?

She didn't understand herself right now. Her thoughts. The wild swings in her emotions.

Turning her head, she stared at the water, the rippling water, bubbling hot from the earth. Had she learned nothing from the horror of her captivity? In this moment, she was alive and Tristan was alive and she deserved this, deserved this moment in time even if she would never be granted another like it.

Had she not learned to seize what joy she might?

Easing her feet from her boots, she watched as he moved into a squat to gather their things from the ground. His back was toward her. Beneath the formfitting material of his pants, the muscles of his buttocks flexed as he straightened with the cloths and sealing agents in his hands. Leaning forward, he put them in the med-tech kit on the rock.

She pushed her pants down her legs, pausing only long enough to kick them free.

"Tristan," she said, clear, fast. Before she could change her mind.

Then she dove into the pool, clothed in nothing but her undergarments.

The water swallowed her, a warm embrace. It stung her cuts and wounds, but soothed her battered muscles and bruised flesh. A trade-off. Wasn't everything always a trade-off?

She ducked beneath the surface and glided deep, toward the bottom, her eyes closed against the sulfur sting, her arms and hands stretched before her. It made her chest ache, diving so deep in a cave beneath the earth, buried beneath yuales of rock and the weight of the water.

At the same time, it made her feel free. Because she *could* do it. Face this, her secret fear of being trapped beneath the earth, a prisoner. But she wasn't trapped. She was free. Free to choose.

After a moment, she surfaced, dragged in a deep breath and decided it was a sinful pleasure, the heat of the water against her skin. Better than a shower and min-dry.

Floating in the deepest part of the pool, she looked up. Tristan stood on the rocks, his body taut, ready to spring. Naked, gloriously naked, his limbs muscled and long and lean. His belly tightly ridged. The thick, hard length of his erection jutting forward.

Whatever modesty had made her keep on her undergarments, he was afflicted with no similar qualms. She found herself very glad of that. For a moment, she could do nothing but stare.

His lips curved in a hard, masculine smile that made her insides dance and writhe, low in her belly.

Peeling off the last scraps of her clothing under the cover of the water, she slapped them against the nearby rocks.

With a grin, Tristan sprang, his body arched in a clean

line, slicing the water as he dove. He swam toward her beneath the surface; she could see the dark shape of him, the powerful strokes. Closer. Closer. She almost vibrated with anticipation.

Bobbing up before her, he caught her arm, drawing her toward him, and for a second she panicked, froze. Because if she gave herself to this man, she would never be the same. She knew that with gut-deep certainty.

"Do you want this?" he asked, floating at her side, her shoulder pressed to his chest, his lips against her ear.

The moment spun out, and then he slid long fingers down her abdomen, lower, lower, so slow and tantalizing it made her breath stop and her heart race. He eased his hand between her thighs, touched her with a firm, slow stroke that made her gasp.

"Do you want me, Ana?"

Wake from a darkened dream and see the beauty that surrounds you.

"Yes," she whispered, so low, she wasn't certain he heard.

He did, and he pulled her against him, gentle, a light stroke of his lips on hers, then harder, his mouth open, taking, his hands pulling her close. Deep and wet, his kiss poured through her, a claiming. She gave herself up to it, to the pleasure and the heat.

The feel of his chest pressed against hers—planes of solid muscle—was delicious. She moaned at the wonder of that, the pure sensation of skin against skin.

Desire coiled through her, a tight helix, a sharp jolt of anticipation. She opened to him, sucking on his tongue, biting his wonderful, lush lips. Her hands tangled in his hair, and she arched against him, her nipples hard and aching. She wanted this. She wanted him.

The water lapped at them, closed over their heads as they sank into the depths, then parted to set them free as they bobbed up, gasping for breath, cleaving to each other.

Sliding his body along hers, he teased her, made her ache, made her moan. Sensations cascaded through her, to her breasts, her limbs, sinking down to live between her thighs, a dull throb, almost pain. She felt empty, hollow.

"I need you inside me." She gasped and slid her hand between their bodies to close her fingers around the thick, heavy weight of his rigid cock. Smooth, smooth skin. He was so hard, straining up into her hand. She loved the feel of him.

He made a sound, a dark groan, and pumped his hips against her, kissing her with lips and teeth and tongue. The taste of him was lush, sensual, stealing her breath, stealing her mind.

Again, they sank below the surface of the pool, the warm water sliding around them, between them, heightening every sensation. Her toes touched bottom, and she realized he had maneuvered them to shallower water, to a place they could stand, slick rocks at her back, the hard wall of Tristan's body at her front.

His hips fit against her own, rocking, leaving her wanting more, wanting all of him.

Running her hands along his muscled back, she groaned, let her head fall back as he cupped her breast. He stroked her nipple, running his thumb lightly back and forth, then pinched, just enough to make her gasp and arch into his touch, instinct screaming for more and more.

He kissed her mouth, her cheek, her neck, and she opened her legs, guided the smooth head of his penis to the folds of her sex. She was ready, nearly feral with need.

With the solid brace of the rocks at her back, he held her afloat and lowered his mouth to her breast, sucking on her nipple, making her cry out as exquisite sensation rocketed through every nerve in her body.

"Please. Tristan, please," she moaned as his teeth scraped over the sensitive peak.

Hushed and dark, he laughed, the sound strumming something inside her, something deep and delicious.

"I like that," he whispered. "The sound of my name. The way you say it."

His breath came in a harsh rasp, so revealing, whispering of arousal and desire. She liked that, liked knowing she did this to him, made him hard and rigid, made him want her.

Tristan bent his head to the side of her neck, nipping gently, careful of her wound. He kissed her shoulder, her collarbone, his groin tightening with sharp need as she cupped her breasts, offered them to him, the nipples dark and swollen. He took what she offered, licking and nipping until she arched and cried out.

"Please, no more play." She moaned. "I want you so bad I can barely think."

Yeah, he knew that feeling.

Because suddenly, he'd had enough play, too.

His cock was throbbing and all he wanted was to be inside her, to take her, make her cry out, make her his. Reaching between them, he pushed two fingers into the slick, hot core of her, just a little at first, but when she moaned and rocked her hips, he pushed all the way in.

Fuck, she was tight, so tight. So beautiful.

He withdrew, pushed his fingers inside her again. She squirmed and pumped against his hand, so ready. She made a low, breathy sound that made his cock jump and his blood pound.

The power of his attraction to her had a life of its own.

It was more than physical, deeper than lust. He knew what it was. He *knew*. And he slammed the door on that knowing, because to acknowledge it now, the depth of his feelings, was to go beyond what he could bear.

Instead, he lifted her, settled her legs around his waist.

Impatient, she reached down, grabbed him, pushed the head of his cock against her opening. With a feeling of euphoria, he slid inside. Home. He slid home, pushing all the way in with a long, slow glide, holding tight to her hips.

Her breath, and his, came in hard, short gasps.

He withdrew, thrust inside, deeper, harder, working them both. She clung to him, moaned, whispered his name, her face buried in the curve of his neck, wet tendrils of her silky black hair wrapping around him.

So tight. So hot.

His. She was his.

"Now. Oh, God. Tristan. Now." A cry. A plea.

Clinging to him, her heels digging hard into his lower back, she bit him, her teeth sinking into his shoulder, her body closing tight around his cock.

She thrust her hips hard against him, and then her body went still, taut as a guitar string, as she came. Her teeth sank even harder into the bulge of muscle at his shoulder. He welcomed that. Even liked it. Because her release stroked him over the edge.

He thrust deep, pleasure ripping from deep inside him, his rough cry echoing in the limestone chamber as he came, his body shuddering with the strength of his climax.

She grabbed his hair, her fingers twining tight, and she yanked his head back, pressed her mouth to his, a rough, wild kiss that told him everything about the way she was feeling.

That kiss reflected the tumult inside him. The wonder. The passion. The animal need.

Then she collapsed against him, boneless, and he understood that feeling, too.

They floated, together, limbs tangled, a desultory kick now and again keeping them on the surface. He had the thought that he would keep her safe. That somehow he would find a cure. A treatment. Something to keep her safe.

Hard on the heels of that thought came the realization that his Ana would likely punch him for the sentiment. He recognized that as part of the attraction.

At length, she stirred, licked her tongue up the side of his neck.

"Ugh."

"What?" He reared back to look at her.

"You taste like sulfur."

He laughed, free, easy. From the first moment, she had made him laugh. *Ana*.

"We should get back," he said, wanting her to disagree, but she only nodded, and kissed him, and swam away beyond his reach.

They slogged from the pool, hand in hand, meaning to hunt for clothes. But they made it only as far as climbing across the rocks to retrieve her wet, sleeveless shirt before they slid back into the water with a laugh and a shout. His laugh. Her shout.

Tristan dragged her under, kissing her beneath the lapping waves created by their commotion, surfacing to gasp for air as she sank down his body and—sulfur taste or not—licked her tongue along parts of him far south of his neck.

Tatiana studied her pants, frowning, the sight of the blood staining the garment a somber reminder of exactly what their situation was.

She glanced up to find Tristan watching her, his expression both tender and fierce.

"I am unfamiliar with the protocol for expressing appreciation of amazing sex," she said. "Exceptionally amazing sex. I have never experienced the like."

He gave a short bark of laughter, and shot her a look of stunned amusement. "That about covers it. Yeah. Um . . . that definitely about covers it." He raked his fingers back through his damp hair, and laughed again. "You are a marvel, Ana. An amazing gift."

A gift. He thought her a gift.

His words made something inside her unfurl, something warm and foreign, and strangely frightening. She glanced away, then back.

"I need to go," he said, his tone different. Harder. More edgy.

Ah, she thought. The mystery of human interaction. At the exact moment she believed herself closer to Tristan than she had ever been to any person before, he thought himself far, far away.

"I know." She ran her fingers through her wet hair, working out the snarls. "We must return to the others, make certain everyone is safe. Formulate a plan."

He shook his head, and his gaze slid from hers.

"Ana, the night we met, at Abbott's. I was there for equipment. Viral samples. Tissue samples. Yasha and Viktor were to steal them for me. I was there to take delivery." He drew on his pants, closed the zip-seam, paying very close attention to his clothing, as though it held some special interest. "I need to find out why they never delivered, and I need to find those goods. That night, I made a choice to return here because I thought I could get by without those lost items, thought I could sneak past the mutated Reavers and continue my experiments with the supplies I had in the lab here." He breathed deeply, blew the breath out in a rush. "But with all that destroyed, I have no choice. I need to go."

"Understood."

His head jerked up, and he narrowed his gaze, studying her with careful interest. "Why do you say that?"

"Say what?"

"*Understood.*"

She shrugged, suddenly self-conscious. "Do I misuse the word?"

"No. It's just . . . it reminds me of someone and I can't figure out who . . ." He lifted the ragged remnants of his shirt, snorted, tucked the cloth into his waistband so it hung down over his hip. Then he lifted his utility harness and set the bands across his naked torso.

Tatiana liked the look of that. There was something dangerously sexy about the gleam of his damp skin in the lumilight and the crisscross of the black harness over each shoulder.

"You intend to go into the Waste," she said.

"Yeah." He looked anywhere but directly at her. "Yeah."

"I can't let you do that, Tristan." She kept her voice soft, even, but a part of her wanted to howl in despair. "You are infected with a plague that could spread through the Northern Hemisphere in a matter of weeks. Perhaps even to the Equatorial Band and beyond. I can't let you leave here."

He drew in a breath through his nose, his nostrils pinching. "I'm immune."

Two simple words. She wasn't certain what to make of them. Wasn't certain she believed him.

Then she asked the most obvious question. "Have you

attempted to harvest your immunoglobulins and create a passive immunization?"

"Yes, and failed."

Too many questions to ask right now. How was he immune? Why could his immunity not be shared with the others? Curiosity was not enough of a reason to delay their departure, so she set it aside and pushed only the main point.

"How do I know you're telling the truth? How do I know you're immune?"

Something flickered in his eyes, and she thought she had injured him, her query too harsh.

Again, she'd failed at the subtleties of conversational interplay.

"Need I explain myself to you?" he asked in a silky tone, all bristling male offense.

"Yes." She shrugged at his expression, then relented. "I know this is hard for you. I understand that you are used to being a dictator"—at his sharp look, she amended her words—"in charge. But we're in this together now. Everyone down here is in this together."

How strange that she was the one to say those words. She, the consummate loner.

Spreading his hands wide in a gesture of surrender, he smiled, a tight curving of his lips that was hard and masculine and sexy . . . and completely devoid of mirth.

"You'll have to take my word, Ana, given that there is no way to prove my claim."

Taking things on faith wasn't her strong suit.

Her head snapped up as sudden recollection came to her. Digging her hand into the large pocket at the side of her pants, she drew forth a small oblong instrument and held it before her like a prize.

Tristan narrowed his gaze. "STD detector." He raised a brow. "Two thoughts . . . first, why are you carrying that around with you? Second, why didn't you produce it before we made love?" He paused, sighed. "I have no diseases, though I suppose it's a bit late to tell you that."

She wondered at his word choice. *Made love*. Was that what they had done? She had thought it was sex, but now that he'd said those words, she couldn't chase away the odd fluttering they evoked.

"Sexually transmitted infections are not of concern right now." She waved a hand in dismissal, choosing not to try and explain that she could neither catch nor transmit any pathogen. "This is an STD *and* blood-borne pathogen detector. If you're infected with the plague, it'll flash red, in which case, you stay behind and wait for me to return."

Before he could begin the inevitable protestation that she was surely infected and that she must remain quarantined, she averted the entire dialogue by shoving her thumb in the hole at the top of the device. The light shone green.

His eyes narrowed then flashed to hers.

"I'm clean. Your turn." She held the box out toward him, her hand shaking slightly, her heart turning over at what was sure to come.

She needed proof, and at the same time, she wished she could remain ignorant.

The device she held would prove that he was infected with a virus that had no cure.

She had only just found him. The thought of losing him . . .

He dropped his gaze to her hand, then looked up once more, a panoply of expressions chasing each other across his features.

Frowning, he took the detector from her and pushed his thumb in the hole.

As the light flashed, she reached out and rested her hand on the rocks, steadying herself.

She felt dizzy, her gut churning, her palms slick.

She'd thought she was prepared for the outcome, that she had steeled her emotions against the flash of red light and all it would mean. That Tristan was infected. That he would die.

But she'd been wrong. She hadn't been prepared at all.

Because the light shone green.

CHAPTER EIGHTEEN

"I'll climb it," Tristan said, his expression taut.

Shoulder to shoulder, they stood in the ancient elevator, staring up at the dark shaft through the open trapdoor in the ceiling. They had made it back to the living quarters, grabbed a meal and a few hours of rest before setting out.

And they'd stolen the moments for a frenzied coupling, hot and hard, limbs entwined, lips and tongues and sounds in the dark.

Just thinking about it made Tatiana's heart pound a little harder.

Their return to the living quarters had found the status quo. No Reaver sightings. No one any sicker than they had been.

Lamia had told them that her equipment detected that a tremor had rocked the facility while they were in the cave.

Now, standing here in the elevator, covered in dust and rubble that had fallen through as they opened the trapdoor in the ceiling, Tatiana had a good idea what that tremor was. Someone had demolished the doors of the elevator at ground level. She had a strong suspicion that someone was Ward.

He had sealed them in. Buried them alive.

She expected the knowledge to shut her down, make her sick with fear. This ancient elevator shaft was the last way out, and Ward and blown it to hell.

Now there was no way out.

That realization brought a tide of cold and bitter fear, but she refused to let it drag her under.

She wasn't Ward's prisoner anymore, hadn't been for months, and she never would be again.

On some level, she had known that ever since she escaped his dungeon. It had just taken her a while to accept it, to come to terms with it.

Now, buried fifty yuales beneath the earth, she decided she was free.

Wasn't she just a contrary girl?

Beside her, Tristan began to strip off his thermal gear.

"Much as I'd love to see you with far less clothing," she said, casting him a sidelong glance, "you might as well leave it all on." She reached for the zip-seam of her parka and slid it halfway open. "I'm the better choice for this task."

"I'm going. You're staying." His tone brooked no argument.

"You won't make it," she said, tipping her head back to watch the laser array crisscross the shaft. He couldn't see it. Infrared wavelength was beyond normal human visual range. But she could. "The laser security grid's been triggered."

He looked up and stared through the hatch into the darkness as though he could see the grid, rather than just relying on her word. His lips thinned. "Fuck."

"Eloquently put."

"Tatiana—"

"Uh-oh . . . you're using my full name. Not a good sign." Undoing her zip-seam the rest of the way, she pulled her parka off, rolled it into a compact cylinder and held it out to him.

He stared at her, unblinking, his indigo eyes glittering.

How much to reveal? As little as possible. Slag, she had no frame of reference for this, no experience learning how to tiptoe through such dangerous terrain as learning to trust. She sighed.

"I'm trained to do this, Tristan. Trained to a degree that I doubt you can even imagine. I have no wish to wound your pride, but the fact is that your chance of making it to the top of the shaft is less than 1 percent. My chances are approximately 15 percent. Statistical probability is in my favor, so I go."

Reaching out, Tristan took the parka from her.

"I don't want you to do this," he said, his stiff tone suggesting that what he really meant was, I want to grab you by the hair and stop you, and I'm barely containing that urge.

She dragged her hair back, out of temptation's way, and plaited it in a single braid, then tucked the length of it into the back of her shirt. The last thing she needed was her hair triggering the laser array.

"Okay," she said, flexing her fingers and rocking up and down on her toes. "Okay."

A huff of air escaped him. He grabbed her wrist, dragged her against him and kissed her, a hard press of his lips, urgent, possessive.

"You want me to stand here and watch you go?" he rasped. "How am I supposed to do that?"

"I have no answers. I know only that this must be done and I am the one to do it." She reached up and stroked the backs of her fingers along the stubbled arc of his jaw. "A good commander chooses the best soldier for the job."

The muscles flexed in his jaw, but he said nothing, only

stared down at her with those wonderful, beautiful eyes, still not convinced.

"The grid is too tight for you to slip through," she said. "I'm smaller than you are." She grabbed the back of his head, dragged his lips to hers and kissed him with the same urgent possessiveness he had just shown. "And I am more flexible and have been through a laser array before." The memory made her shiver, the sounds of the man at her back screaming in agony as the array sliced him to bits still sharp and clear in her thoughts. "I am the logical choice to go."

His expression was a play of emotions, leaving her no question of exactly how hard this was for him. He wanted her behind him, wanted to place himself first in harm's path, to shield her, protect her. She knew that.

Letting her step up beside him, equally vulnerable, equally at risk, was difficult for him. Letting her take the most dangerous position was nigh impossible. She knew that, too.

"Go," he said, his voice a rough rasp, the word torn from him.

He freed his hold on her, his fingers uncurling in an abrupt rush, as though he needed to let go quickly or not at all. She turned away, only to pause and look back at him over her shoulder. One glance.

"I *will* be fine, Tristan." There. She'd said it. Maybe that would make it true.

"Ana, I lo—" He broke off, locking whatever he had been about to say behind clenched teeth and a grim expression. "Stay safe, Ana."

She rolled her shoulders and flexed her fingers once more. "I intend to."

Tilting her head back, she looked through the opening and studied the shaft that rose above her. Darkness ascending. No sound. No light. Just four walls forming a rectangular shaft that seemed to go on forever.

Crisscrossing the shaft were thin lines of red light.

Red death.

"Wait!"

Tatiana froze, then turned.

Lamia was tearing across the wide space toward the elevator, the dark curtain of her hair flying behind her. She skidded to a halt, worry and strain etched on her features.

"Promise . . . you'll come back," she gasped between breaths.

It was a plea for so much. For them to return safely. For them to return with a cure, or at the very least, with hope. Locked down beneath the ground by Tristan's security measures, these people were trusting their lives to him.

And they *did* trust him. Not one had argued against the plan he had presented when they returned from the cave. Each one in turn had used Tatiana's blood-borne pathogen detector, and each one in turn had made it flash red.

Except Tristan and Tatiana. So they were the only ones to go.

"Promise me." Lamia stepped closer, her arms hanging loose by her sides, her gaze shifting first to Tristan then Tatiana. "And promise me you'll stay safe. Both of you."

Throwing her arms around Tatiana, she hugged her, hard. Tatiana stood there, feeling uncomfortable and a little appalled, as she had the day she returned the ring to the old man, uncertain how to respond, where to put her hands.

And then something shifted, a place inside of her that didn't feel odd, but instead felt . . . warm. With a sigh, she wrapped her arms awkwardly around Lamia and gingerly patted her on her back.

"Stay away from the access tunnels," she said, her gaze

meeting Tristan's over Lamia's shoulder. *Pat. Pat.* "If you hear anything, even a whisper of Reaver presence, set charges and blast them again." *Pat. Pat. Pat.*

"I know," came Lamia's watery whisper.

"If anyone declines rapidly, lock them away. Don't hesitate. Don't feel remorse. Do what you need to do," Tristan ordered.

"Is that your version of an affectionate good-bye, Tris?" Dropping her hands, Lamia turned to him and offered a weak smile.

They stood there for a frozen second. Then Tristan reached out, laid his hand on Lamia's head and ruffled her hair.

"Go," he said.

Lamia nodded, blinking back tears. Then she glanced at Tatiana and said, "See you, my friend."

My friend. Yes, Tatiana realized, her chest grown tight, her heart constricting as though compressed by a vice. They *were* friends.

Without another word, the girl spun and ran off, the sound of her footsteps echoing and finally fading completely away.

Her gaze sought Tristan's. In his eyes was a depth of emotion so deep, it would drown her if she let it.

Too much. Too much to deal with.

So she shut down, let her emotions drop into a cold, dark place inside her, and focused only on the task. The job.

Looking up, she took a moment to study the laser array, to time the pulse of the beams as they sliced the darkness in a random pattern. She could hear the hum of radio frequency jacking the current.

This security grid wasn't meant to deter. It was meant to kill.

Blindly climbing into a death trap wasn't usually first

choice on any intelligent person's activity log. And since she had every intention of going up there, what exactly did that make her?

"What type of laser?" she asked Tristan. "Nd:YAG?" Neodymium-doped yttrium aluminum garnet laser, solid-state, short pulse. A viable choice, but she didn't think so. From what she'd seen so far, she was guessing the highly efficient carbon dioxide laser.

Efficiency is a virtue.

The second the thought crested, she shoved it aside. That was Ward's motto, and she slagging well didn't want him here—not even an imaginary him—riding shotgun on her every move.

Her gut clenched. She didn't want to do this. Didn't want to climb that cable hanging there in midair, in the middle of nowhere, with the walls closing in on her from all sides. She definitely had a thing about confined spaces.

But staying down here, locked in the bowels of the earth, no way out, no light, no hope, just waiting for everyone to die, people she had begun to care about—that was worse.

She sucked in a deep breath, let it out. She had a job to do, and no amount of psychological baggage was going to stop her from doing it.

"Carbon dioxide laser," Tristan said, stooping low and lacing his fingers to offer her a leg up.

She put her foot in his hands, her hand on his shoulder, and vaulted up to grab the sides of the opening. On a sharp exhale, she swung herself up and through the hatch, immediately falling flat against the roof of the elevator.

Directly above her face, a slash of infrared light cut the darkness, then another an inch higher, then another at the same level but from a different direction. She could hear the sound of her own breaths echo back at her off the walls.

"It had to be a slagging carbon dioxide laser," she muttered.

"Pumped with a radio-frequency resonator, diffusion cooled with a static gas field," came Tristan's voice through the hatch. Then came his hand, passing her the little metal box of cytoplast. "When you get to the top, set the cytoplast and the trip wire. You won't need much to blast open the mess Ward made of the doors. Only a bit about the size of a tooth. Don't use too much or you might collapse the whole shaft and trap us down here permanently."

"Understood."

"Ana, getting up there is only half the battle. You'll need to get at least halfway back down before you trip the wire. Once it blows, I'm hoping it'll take the control panel for the laser with it, and then it'll be a quick climb for the both of us."

"Understood."

"Ana—"

She waited for his next instruction.

"Come back to me."

The emotion in those four simple words nearly overwhelmed her. For a second she just lay against the cold metal of the elevator, watching the red beams dance across the darkness.

Finally, she spoke, low and tense. "Understood."

Then she turned her thoughts to the execution of the task. Carbon dioxide laser. It was precise, neat, using high-intensity light to generate electrically charged gas plasmas. If a beam contacted her flesh, it would collapse in a microexplosion and tear her molecules apart.

That laser would cut her in half if she let it.

So unless she wanted to be sliced, diced and minced

like sim-steak ready for the cooking pot, the best thing would be not to let it.

The seconds ticked past as she studied the laser cutting across the elevator shaft again and again. No pattern. No rhythm. No way for her to guess where the next beams would travel, which meant she had no way to plan her climb to avoid them.

She was about to rethink her position when she spotted the flaw. The pattern of crisscrossing beams rebooted and started over again, like a wave. Someone had gotten sloppy when they put this program together, looping it back on itself in an infinite feed rather than programming a continuous unique and random run. They had taken the cheap way out.

She smiled. Greed was a lovely thing.

There *was* a pattern here, barely discernable, but a pattern nonetheless. And that meant she could predict where the beams would hit and figure a way to avoid them.

Just to be certain, she waited out another pass of the program, start to finish, and then one more, until she was confident she'd memorized the pattern.

If she miscalculated, drew her legs up too slowly, twisted to one side when she needed to go to the other, the beam would cut her in two. Or three.

Hand over hand, she began to climb, contorting her body right, then left to avoid the laser array.

She calculated distance and angles, pushed herself to the limit, at one point hanging flat horizontal, perfectly still, toes pointed, chest and abdomen pulled inward to minimize herself as a target. Her muscles screamed as dual beams sliced within centimeters of her back and belly to hit the walls of the shaft on opposite sides.

Halfway there.

A beam shot past her, less than a centimeter away from the tip of her nose.

Reaching up, she grasped the cable, moved a millisecond too slowly.

The cut was sharp, fast, the laser cauterizing as it sliced, so there was little blood. The beam cut through the front of her wrist, through skin, muscle and tendon, leaving her hand useless and numb. A hiss of shock escaped her as her mind screamed *grasp*.

Her fingers simply refused to obey, and the cable slid away like water.

She barely had time to register the thought before she was falling through the darkness and the woven mesh of deadly red beams. The laser caught her in the calf, then grazed her shoulder as she spun through endless black space.

Fifty yuales was a long way down.

Panic surged and she locked it down tight.

Flailing, she reached blindly, snagged the cable with her good hand. Her own weight dragged her downward with a momentum that nearly jarred her shoulder from the socket as she twisted and lurched, desperately twining the cable and her forearm.

She jerked up hard at the hips, ankles together, raising her legs to the horizontal as a beam grazed her thighs. Any slower, and her legs would be tumbling to the bottom of the shaft without her torso.

Okay. Okay. So now she was scared enough that even her enhanced physiology couldn't maintain the facade of calm.

Breathing hard, she hung there, heart pounding, abdominals cramping, every nerve and cell in her body on high alert. Just above her head, a thin red beam arrowed through the darkness, shredding the last of her calm. Her palms were slick with sweat and a bead trickled down her forehead into her eyes. Her heart beat so hard she was nauseated from the force of it.

It was either laugh or puke. She remembered Tristan telling her that.

She made a short, hushed laugh, tipped her head back to study the shaft.

She needed to finish this climb and she had only one hand to do it with. Not good.

But not impossible.

Above her, below her, the laser grid spun its deadly web. She caught the rhythm of the pattern, and once more began her ascent—one handed—thinking only of her next grasp.

Her right ankle and foot wound around the cable creating a makeshift step, helping do the job that her injured hand was now worthless at. She bent her left knee, wound her left foot through in the same way several centimeters higher. Reaching up, she grasped the cable with her functioning hand and hauled herself up a few centimeters as she unwound her lower foot.

Grab. Unwind. Rewind. Reach up and grab again.

Her entire world narrowed to three of her four limbs, and the need to move them in perfect precision.

And all the while, she calculated where the next beam would hit.

She contorted and twisted, forcing her body to unnatural angles, trying to make it to the surface without losing too many bits and parts of herself.

Meters felt like yuales.

Her glove was torn clean through, her skin rubbed raw by the cable. She was bleeding now, hot, wet blood, dripping down her wrist, her forearm.

That was fine. She would heal.

Her bigger worry was the severed tendons and nerve that had been cauterized as the laser passed through them. Cut tissue healed more efficiently than burned tissue, especially laser-burned tissue where the microburst caused all sorts of nasty damage at the cellular level.

Which meant she would likely heal at a slower pace than was her norm.

Slag.

The pain was starting to kick in now, or maybe it was just the build of apprehension because she knew it was going to hurt.

At some point, it was going to hurt like hell.

She let out a sharp huff of air as she came level with what was left of the topside elevator doors. There were steel beams that had once reinforced the small building, collapsed inward now, twisted from the force of Ward's explosives.

The destruction was haphazard. No evidence that he had planned the placement of the explosives. One corner of the shaft remained untouched.

If she'd been the one doing the job, she'd have made certain nothing remained.

Dragging herself up a little higher, she noted that the laser grid didn't extend the full length of the shaft. It stopped just below the jutting lip that marked where the door had been. Again, she was glad that the laser-grid designer had been lazy, or greedy, or both.

She assessed her options. There were no handholds in the bent and twisted remains of the elevator doors. None in the mangled frame. None in the wall.

And she needed to get close enough to set the cytoplast to blow a hole big enough to get them the hell out of here. Her breath came in harsh panting gasps, the sight of the demolished doors ramming home the fact that they were trapped.

She had one working hand, and she needed to use it to hang tight to the cable. At the same time, she needed to use it to free her knife and hack it between the crumbling wall and the mangled metal frame of the door, dig it deep to give her something to hang on to while she set the cytoplast and the trip wire.

With one hand. Nice.

Okay. She could do this. One small step at a time.

The muscles of her arm screamed as she hauled herself a little higher. Then bending so her torso hung below her hips, both feet twisted in the cable, one above the other, she freed her hand, and pulled her knife from its sheath.

On an exhale, she eased back so she hung completely upside down. Twisting at the waist, she sent her weight to one side then the other. Getting a momentum going as she swung back and forth, she hung suspended fifty yuales in the air with the bottom of the elevator shaft a long, long way down.

The cable had little give. She would have to rely mostly on just her body, arcing like a pendulum side to side.

She would need to time this to perfection. One wrong move and her knife would go tumbling away, and with it, her hope for getting the hell out of here.

Worse, she would go tumbling away to spin through the air and the laser grid. Not her preferred outcome.

Wrenching her body to the side, she increased the swing arc, back and forth, back and forth.

Almost there. Almost—

"Aaarrgh!"

She hauled back her arm, threw all the force she had into the swing and slammed the blade home, sinking it deep into the tiny space between a fallen girder and a twisted pile of rock and metal that had once been a wall.

The handle oscillated with the force of her thrust.

Tears clogged her throat. Slagging tears. She was furious at herself for feeling such relief.

There was no place for emotion here, no place for anxiety or fear.

She just needed to get the job done.

Using the remaining momentum of the swing arc she'd generated, she lurched from side to side to widen the angle.

Her ankles ached where the cable ate into them. A good pain. It meant she was still alive.

Back and forth. The cable creaked as she moved, inching ever closer to the knife with each pass.

One more—

She swung in, caught the handle of the knife, tested its strength, then let go before she dragged it free as the cable pitched away once more.

The blade was in there, nice and solid.

Unwinding one foot, she hung like a drop of water quivering at the edge of a tap, her entire weight suspended from one ankle.

On the next pass, she caught hold of the knife and pulled her foot free. Her legs fell. Her arm jerked up, spinning her upright with dizzying speed. The fingers of her good hand curled desperately about the knife hilt, her feet dangling into nothingness.

Her heart clutched tight and she felt the cold edge of sheer terror as, with a discordant rasp of metal against metal, the knife dragged down in the groove that held it, tipping from horizontal to a sickening oblique. Her fingers slid an inch down the hilt.

Panting, she tightened her grasp, hung there assessing her options—which were looking so sparse they bordered on bald.

She thought of Tristan, of the way he'd left her, his mouth hard and demanding on hers. The words he had almost spoken before he cut himself off. Words of caring. She was certain of it. She could have told him how she felt. Could have found the strength to trust him with her emotions.

As he had found the strength to let her do what she needed to do.

Could have. Should have.

She couldn't hang here forever. But she couldn't quite figure a way to get herself into a different position.

She glanced down.

The shaft fell away in a rectangular well of endless darkness cut by beams of deadly red light.

Above her, the knife shifted a few more degrees, sliding toward the vertical. She exhaled sharply, tightened her grasp.

It didn't help.

Her fingers slid another centimeter down the blood-and-sweat-slicked hilt.

CHAPTER NINETEEN

Tatiana hung by one hand in the dark shaft, listening to the sound of her own breathing, focusing on that, the steady push and pull. The knife blade was wedged tight for the moment, but she knew it could pull free at any second and send her tumbling fifty yuales down the shaft. Fifty slagging yuales through the laser grid of death.

She doubted that even her enhanced ability to overcome traumatic injury would survive that. Likely, she'd end up julienned like Gemma's carrots. She wasn't in the mood to test that theory.

Like a hungry shark, fear sank rows of jagged teeth deep inside her, razor sharp, biting out hope and confidence. Her breath came in harsh rasps. Her heart slammed hard against her ribs.

Fear was her enemy. She needed to block it out, to stay calm, stay in control.

Choices. Choices. She had very few here.

Glancing around, she searched for options. Then she saw it, right out in the open, untouched by the destruction that surrounded it—the control box for the laser grid.

All she needed to do was figure out how to swing herself up, open the titanium lid, and use her plasgun to disable the system. Then Tristan could climb the slagging hell up here and set the cytoplast himself to blow them a doorway out of the shaft.

She felt a flicker of hope. It was a viable plan. The challenge would be to execute it with only one good hand and her weight balanced at the end of a knife that was doing a slow slide down the crack she'd jammed it in.

No quick moves. No hasty, panicked actions. Everything needed to be timed to perfection.

On a slow exhale, Tatiana contracted her abdomen, curling up, using the knife as a fulcrum to rotate her body into a better position. This was insane. This was impossible.

This was her one hope.

Crying out for impetus, she swung herself up until she was completely upside down, balancing her entire weight on one arm, one hand. She'd seen holo-vids of gymnasts in Neo-Tokyo. She figured she looked like one of them, only they were a lot more graceful. Locking her legs around a girder that was twisted and mangled by Ward's mines, she pressed so tight that her thighs ached where the metal edge dug into them.

The pain roared through her lacerated wrist, through her muscles, even her joints, bright, hot. She hung there, panting as adrenaline rocketed in her blood. Hung there upside down like a bat.

The thought made her want to laugh, giddy and wild.

Not good. Lock it down. Lock down emotions and focus only on the task.

Ramming the forearm of her injured limb against the side of the wall for extra balance, she gritted her teeth against the pain and tested the knife, only to find it jammed in solidly. She decided to sacrifice the weapon. She had another in her boot, and time was melting away.

She needed to get to the slagging control box. Problem

was, a plas-shot to the outside might do the trick, or it might just char and bend the metal, but not expose the controls for the laser grid. Even worse, in these close confines, there was a risk that the metal of the closed lid would reflect the plasma blast back at her. She needed to use her blade to jimmy the lock so she could blast the innards.

Using her one good hand and her legs, she shimmied along the girder. The metal groaned and shifted, and she focused only on her goal, because if she thought of the beam tearing away from its damaged moorings to tumble end over end down the shaft—and her with it—then she would freeze in terror, like a caribou caught in the headlights of a gun trucker rig.

Centimeters felt like meters.

When she finally reached her goal, she almost sobbed in relief. Lowering her torso once more, clinging to the girder with only her legs, she dragged the knife from the sheath in her boot. She was hanging a hiccup away from a brutal death.

Don't look down. Don't think about down. Just do what you need to do.

Jamming the tip of the blade in the lock—an old-fashioned key-based item that spoke to how ancient this facility was—she worked slowly, methodically, until, with a soft snick, the control panel swung open.

"*Huh-huh.*" Her breath slid free in a rush of relief.

The inside of the box was definitely a control panel, and it appeared to need two specialized keys to initialize deactivation. Lacking those keys, her plasgun would have to do.

She jammed her knife back in her boot and wriggled back along the girder until she was a safe distance away. Then she flipped her Setti9 into position and blasted the hell out of the laser grid control. Bits of metal and electrical wire sprayed in all directions, pinging off the metal girders, then falling away down the long, empty shaft.

She let her head fall back, turned her face to the side and watched as, below her, the crisscrossing beams died. Abrupt. The thin threads were there, then gone in a millisecond.

She stared down the pitch-dark shaft, thought of Tristan, alive, safe, because she'd climbed the shaft and done what she needed to do, and she blinked against the sting of tears. *Tears*.

What the slagging hell was wrong with her?

Wincing at the pain, she used the back of her damaged hand to push her lip-com into position and switch it on.

Tristan would have to pick up the slack. She'd done her part.

"Laser grid disabled," she said into the com, the words grating like broken plastiglass.

"I see that."

His reply left her with a momentary disorientation. Infrared was beyond the wavelengths visible to the normal human eye.

Suddenly she recalled the way he had been so evasive about the goggles that day at the Maori Talisman, refusing to offer a straight answer when she'd asked if they were telescopic. Because maybe they weren't. Maybe he *could* see infrared, and telescopically. Maybe—

"Status report?" His voice carried to her through the com, jerking her back to the moment, making her realize how outlandish her thoughts were.

He wasn't asking about the status of the mission. He wanted *her* status. She could hear the worry and strain in Tristan's voice, his wonderful, beautiful, sexy voice, and she had never been so glad to hear anything in her whole life.

"Status? I'm alive."

Silence, then, "Have you set the cytoplast?"

No. The word caught in her larynx, a hard knot, and she almost couldn't force it free. She had spent so long alone, so long with no one but herself to rely on, to trust. That made it very hard to ask for help, to depend on someone else to act as a partner in her fight for survival.

Logically, she knew her response was inappropriate, knew that she needed help, and she needed to ask for it.

So why didn't she?

Her gaze slid to the warped and misshapen remains of the elevator doors, then to the cable that led back to the earth. She couldn't do this. Couldn't set the trip wire and the cytoplast and rappel back down before setting off the blast. Not with only one functional hand.

And she didn't have to.

Because Tristan was there, ready to stand beside her.

"Hey," she said into the com, each word coming easier than the last. "How fast can you climb? I need you."

They rappelled down the wall of the shaft, moving swiftly. Tristan noted that Ana was favoring her right hand. Hell, she wasn't using it at all. He figured that was the reason she'd asked him to climb up to set the cytoplast.

"What's with the wrist?" he asked through the lip-com.

Her hesitation was brief, but it was enough to tell him that she was downplaying things big-time when she replied, "Just a sprain."

She reached the bottom first, unhooking her line and maneuvering through the open trapdoor in the roof of the elevator, her right arm pressed tight across her abdomen.

Once they were both through the hatch, they moved into the wide space of the gallery that overlooked the ancient generators, then rounded the edge of the wall for additional cover. Instead of a trip wire, Tristan had set a timed fuse for the cytoplast, and now they waited for the explosion topside.

Moments later, a massive roar reverberated down the shaft, shaking the walls and the ground beneath their feet. Tristan turned his body to act as a shield, curling instinctively around Ana's frame.

The fact that she didn't shove him off made him uneasy. He figured she wasn't in good shape if she was meekly letting him slide into the role of protector.

When the noise and the tremor subsided, he put his hand on her shoulder, gently turned her to face him. Reaching out, he stroked a strand of hair off her cheek.

"That was the longest hour of my life," he said, barely able to hold himself back from grabbing her, hauling her against him and pushing his tongue in her mouth. Kissing her, tasting her. Proving to the primitive creature at his core that she was here and she was safe.

"An hour? Is that how long it took me?" Her gaze slid away, and he got a bad feeling in his gut. Her cheeks were white, her lips faintly blue, bracketed by lines of tension. Everything about her demeanor screamed pain.

"Let me see the wrist," he ordered.

"It's a sprain." She shouldered past him, went to the pack that held some water and food rations and a medtech kit. "I'll just patch it up. We need to go. You have enough cytoplast left to reseal the shaft once we're out?"

"Yeah." He felt sick at the thought of setting that second blast, sealing his friends in the earth.

What the fuck were his choices? Leave an opening for even one infected person to claw free, and the whole world would pay the price.

It was a damned expensive price for others to pay for his mistakes.

But he still had a little time to make things right. Based on the disease progress in the Reavers, he was guessing maybe five, six weeks before the researchers deteriorated beyond possible recovery. If he could just get the viral samples and the tissue samples that Yasha and Viktor were supposed to have delivered, he could work with that. Formulate, if not a cure, at least a control to buy him additional time.

To save the people he cared about. The people he'd as good as murdered.

As the anger flared, the hate, the guilt, he closed his eyes for an instant, sought a plateau inside himself, a meditative plane that he had trained so long to reach. He found it, clung to it, held on by his fingernails as he felt himself slipping away from the plateau.

He scrabbled for purchase against the sucking mire of self-recrimination and rage.

These were unnecessary emotions that he created in his mind.

This moment was exactly as it was supposed to be. All he had done and would do were exactly as they were supposed to be.

He needed to believe that, needed to hold fast to it.

Opening his eyes, he looked at Ana, frowned as he watched her struggle, one-handed, to drag the med-kit free. If anything, she'd gone a whiter shade of pale, her right arm tucked inside her parka, her face pinched with pain.

"You sure you're all right?" he asked, squatting at her

side to brush her hand away and take the kit out for her.
With the urgency to remove themselves from the blast
radius, there had been no opportunity to see to her wounds
when he climbed topside, but he figured it must be bad if
his tough-as-tundra Ana had asked him for help in the
first place.

"Just a sprain," she mumbled, her gaze sliding away.

"Let me look."

She shook her head. Rising, she stepped away.

"It wasn't a request," he said, following her, taking hold
of her forearm and turning it with care.

"Listen. It looks bad," she mumbled in a rush. "Looks
worse than it is. I heal fast. Don't—"

"Fuck." He stared at her wrist in horror. Through the
edges of the cauterized wound, he could see that the laser
had cut clear through to the bone. The superficial and
deep flexor tendons were completely severed, along with
the median nerve. Only sheer luck and the placement of
the cut had saved the radial and ulnar arteries.

He felt her trembling beneath his touch.

"Ana—" His gaze shot to hers. He could fix this. Yeah.
If he had a surgical theater and about ten hours to work
on her. But he didn't. All he had was a ticking clock, an elevator shaft they needed to climb, and the frozen fucking
endless Waste. No way to help her. Nothing to offer.

The nearest medical facility that could handle this type
of injury was in Liskeard.

Scattering all his enlightened efforts of moments past,
fury reared inside him, a multiheaded, fanged monster.
This was why he had come to work for Ward in the first
place. For the chance to create an injectable, virally infected
bacterium that would induce a set of temporary symptoms—
aggression, sleeplessness, abnormal strength—that would al-

low the injured individual to make it to a distant facility for treatment.

Only everything had gone wrong. So goddamned wrong.

He swallowed, raised his gaze from the horrific wound, studied her face.

She would never recover full use of this hand.

And his brave, beautiful Ana was standing—*standing*—by his side, ready to fight for the lives of a group of people she'd only just met.

What the hell was he supposed to say to her? How the hell was he supposed to tell her?

No, he realized. He didn't need to tell her. Anyone could see how horrific the damage was, and she was living it, feeling it. She had to know—

"We need to move," she said. "Just patch it. We need to go."

She was right. And she was so focused, so valiant . . . she humbled him.

Suddenly, his anger and rage and self-castigation—the emotions he battled always in the darkest corner of his soul—paled in the brightness of one clear, shining truth.

"I'm in love with you." The words tore free in a low rasp, tumbling into the silence like a massive chunk of ice crashing away from the glacier. The declaration was out there now, lying between them, and he couldn't haul it back, didn't even want to. "I'm in love with you, Ana."

She stared up at him, her mercury-gray eyes so bright against the fan of dark lashes. There was pain there, so much pain, not from her injury.

From his words.

He sensed that. The pain came from old, deep scars upon scars. In her soul.

She wet her lips, a roll inward, a swipe of her tongue.

"You've known me for three days."

Her words made him smile, because the flare of hope in her eyes, the parting of her lips, the softening of her gaze made him believe that only her logic, not her heart, forced her to decry his admission.

Carefully, he applied a pain medication to her open wound, then the biotech sealing agent. At least the antiseptic in the sealer would stave off infection.

"Three days is enough. We do not learn by experience, but by our capacity for experience," he said quietly.

She laughed, the sound hard-edged and a little desperate.

"Which means what? That you love me because you have the capacity to love me?" She dragged away from him, frustration and anxiety in every jerky move. "What if I don't have that capacity, Tristan? What if I'm frozen inside? Broken? What if all I am is built on the stolen emotions of others with none of my own? *None*."

She was in pain, and he had caused it, and he had no idea why or how. The realization of that was terrible. He didn't understand her questions, didn't have the answers.

"How can you love something so fatally flawed?" she whispered.

At last, a question he understood.

"Ana, love, you exist freely in the fullness of your entire being. There are no flaws, only different ways of self. A person without defect is not human."

Stepping close, he drew her into a loose embrace, just held her, resting his chin on her crown, feeling the tension in her muscles, willing her to let go of even a little.

After a moment, she sniffled and said, "You always say the strangest things." She sighed. "I'm a literal thinker. Not very good at philosophical concepts. Tell me in linear terms what that means."

"It means that I love you as you are. It means that three days was enough. For me, three days was all it took to lose my heart. And if you add our meeting at Abbott's, it's been longer," he offered, struggling for a lighthearted tone and failing dismally.

She snorted. "I barely spoke to you at Abbott's."

True enough.

"How much time do you believe is enough, Ana?"

"What?" Her head snapped up. She was less pale now. He figured the pain med was doing its work.

"How much time needs to pass before you believe I can love you?"

She shook her head. "I don't know." She sounded panicked. Overwhelmed.

His timing sucked.

"When you feel that enough time has passed, tell me." He brushed his thumb across her lower lip, and she stared up at him, wide-eyed. "Three days . . . three months . . . three years . . . I'll wait. And then I'll tell you again when you're ready to hear it, because no matter how much time you need, I will still love you."

For an endless moment, they just stared at each other, locked in a tableau. Then from the elevator shaft came the sounds of debris falling free and tumbling down to the bottom.

Ana glanced over her shoulder, then back at him, her demeanor changed, her expression cool and remote, her fail-safe mechanisms firmly in place once more.

"We need to go. Get the pack." Her words were ice, and her eyes shone like liquid mercury.

That was fine. He could wait. He had learned how to wait.

Then she made a sound, barely a moan, and stepped in, close to his body so he could feel the brush of her thighs against his own and the press of her breasts to his chest. She rose on her toes and kissed him, her mouth on his for a bare instant.

But it was enough.

And he thought, If I cannot find the truth right where I am in this moment, where else do I expect to find it?

CHAPTER TWENTY

Tristan had a truck. In a manner of speaking.

It wasn't a bright and shiny rig with a long trailer and living quarters in the back of the cab like the trucks that trolled the ICW. It was an odd-looking thing, small and sleek, the tires three times taller than the vehicle itself and cased in caterpillar treads that chewed up the ground like a chain saw.

He'd kept it concealed beneath a white tarp and a carefully applied dusting of snow. *Just in case*, he'd said. She'd been speechless when he uncovered it with a proud flourish.

"Where exactly did you find this thing?" she asked now, the words rattling around as the movement of the vehicle shook her whole body.

"Built it. From scrap." He shrugged and winked at her. So handsome. Strong and solid and true. "It's a hobby."

Strange man.

Wonderful man.

No matter how much time you need, I will still love you.

How was she to answer that? What she knew of love was taken in snatches from the thoughts of others. She had stolen their emotions like a thief.

And even if that wasn't the case, even if she knew everything of love . . . every person she'd ever cared about was dead, and she had had a hand in killing them. Yuriko. Wizard. Raina Bowen.

Given her track record, she figured Tristan was a hell of a lot safer if she didn't love him.

She cut him a sidelong glance, to his hands, solid and strong on the wheel. Capable hands. Her lover's hands.

Disconcerted, she looked away, out the front window. The moon was an enormous yellow disc hanging in a blue-black sky, its bottom edge serrated by the dusky purple peaks of distant mountains. Behind them stretched a flat plain of solid ice, a thick crust floating atop the inky dark and frigid ocean. She knew that somewhere to the far right lay the floe edge, the end of the ice, and beyond that, the dark swells and waves of the sea.

There was beauty here in the Waste, even here in this place of frozen danger and death. She supposed one could find beauty anywhere, if they chose to look.

Wake from a darkened dream and see the beauty that surrounds you.

Was that what she had done? Wakened from her darkened dream?

Her gaze slid to Tristan once more, then away. Did she dare to love him, to allow herself that beauty? Right now, at this moment, she had no answers.

With a sigh, she turned her gaze to the horizon, where endless star-dusted darkness met the barren ice. Too much open space. It made her belly cramp.

What the hell was she doing out here chasing a fantasy?

She should simply kill them all. *Simply.* That was the key concept in the whole mess, because there was nothing simple about it.

Annihilating anyone who had been exposed to the pathogen was the most efficient way to ensure containment, but the thought of it . . .

She *knew* them. Had shared meals with them. Conversations. Laughter. Shayne. Kalen and Gemma. Lamia. They were *people*. She had formed relationships with them, strange and awkward though they might be. Even she, with her limited experience, understood that these people had become her friends. *They had become her friends.*

So how was she to go about killing her friends, then walk away and go on with her life?

The knowledge that sacrificing all the researchers and support staff would ensure the safety of the entire world didn't make the prospect of those thirty-seven deaths sit any easier in her thoughts or her heart.

She remembered the day Gemma had stabbed the rapist out on the ice. She had thought that she had no place stepping into that scenario, while at the same time she had been convinced that it was both her right and her responsibility to end the man's life in a merciful way.

Didn't that same logic apply here?

Her sentimentality could doom millions—no, *billions*—of people. She needed to go back, terminate the thirty-seven researchers and the Reaver test subjects. Incinerate their bodies. Blow the lab with a nice combination of cytoplast and phosphorous mines.

There wouldn't be any possibility of the virus getting out then.

Sacrifice a few to save the whole slagging Waste, maybe even the whole slagging world. That was the safest, smartest route. Do the deed and live with her conscience.

So what the hell was she doing out here, tearing across tundra and ice on a futile mission with an almost definite outcome? She and Tristan were chasing dreams, chasing the hope of finding a cure.

What had Lamia said her father called them? Pipe dreams.

They would fail. How could they not? The statistical probability that they would find the stolen equipment, find the missing viral samples, and find whatever secret edge Tristan believed the stolen goods contained was impossibly low. The likelihood that they could create a treatment or a control or a vaccine in time to save anyone was equally ridiculous.

The researchers in that lab had had months, perhaps even years, to do exactly that, and all they had created was death.

The desperation that touches my insane companion, touches me. Only this time, he was the insane companion, and she was the one searching for enlightenment.

"This isn't just a futile mission," she said. "It's a suicide mission. We're going up against Ward, and he's likely protected by an army."

He smiled, a dark, mirthless curving of his lips. "Let's just say I hope to have some allies. Lamia worked her comm magic before we left and set up a rendezvous. We should be there in a few hours." He was silent for a moment, the engine roaring and vibrating through them, then he cast her a glance and finished, "Besides, we make a great team, you and I."

"That, and . . . three hundred interdollars might buy you a hydrogen fill."

"Do I detect a note of sarcasm?"

She shrugged. Great team or not, there were only two of them.

Yeah, she was genetically enhanced, which counted for something.

She glanced down at her injured wrist, tried—and failed—to flex the fingers of that hand.

Yeah, she healed quickly. But death was death, even for her. Ward had numbers in his favor.

No matter what, she needed to stay alive, at least long enough to make it back to the lab. Because, in the end, if Tristan's mad—and as yet unrevealed—plan failed, she would have to go back into the ground and do what needed to be done, murder her friends and bury the last of her humanity fifty yuales beneath the frozen tundra.

Her gaze slid to Tristan, then away. She could talk to him, if she chose. Talk to him about the confusion and the pain and the uncertainty roiling inside of her.

She didn't. Couldn't. The words choked in her throat.

Yeah, that whole human interaction thing still needed some work. She really had no idea what to say.

"Stop," she ordered, and was a little surprised when he did exactly that, skidding to a stop on the ice, the tail of their vehicle spinning out at the abruptness of the move.

"What?"

Just ahead was an opening in the thick crust of ice that floated upon the black, frigid depths of the ocean. It was about as long and wide as a Janson truck, the dark water shimmering and dancing with the reflection of the overhead moon and stars.

Without answering him, Tatiana pushed open her door and clambered down from the rig. She stalked across the ice to the hole, the slam of a door echoing through the still night as Tristan followed her.

"What?" he asked again.

As they approached, the smooth curved back of a white whale—a beluga—broke the surface in a slow roll, the head and flukes never clearing the water. A geyser rose high as the creature took a breath.

Tatiana watched as the arc of the whale's back flowed, then disappeared beneath the dark cold water.

A moment later, a second whale took its place, rising to the surface for a life-giving breath, then sinking into the deep dark once more.

As Tristan moved to stand by her side, shoulder to shoulder, she noticed that the edges of the hole were raised, built up by the splash of waves and the spray generated by the movement of the whales, frozen to a solid raised rim. They had been here for a long time, these whales. Weeks and weeks.

Narrowing her eyes, she twisted to look to her right. Flat white. There was nothing to see but flat white and swirling snow lifted by the wind. The ice floes had tightened to a solid pack and there was nowhere else in sight for the whales to surface and breathe.

They were trapped here. Trapped by the ice.

The horror of that made her throat tighten.

Walls of stone on three sides and a shatterproof plastiglass wall on the fourth. The illusion of freedom. A glimpse of the world beyond her cell, but no way to reach it.

Her belly did a sickening roll.

"Ana, what is it?" Tristan asked, his voice gentle.

"The whales. They're trapped. Prisoners of that tiny hole."

He turned slowly, looking to each side, saw what she had already seen. "There are no other breaks in the ice. How long until they need to breathe again?"

"Twenty minutes maximum. That's the longest a beluga can hold its breath before it needs to draw more. And there's no food here for them. They're trapped swimming beneath the ice, no more than ten minutes out in any direction, and ten minutes back, using up their stores of fat, and if they're lucky, surviving until the thaw. They'll be here for months, swimming up and down to this hole until the ice breaks up." Her tone was cool, calm, but inside she was screaming, railing against their fate. Her fate. Trapped, unable to break free.

She waited for him to say something. What? To berate her? They were trying to save people, save their friends. Time was sliding away from them like ice melting in the sun.

And she wanted to stop and talk about the whales.

Why? What was she thinking?

She had no idea. She only knew that the sight of that sleek, curved white back and the desperate sadness of the creature's predicament left her feeling broken inside.

"Tatiana." Tristan was very close to her now. She stood, trembling, staring at the break in the ice, so small and isolated in the face of the stretch of flat, white plain that went on and on as far as the eye could see.

No way out. Trapped. No hope.

Tears stung her eyes, and she couldn't explain that, couldn't say why she felt so incredibly sad.

"Tatiana," he said again, and she thought he would tell her to get back in the truck. Move out. Of course. They needed to move. Time was so short and they had a long way to go.

Reaching up, he dragged his gloved thumb along her cheek. For a moment, she didn't understand. And then she did, and she was mortified and horrified. She was crying.

Crying.

For the whales.

For herself. For the years she had spent trapped as they were trapped.

"We need to move, Ana. Standing here does them no good. Let's go." He waited a heartbeat, and when she remained where she was, staring at the shifting surface of the frigid, dark water, unable to tear her gaze away, he said, "Now."

Ever the dictator.

And always right. They did need to move and her inexplicable sentimentality had no place here.

Swallowing, she nodded and walked to the truck, climbed inside, a cold, sick knot sitting heavy in the center of her chest just below her ribs.

Tristan turned his head toward her. She couldn't see his expression, and she was glad for that.

With a sharp nod, he faced forward once more and drove out. Tatiana stared straight ahead, tears trailing down her cheeks to drop onto the backs of her hands where they lay in her lap. Silly. But she couldn't seem to make them stop.

Turning, she watched another geyser of water shoot skyward, the huff of the whale's exhalation through its blowhole.

Some fifteen minutes later, Tristan drew to a halt, dug beneath his thermal gear, and hauled out the small metal box of cytoplast.

No, he couldn't be thinking—

But he was. Vaulting from the truck, he gouged a tiny indentation in the ice with his knife, dropped the cytoplast in the hole and set the fuse. His actions were deft and precise, not a second wasted.

As he climbed back up behind the wheel, his gaze met hers, and he grinned, white teeth, the front two overlapping ever so slightly. She had never seen anything more wonderful than that smile.

Leaning toward him, she grabbed his coat and dragged him close enough to kiss. His lips were cold, his tongue warm.

"See," he murmured against her lips. "It wouldn't be so hard to love me."

No, she thought as he put the truck in gear and drove out, not so hard to love him at all. And somehow, that thought was less frightening than it had been before.

An instant later, the explosion rocked them, punching the vehicle forward with an invisible fist. A shower of pulverized ice rained down on the roof.

They drove on, with Tristan repeating his actions again and again, blowing breath holes in the ice for the whales that followed them, veering their vehicle toward the floe edge in a steady curve.

Climbing from the truck, Tatiana watched Tristan work at setting yet another charge. She stood out on the ice, with the stars glittering overhead, and the wind howling along the open, flat terrain. She turned to look behind them, and in the distance saw glittering fountains of water reaching toward the night sky, reflecting the light of the bright moon as the whales surfaced in a newly created hole.

"They're following us," she said. "Slowly, but they *are* following us."

"The noise of the explosions makes them wary," Tristan offered.

"But they know where the holes are." Relief sifted through her, freeing the vice around her heart. "They'll come along eventually."

"How do you figure they know where to go?" he asked, his head bowed, his hands working with quick efficiency.

"Echolocation." She could hear the faint sounds of his knife scraping on the ice. "They bounce sound around under the ice and off the ocean floor. It's the same principle they use to find food. Whatever echoes back at them tells them about the thing the sound wave bounced off."

"What are you . . . a whale specialist?"

She could hear the smile in his voice, and felt the

answering smile unfurl deep inside her. "Something like that, yeah."

Staring into the distance, she watched for another sign of the whales.

"It must have been terrifying for them," she said softly, "being trapped like that with no way to break through, no way to break free."

She glanced at him over her shoulder and saw that his hands had stilled. Raising his head, he stared at her for a long moment, his eyes glittering like the star-flung sky. He saw too much, things she wasn't ready to share, and it was all she could do to hold his gaze, to hold herself steady in the face of her surging memories.

Then he set the cytoplast in the dent he'd gouged.

"Time to go." He rose and walked toward the truck, and she ducked around to the passenger side and climbed in.

The sound of yet another explosion followed in their wake as they pulled away.

"Why do you hate tight spaces, Ana?"

His abrupt query caught her off guard. She felt bare, exposed, as though sharing a bit of herself with him only put her more firmly in his thrall. There was danger here, but also the promise of something safe. She was wise enough to recognize that.

"I"—she hesitated, uncertain she would be able to explain, uncertain if she *ought* to explain—"I spent a very long time in a very small space."

"You were a prisoner." His fingers tightened on the wheel, a small thing, but so telling.

His observation, his conclusion, were inevitable. Her reaction to the whales had betrayed her. That he read her so easily was frightening . . . while at the same time freeing. He understood. How strange that he understood.

Or perhaps not strange at all. Tristan had his own tragic

tale to share. She didn't need a window into his thoughts to know that. The question was, was she brave enough to share her story, brave enough to ask him for his own?

She swallowed. "I was a prisoner of . . . Duncan Bane. Half my life was spent in a cell under his offices in Port Uranium."

Tristan's grip on the wheel grew tighter still, but he said nothing.

"Bane believed I could tell the future. He believed I was his oracle, his secret weapon. He believed that my predictions would make him ruler of the world."

Cold fear slapped her. Why had she said that, divulged so much?

Tristan turned his head, his eyes glittering in the darkness, and there was neither censure nor disbelief in his gaze, only quiet understanding.

"Bane was a snake and a bastard," he said, "but he wasn't stupid. If he believed you could tell the future, there had to be a reason."

"A reason." She made a choked laugh. "Do you think I can tell the future? Do you think such a thing is even possible?"

"I think that you could do something that made Bane believe it."

What harm in telling him? What could he do with the knowledge? Besides, harm or no, she *wanted* to tell him, ached to set the words free. Set herself free.

"I can read thoughts. Read emotions. Not everyone's, but most people's." She turned her face to the window, stared out at the moon and the ice, endless ice, the open space leaving her wary and on edge. "I read enough of Duncan Bane's thoughts to tell him likely outcomes of his business dealings and political machinations. He thought that meant I could see the future, and since that belief kept me on this side of the curtain between life and death, I let him believe whatever the slagging hell he wanted. If he'd known I could read his mind, he'd have killed me." She drew a deep breath, and told the rest of the sordid truth. "In my mind reside the horrors of so many of his crimes. Not all—some things he kept hidden—but enough that they haunt me. The murders. The tortures. The mass destruction. I know them. I see them. And I never did anything to stop it. Maybe, with the advice I gave him and the things I told him, maybe I helped make it all happen."

There. It was out. One of her secrets.

Let's see if he would love her now.

He glanced at her, held her gaze, and said, "If tears come to you for the suffering of others, any others, those known to you, or unknown, then you are compassionate. If you cry only for the suffering of those you love, for their death, for your own loss, then you are selfish." The words crossed the space between them, darkly soft. "Have you ever cried for yourself, my Ana?"

His tone implied that he already knew the answer, knew that she had never cried for herself. And loved her for it. That took her breath, stole it from her lips, and left her aching inside in ways both painful and wonderful.

"What benefit tears?" she asked, just to fill the silence.

There had been no avenues open to her. There had been only the focus on survival, on making it through each night, each day. If she had cried, it had been for those in the cells the bordered hers, for their suffering, their heartache, their emotions becoming her own.

"Look," he said, pointing out her window.

She turned and saw that they were driving parallel to the floe edge. Beyond the ice was a vast expanse of water, smooth as plastiglass, black as the overhead night sky. Large chunks of ice rose from the surface, ghostly white.

And then she saw something else, something wonderful, the white, smooth curve of a whale's back. Free. They were free.

She laughed, spun and launched herself at Tristan across the space that separated them. With his arms wrapped tight about her, their bodies arched and twisted to meet halfway between their seats, they both turned their heads to watch the whales swim free.

After a moment, they were gone, disappeared beneath the black surface of the water.

"Can you read my thoughts?" he asked, a little wary.

She disengaged from his embrace, shifted back to her own seat and shook her head. "No. And I had trouble reading Lamia and Gemma and Kalen. I think that might be because of their infection, because the virus is changing their thought patterns, altering their consciousness."

"Makes sense." He was silent for a long moment. "How do you do it?"

His tone made her smile. "Ever the scientist, huh?"

He laughed.

"Electric currents. I have heightened sensitivity to the electric currents of thought waves."

"You pick up the residual of the action potential traveling along neuronal axons?"

"Yes, exactly."

"And what is the rest of your story, Ana? What happened after Bane was killed?"

Apt questions, they cut straight to the heart of the matter. The rest of her story. He seemed to sense that, as bad as the part she had told him was, there was something even darker beneath that surface layer.

She tapped her index finger against her thigh, a slow, steady beat, and said nothing. Nothing at all.

Narrowing his eyes, Tristan dropped his gaze to her fingers, his brow furrowing in a slight frown.

"You're moving your finger," he said, clearly bemused.

"Uh-huh." She kept tapping her finger for a moment, small movements of flexion and extension, before realizing what was confusing him.

It was the finger of her damaged hand, the one that he probably figured she'd never be able to use again. And here it was, already repairing itself to an amazing degree. Catching her lower lip between her teeth, she tried to figure out what to say, how to explain.

"I—uh—I guess it wasn't as bad as we thought."

The look he sent her spoke volumes.

But to her surprise, he didn't press. Didn't ask a single thing.

"Ah," he said softly, as though he'd had a revelation.

"Meaning what?" But her question only earned her a secretive smile.

So although she was the one who hoarded a chunk of her secrets—not quite ready to bare the entirety of her soul—she was left feeling as though she ought to be asking some questions of her own.

CHAPTER TWENTY-ONE

"Are you crazy?" Tatiana demanded hours later, her heart slamming against her ribs as they drove closer to the lethal rows of ice pirate rigs parked at the base of the mountains. Each truck boasted thick caterpillar treads, layers of metal scaling, and gun turrets, armed and ready.

She only wondered why they hadn't fired yet. Reavers weren't known for their restraint.

There were three plascannon rigs, and a dozen slightly smaller plated metal trucks . . . though in this case, *small* was a relative term. And snowscooters. About twenty of them.

The Reavers on the scooters each wore a miniarsenal—double harnesses with massive AT950s front and back, and holsters at their hips, buckled over thick layers of matted furs. She figured they had wrist holsters as well. Maybe even guns in their heavy boots.

"Slag, each one of them has enough firepower to take down a city," she breathed. "What the hell are you doing, approaching them like this?" She held up her hands, palms forward, when he cut her a sidelong glance. "No, no, don't say a word. I know. If I understand, things are just as they are. If I do not understand, things are just as they are. Right?"

Tristan inclined his head, his lips curving in a glimmer of a smile. "Precisely."

"I could hit you."

"You could," he agreed, all amiable and content, as though they weren't driving toward certain and brutal death.

"They eat their victims."

"You are no victim, Ana," he said, very quiet, very sure. "And neither am I."

His words sank through her, buoying her, making her feel so close to him. He saw her. He *knew* her. She had been a victim for a very long time, Bane's victim and Ward's, and then slowly, something had changed. She understood that now. Not her circumstance. She had still been locked away in a cell.

No, it was her state of mind that had changed.

Aside from all the budding genetic enhancements that had begun to appear, making her physically stronger each day, it was her mind that had grown stronger.

She would never be a victim again.

"Besides, we're expected," he continued.

"Being expected might not be a good thing." She narrowed her eyes and studied the jagged peaks of hills nestled at the feet of the larger mountains that rose to touch the sky.

At this distance, Tristan wouldn't be able to see the threat that lurked there, hidden by distance and careful placement, but she could see them. Reavers.

"There are snipers, positioned there . . . there"—she pointed to each place—"and there."

"Strategic placement." He didn't sound particularly concerned.

"Now might be a good time to let me in on your grand plan." Her heart gave a solid thud in her chest, and after a few seconds of silence, she realized she was holding her breath. It was inordinately important to her that he trust her with this, that he share his plans. That he accept her as an equal partner.

"My grand plan . . ." Tristan geared down and slowed their vehicle, his tone even. "Did you wonder where the Reaver test subjects came from?"

"Actually, I hadn't thought of it before, but now that you ask the question, I do wonder. . . ."

"They were volunteers. Ward went to their leader, Belek-ool, promised a massive signing bonus to every volunteer. Extra drugs. Even women. He promised they would be stronger, faster, more brutal when the experiments were done. And he promised that there was little risk." He glanced at her, his mouth pulled taut with tension, a muscle working in his jaw. "He promised them power, and all along, he meant to kill them, knew exactly the sort of death he planned for them. He knew what he intended to do with my research, how he would twist it from something good into something evil. And I was so blind, I let him." He slammed his open palm against the steering wheel. "I was so fucking blind, that I let him."

"They're killers. Rapists. They eat the dead," she pointed out, though for some reason, it didn't make what Ward had done any more palatable.

"Then they should be subject to laws and justice. It is not Ward's right to determine that they are less than human, that they were expendable. And they were only the first, not the final stage. He infected my friends, and he intends to use my research to kill millions."

"You cannot carry the responsibility of what Ward did."

"No, I can't. But I can carry the responsibility of what *I* did, and I can try to set it right." Tristan parked the rig, set the brakes, and he turned to face her, all expression wiped clean. "Belek-ool sent his sons to Ward. All three of his sons. The youngest was nineteen. They were among the first to die."

His words punched her hard, the thought of a Reaver prince sending his sons to die like that. Emotions coiled through her, twisting in her gut, and she wondered that she could feel for the suffering of an ice pirate who was himself a murderer.

Slagging emotions. She was going to have to learn to deal with them because they weren't always neat and tidy, and they didn't always make logical sense.

"Does he know they're dead?" she asked. "Does he know *how* they died? What Ward did to them?"

Tristan leaned close to her, until his lips brushed her ear, and he spoke low, as though sharing a confidence, though there was no one else in the vehicle to hear. "That's what we're here to tell him."

She drew back and stared at him, both horrified by the prospect of bearing bad tidings to a man who would as soon hack off someone's head as speak to them, and awed by the simple genius of Tristan's plan.

"You were worried that this was a suicide mission, that Ward has an army and we have none?" His gaze slid to the front window. A stocky man with ice-pale eyes and a jagged, raised scar that marked him from brow to chin walked toward them. "That, Ana, is Belek-ool. And once he hears what I have to say, I suspect we'll have his army as our own."

Tristan didn't delude himself into imagining that Ana agreed with anything he was doing here. She hadn't liked that he'd come to the Reavers for help. She hadn't liked that she had to stay in the truck with her hood pulled up and her face obscured. And she hadn't liked that he stepped out to meet Belek-ool alone and unarmed, save for the knife at the small of his back.

But Ana wasn't one to let personal preference sway the outcome of a mission. Once she had said her piece, made her arguments and counterarguments, she'd closed her mouth with an annoyed snap and drew up her hood.

Then she'd cracked the window enough that she could aim her AT450 directly at Belek-ool's head.

And he loved her for that, for doing what needed to be done even though she thought he was dead wrong.

Tristan strode from the truck, keeping his gait slow and even, his attention split between Belek-ool and the snipers on the ridge. Ana had his back. Guess she'd changed her mind about watching no one's back but her own. She'd made a recent habit of watching his. But after this, maybe she wouldn't anymore. Maybe this decision to ally himself with the Reavers—one she vehemently opposed, with damned good reason—would push her beyond his reach.

He wanted her to love him.

But how could she if he showed her his deepest truths and secrets, bared the ugly part of himself that could find a way to partner with killers? That was far more likely to make her hate him.

And, yeah, he'd have to live with that, too. This wasn't about her or him or what he wanted. It was about the entire Waste, maybe the entire world.

Belek-ool sauntered forward, then stopped some ten meters away. A statement. He expected Tristan to come to him.

Fair enough. He'd come this far. What were another few steps?

"Belek-ool," Tristan greeted, his tone even. The bitter wind howled across the open plain and swirled at the base of the mountains.

Tristan gritted his teeth. Just standing here cost him. Because he was planning to ally with monsters against a monster, an alliance that dragged him one step closer to being one of their kind.

Then again, he'd been one of their kind for a very long time. He'd killed his own family, then conjured a new type of death. The number of people his work would kill was vastly greater than the number who would die at the hands of every Reaver in the Waste.

Somehow, he had to find a way to reconcile what these men were with what he needed them to do.

If adding more filth to his soul by asking a man who murdered others for entertainment and tormented innocents for his pleasure was the only way to stop Ward and eradicate the plague, then he would do it. Because there were gradations of evil, and if he needed to overlook the lesser in order to overcome the greater, he would have to find a way to reconcile that, too.

He would do whatever it took; too many lives were at stake for him to make any other choice.

"You are Tolliver?" Belek-ool made a subtle gesture, and the Reavers standing just behind him angled their plasguns until they were aimed at Tristan's chest. The mountains loomed at their backs, dark purple, snow-capped crags.

"I am."

"Why have you come here?"

"For your help."

His words were met with a startled silence, and then Belek-ool threw back his head and laughed, a rusty dark sound that scraped like a dry razor.

"You are either very brave or very stupid, Tolliver." His ice-pale eyes narrowed, and he glanced around at his men with an expression of blatant amusement. Returning his attention to Tristan, he opened his mouth to say more, but the only sound that issued forth was a garbled grunt.

Everything happened so fast that Tristan wasn't certain where she came from or how she accomplished it, but Ana was there, her arm around Belek-ool's throat, her knife poised against the pulse of his carotid, pressing hard enough to draw a bead of blood. With her other hand, she held her Setti9 against his temple.

There were mutters of shock and anger from the onlookers, but apart from snarls and a few lurching steps forward, none challenged Ana's sincerity when she barked, "Stay, or I slit his throat."

Belek-ool neither flinched nor moved. His scarred face was completely devoid of expression, though Tristan suspected he was battling a killing rage. Being overpowered in front of his men must be a bitter pill.

Being overpowered by a woman probably turned the bitterness to poison.

Ana spun him like a doll—a guy twice her size and weight—so that his body shielded Tristan from the array of plasguns. If they fired, Belek-ool would be the first to die.

"Guns down," she ordered, sharp and hard. "Or I take you out. Your men might kill me, but not before I kill you. You have three seconds to decide."

He nodded, a spare movement of his head. Ana eased the pressure on his windpipe only enough that Belek-ool could order his men to lower their weapons. Then she pressed the knife in tight once more.

Tristan rapidly readjusted his plan. Ana had just blown a huge curve in the road. Given that she'd been right and he'd been wrong—and that without her intervention he would probably be dead right now—he wasn't planning to complain about the alteration.

"A woman. You set a woman against me?" Belek-ool sounded affronted and disgusted. And maybe a little intrigued.

"Actually"—Tristan shot a look at Ana, but she kept her focus on her prey—"she set *herself* against you." He knew that he wasn't furthering his cause by saying more, but he continued anyway. "She has a mind of her own. Guess she didn't like the two snipers who were getting ready to gun me down."

"Didn't know you saw them," Ana murmured.

"Saw them. Figured you'd take them out if need be." He paused. "Figured you'd take them out from the safety of the truck."

She snorted. "Nothing safe about that truck. You need to practice your skills with a fusion welder."

In the background, the Reavers shifted restlessly, but none dared move forward or make a threatening move. Belek-ool was too important to their continued success as a strong and dangerous band. He was what unified them, and none dared risk his life.

Not yet.

That might change at any moment, though. Reavers weren't exactly known for their loyalty.

"So we were about to discuss an alliance," Tristan said.

"Alliance?" Belek-ool huffed, bristling with affront. "You come to ask for my *help*, but you hold a blade at my neck. Your tactics are underhanded."

"Fair enough." Tristan decided it was counterproductive to the negotiation process to point out that he wasn't the one holding the blade. "But that makes them tactics that you admire."

"Hnn." Belek-ool tensed, testing Ana's hold.

She pressed the plasgun harder against his temple and shifted her stance, sliding her knife hand down his chest, then his belly, to the top of his thigh. The point of her blade was strategically positioned at his fly.

"Try it," she whispered, darkly soft. "Please. It would be a joy to substitute a particular part of your anatomy for the sim-protein in my next meal. Heard tell it's the *tender* part. Never tried it, but there's always a first time."

There was enough venom in her tone that, for a millisecond, Tristan actually believed she would do exactly what she threatened. And from the way Belek-ool froze, it appeared that he leaned toward believing it, too.

In that instant, one of the Reavers behind Belek-ool moved, a tiny shift, but enough to show his intent. Tristan yanked his blade free, his right foot automatically sliding forward, his weight shifting to the ball of his left foot. With his knife held in a hammer grip, wrist perfectly stiff, he brought his arm in a trained arc, shifted his weight to the front foot. The knife flew, hit the Reaver in the throat, and the plas-shot that had been aimed at Ana went wide.

"You killed my man," Belek-ool observed without inflection as the body hit the ground with a dull thud.

"Because he meant to kill mine." Tristan centered his thoughts, his emotions, drawing on years of training to maintain a calm facade. The bastards had meant to kill Ana, and if they had succeeded, he would have had her death to add to his long, long list.

Whatever dark deeds lay in his past, he had managed to stay sane, to hold back the flood of his self-hate just enough to go on. But if Ana died here tonight, the dam would burst.

"Enough," he said, looking at the Reavers, his tone no

longer conciliatory. "Yeah, I need your help, but you need mine as well. And if you deny me that help, you *will not* live. Let me tell you about Gavin Ward and what he did to your comrades, your fellows"—his gaze shot straight to Belek-ool—"your sons."

He spoke loudly enough for all to hear, his words echoing through the silence that greeted them. He kept his descriptions clean, concise. But it was enough. When he was done, he looked back to Belek-ool and waited.

"My sons are dead," Belek-ool said. He raised his head, and Ana slacked her hold enough to let him. "My sons are dead," he roared.

Tristan held his hand out to Ana, and she stepped away from Belek-ool to his side.

The Reaver stood rigid for a long moment. No one spoke. No one moved.

Staring straight ahead, he took his knife from the harness that crisscrossed his chest. With slow controlled movements, he shed the layers of furs and thermal gear that clothed him, right down to his skin, the bitter wind slapping at him.

His jaw set, his expression savage, he cut a deep groove lengthwise down his left biceps.

"For my sons," he boomed.

A chorus came back at him, "For your sons."

Tristan saw that a dozen other men had bared their torsos and were cutting similar grooves in their flesh.

Belek-ool cut another groove. "For my sons," he called, louder, and waited as a roar echoed back at him.

With a deep breath, he cut a third groove, parallel to the other two. "For my sons!"

All the Reavers stamped their feet and called back at him, "For your sons!"

Then Belek-ool turned his gaze to Tristan and said, whisper soft, "What need have I to ally with you, Tolliver? Vengeance is mine. Vengeance must be mine."

"Understood," Ana said, stepping forward. "But remaining alive after you kill Ward must be part of that vengeance. If you do not ally with us, then there will be no one to find a cure, no one to protect the denizens of the Waste. Then your vengeance will be for naught. You will die. Your comrades will die. Any other sons you have will die."

With her gaze locked on Belek-ool's, she shoved up her sleeve and cut a deep groove in her forearm. Tristan jerked forward, but she shot him a glance that made him freeze.

She had trusted him to follow the path he thought best, though she disagreed with his choice. Now she expected him to do the same for her.

How could he offer her less than she offered him?

Fisting his hands so tight at his sides that he thought he might turn his bones to dust, he stayed where he was as she turned her face back toward Belek-ool.

"For your sons," she said. Then she cut another groove beside the first. "For your sons," she said, louder, and raised her knife to cut a third groove, but Belek-ool caught her wrist and did the deed himself, slicing a deep, bloody line in her forearm, the blood from the cuts he had made on himself mixing with hers.

"For my sons!" he roared, and the mountains echoed with the answering cries.

"Ward is mine," he said when the cacophony finally died down. "The killing blow is mine."

Ana took a deep breath, and leaned in close, murmuring something that Tristan couldn't hear.

Belek-ool reared back and stared at her, his entire body so still it seemed to oscillate in the cold.

"Yes," he agreed. "Yes. That is the right way. The killing blow will be yours, Woman-who-should-have-been-a-man. The killing blow will be yours."

And as Ana raised her head and shifted her gaze to meet his own, Tristan felt a chill of dark premonition.

CHAPTER TWENTY-TWO

It took them two days to find Ward's convoy. Belek-ool's contacts throughout the Waste were incredibly forthcoming, and Tristan stayed in close contact with Lamia, who used her comm and satellite links to hunt down information from every trucker and settler she could contact.

The Reavers favored an ambush, so a day later, with the frigid wind whipping down on them and the night sky dark with low, gray clouds, they laid their trap, held their positions and waited.

Tatiana lay on her belly on an icy ridge five hundred yuales south of Gladow Station. Monstrous chunks of ice and snow reached skyward, and on each was a strategically placed sniper. Belek-ool's men.

With practiced ease, she ran a checklist on her AT450, double-checked the plas-shot cartridge. Full. Then she scoped her escape route. The side of the ridge was smooth and slick, angled at a nice incline. She could slide down it and hit the ground running if Tristan needed her.

Or if she had the chance to get to Ward.

No, not if. She *would* have the chance to get to Ward, because she meant to be the one to kill him. It was the only way she could ever be truly free.

Justice. Not vengeance. Justice.

It was her right. More than that, it was her responsibility.

From this vantage, she had a clear view of Tristan. He was just below her on a borrowed snowscooter, armed with borrowed weapons. His tattered thermal gear stood out against the fur garments of the ice pirates, but even without that marker, she would have been able to pick him out among a sea of men.

Because he was hers. Her man.

And neither of them better die tonight because she had things she needed to say to him.

She flipped her Setti9 from her wrist holster and, though she'd already done it a dozen times, ran a checklist on that as well. Glancing at her injured hand, she flexed her fingers. They were a little numb, and they felt heavy, clumsy, as though they'd swollen to twice their normal size. But they were functioning. A boon when she needed it most.

Tension coiled through her. They'd needed an army. She knew that. And while she didn't love Tristan's method of gaining them one, she couldn't fault its efficacy. Problem was, as soon as Ward was dead, the ice pirates were just as likely to kill her and Tristan as let them go.

Perhaps her show of solidarity with Belek-ool, the three cuts she'd gouged in her flesh, would make him more inclined to let them go about their merry way. Perhaps.

More likely, if he did set them free, it would be because the main reason the Reavers had agreed to the alliance in the first place was to ensure that Tristan had the opportunity to engineer a cure. If they incinerated him here in the middle of the Waste, it would sort of defeat the purpose.

Still, she was wary. Reavers weren't exactly known for either loyalty or reliability. If Belek-ool died today, his successor wasn't guaranteed to honor any bargains he'd made.

That was the part of the plan that didn't work so well for her.

Her head jerked up. Before any of the others, she heard it, the distant roar of the powerful truck engines. Her gaze slid to the horizon where a faint dark mass was moving across the frozen terrain.

Turning her focus to Tristan, she stared down at him, willing him to turn. The seconds ticked past with agonizing slowness. Then he did turn, his head tipping back as he looked to her position, and she nodded once, a signal to let him know what she saw.

In the distance, four sleek, black trucks came into view, barreling toward them, unaware. The monstrous engines roared, the sound carrying up and bouncing off the high, straight walls of the icy crags.

Suddenly, six snowscooters closed in behind Ward's rigs, peeling out from the cover of the massive chunks of ice that had obscured them from view. They closed in fast, their blades screaming over the ice.

Massive flares of plas-shot erupted from the ice pirates' weapons, harrying the rigs as they wove side to side in avoidance.

There was a flash of light, so bright it was blinding. One of the scooters erupted in flames, and the remaining five closed ranks.

Then the first of Gavin Ward's four trucks hit the line of phosphorous mines that Tristan and Belek-ool had planted in the snow. The explosion rocked the ground, sending twisted bits of truck in all directions, spewing churned-up chunks of ice and frozen tundra like a thick cloud. The flames were so hot that Tatiana felt the wall of heat come at her even from this distance.

Her gaze sought Tristan where he barreled across the snow. One of Ward's men leaned out the rig's window, took aim. Her breath locked in her chest. She swung her AT450, took a bead on his head, breathed halfway out and blasted him to hell.

No one was taking Tristan down. Not on her watch.

From all around her, plas-shot rained down on Ward's rigs, but they were anything but helpless. One by one, they picked off each of the scooters that followed them, then turned their sights to the crags and the snipers.

A chilling scream came from far too close as one of Ward's men hit the ice arch just behind her, crumbling the top of the massive structure, sending the Reaver who had been firing from that position flying through the air to land with a dull thud on the ice.

Below her, plas-shot from Ward's men hit an ice pirate as he whizzed past on his snowscooter. The firepower was enough to incinerate his torso while his legs were left twitching on each side of the saddle.

Grabbing her opportunity, Tatiana shoved off the edge of her perch, squatting low for balance, her arms outstretched on either side. She careened wildly down the slope toward the frozen tundra below. Just as she'd planned, she hit the ground running, skidded toward the scooter of the man who'd just died and shoved his remains off onto the snow.

Steeling herself to ignore the spray of blood that left the saddle slick, she threw her leg over, gunned the engine and leaned in, tearing across the ice toward Ward's rig. Tristan was already heading in that direction. She'd seen him take off with two of the Reavers.

They were just ahead of her, weaving back and forth to avoid the plas-shot.

All the Reavers were sticking to the plan. No one was

firing directly at Ward's rig. They couldn't risk it. Couldn't chance destroying the rig, and with it the viral and tissue samples they so desperately needed.

Scanning the vicinity, Tatiana spied an icy rise with a gentle slope up one side and a sharp drop on the other. Ward's rig was approaching it now, ready to pass right next to it, and she didn't think, didn't plan. She just moved.

Her heart pounded wildly as she gunned her engine and sped up the slope, never slowing, never pausing, just flying off the far end so she was soaring, she and the scooter high above the earth, just as Ward's rig passed below her.

She threw her body to the side, flinging herself from the saddle to land with jarring force against the roof of Ward's truck. Her scooter kept going until it slammed to the ground with a violent rumble and erupted in a ball of flame.

Beneath her, the rig swerved to one side, and she skidded wildly across the roof, whipping off the far edge, her body swaying erratically as she grabbed hold of the raised lip. She clawed at the metal, her fingers screaming in protest, sliding beneath the rim, grabbing hold tight enough to keep her from falling free.

Slag. She was slipping. She was falling.

With a wild cry, she hauled back her hand, pressed her fingers tight together, and chopped at the metal. Pain slammed her, but to her shock, her efforts paid off. A narrow, deep groove offered a perfect handhold, and she grabbed it, steadying herself as the rig swerved in the opposite direction.

Guess it worked on trucks as well as Viktor's hand.

She saw him then, Tristan, leaning low on his scooter, the black, rippling flag of his thermal gear flying as he roared through the night toward her.

All around her were screams and fires, explosions and plas-shot. Two of Ward's rigs were destroyed, as were about half of the ice pirates' scooters.

Scrabbling back up the side of the rig, she flattened herself against the roof and shifted forward like a crab.

Two quick huffing breaths were the only preparation she allowed herself, and then she shot out the driver's-side window, taking the driver with it, and swung down feet first into Ward's cab.

No sooner was she in, when the door was yanked open behind her, and one of Belek-ool's men clambered off his scooter and swung up to throw the dead driver from behind the wheel and climb into position himself.

She didn't wait to see where he would drive to. She turned and yanked open the door from the cab to the back of the rig and stepped through into the pitch dark.

Instinct made her drop. A wise move. Plas-shot whizzed over her head, shattering the front window of the rig. Belek-ool's man cried out and went limp.

Tatiana slithered forward as Ward's man kept firing blind. She could see in the dark. He couldn't. A distinct advantage. One she'd have liked to keep. So she didn't fire at him, lest the flare of her plasgun give away her position. Instead, she eased her knife from her boot, ready to slit his throat.

She heard a whoosh and a grunt, and Ward's man sank to his knees, the hilt of a knife protruding from his throat. Glancing behind her, she saw Tristan outlined in the open passenger door of the rig for a mere instant before he ducked behind the cover of the seat.

On her belly, she crawled forward, taking care to make no sound.

Then she saw him, in the far corner. Gavin Ward. His silver hair was mussed and standing up in places, his eyes darting wildly about. At the sight of him, something inside her clicked and froze.

Here he was. The monster from her nightmares, pared down to just a man. A terrified, mortal man.

That made it worse, what he had done. He was only one man, and he had done such terrible things, incited others to follow him into the horrors he perpetrated.

Just a man.

"Hello, my darling girl," he crooned, and just the sound of his voice and those simple words made a chill ripple down her spine.

My darling girl. My precious girl. He had called her that as he sliced bits and pieces from her body. Called her that as he tortured others right in front of her, forcing her to absorb the emotions that burst from them.

"I can't see you, but I know you're here," he said. "We're connected, my precious girl. I always know when you're about."

Connected.

She wanted to argue, to rail at him and shout against him. But that was exactly what he was after. He wanted to bait her, to rile her, to force her to make a mistake.

Instead, she lay where she was, cloaked in darkness, and scanned the rig for the most likely location of the viral and tissue samples.

There. A laser-locked temperature-controlled box with an independent energy source and a backup pack on the side. Ward wasn't taking any chances.

Edging forward, she closed her hands around the box, tested its stability to see if it was bolted in place. It was.

She was about to withdraw, when she felt the barrel of a plasgun press against her temple. Her belly dropped and cold sweat beaded her lip.

"I know you so well," Gavin whispered from right

next to her ear, "I don't even need to see to be able to track you."

She could hear the sound of her own breathing harsh in her ears, and her heart slammed so hard in her chest that she felt sick with it.

"Do you know me?" she asked. "Do you?"

He laughed.

Reaching into the inside pocket of her shirt, she withdrew the vaccination gun she'd brought with her, the single-use capsule filled with Lamia's blood.

She could hear Tristan stealthily moving forward, and she didn't wait, couldn't wait. It needed to be this.

Gavin Ward needed to die the same way he had killed others. He needed to feel what they had felt. He deserved to know the horror.

This was what she had promised Belek-ool to convince him she was the one to deliver the killing blow. This was what she had promised herself.

And she meant to deliver.

Lurching to the side, away from his plasgun, she jammed the vaccination gun against his thigh and shot the dose.

He yelped, jerked back, his plasgun erupting in a bright flare. Pain roared through her.

She was hit. With a snarl, she kicked the gun from his hand, sending it spiraling through the air to clatter against the far wall.

"What have you done?" Ward cried. He stumbled against the wall, flicked on a lumilight, staring down at the vaccination gun in her hand.

She watched as the horror of understanding reflected in his eyes.

"That's how you'll die," she whispered. "Like one of your test subjects. I'll monitor your demise and document it every step of the way."

Reaching out to catch hold of his baby finger, she gave it a tug. "What part do you think will fall off first? A finger? A toe?" she snarled, emotion pouring through her. There was a loud roaring in her ears and her vision had tunneled until she saw only Ward. "A part of your dick, you slagging bastard?"

Ward gasped, stumbled back, his mouth opening and closing, no sound issuing forth.

Pressing her hand to her shoulder, she lurched to her feet, tears stinging her eyes as she felt Tristan move beside her.

His gaze slid from her face to her shoulder, back to her face. Apparently satisfied that she would survive, he stayed silent.

"The samples you need are there." She indicated the climate-controlled box.

He caught her gaze for an instant and offered a whisper of a smile. "Understood."

"She's infected me with the virus," Ward cried. "Tolliver, help me. You need to help me." He slid slowly down the wall, his legs giving way beneath him.

He was sobbing now, and as Tatiana stared at him she felt a sick horror for what he was and what she had endured. What so many people had been forced to endure at his hands. Ward was nothing. He was less than nothing.

"I will help you," Tristan said, in a cool, calm voice as he took a step forward.

Tatiana made a sound of protest, and Tristan turned his head, his gaze meeting hers, cold and deep as the ocean, and she knew. She knew.

"No. It's not your right," she whispered. It wasn't his right or his responsibility, but a part of her insisted it was both.

"Let me, Ana. If you finish this the way you intend, it will haunt you forever. Let me take it on my soul."

"No."

Ward sobbed openly now, clutching his thigh where she had injected him with Lamia's tainted blood.

Brushing her cheek with the backs of his fingers, Tristan looked deep into her eyes. "Some things are not about rights. They are about what *is* right."

Yes, she knew that.

"I'm damaged," she said, the words laced with all the pain in her soul. "I will always be damaged."

"And I will always love you."

Yes, she knew that, too. He expected her to be nothing other than she was, wanted her to be nothing other than she was.

Ward pushed himself up, and snarled, "Do you know what she is, this creature you claim to love? Do you know?"

Tristan's eyes never left hers. "I know."

Cackling madly now, Ward shook his head. "You don't. But I do. She's not human. She's—"

"TTN081," Tristan said. She felt as though she'd been stabbed, the shock of that cutting deep. He knew.

"How?"

"Every tissue culture was labeled. And the clues were easy once I had the first few. You scabbed over within minutes of your shoulder being torn open. The injury that should have cost you the use of your hand healed within days. Tatiana . . . TTN . . . The answer was there for any who cared to look." The corners of his mouth lifted in the whisper of a smile. "And I cared."

His words made something ease inside her. He knew exactly what she was, and he loved her still.

"Let me take this on my soul," he said again, slamming his foot down hard on Ward's chest as he tried to scrabble away.

She shook her head, her heart banging so violently against her ribs that she felt sick. "I don't want his death on your conscience. I don't—"

"I killed my family." He cut her off, his voice low and tormented. She gasped, froze, barely able to assimilate his words. "I brought *Yersinia pestis*—the plague—into their home. Carried it to them because I had volunteered for a government experiment without understanding the consequences. *I* couldn't get sick, but *they* could. It didn't even dawn on me to determine if somehow I transported the disease. I didn't even think that was possible. I never knew I'd been exposed until it was too late."

She swallowed, feeling the depth of his pain. Shredded by the depth of his pain.

Her head was spinning with the things he was saying and the emotion of the moment and the hate and rage that boiled in her blood, the urge to make Ward pay.

Yersinia pestis? The plague outbreak of 2037? But that had been sixty years before. She shook her head.

Ward was mewling desperately, grasping at Tristan's ankle, trying to get free.

"I am responsible for so many deaths already," Tristan continued. "I created the template for this new plague, created the framework for Ward to build upon. So many black deeds. Let me take this one, too, my Ana." He made a self-denigrating sound. "Maybe it will help me to live with the rest."

For a long moment, she stared at him, feeling the emotion pulsing from him in waves. And suddenly, she understood.

He did love her. Truly loved her. Enough to kill for her. Enough to die for her. Enough to walk away from this if she asked it of him.

If she loved him, she needed to let him do this. Whatever twisted absolution he would gain from Ward's death, she needed to let him take it.

"I am damaged," he repeated her own words back to her, a low rasp. "I will always be damaged."

Her heart twisted. Such a terrible place to say the words, but there was no other option, because they *needed* to be said.

She needed to say them.

"And I will always love you," she whispered, and stepped away, freeing him to do what he must do, to kill a man out of mercy.

A man who deserved no mercy.

"The sun that shines on me shines on my enemy. The breath he exhales, I inhale." Tristan's exhalation came in a harsh rush. "His pain is my own."

Closing his hands about Ward's neck, he twisted, sharp and fast.

Tatiana held tight to Tristan's waist as they sped from the battle on a borrowed snowscooter.

She had incinerated Ward's body while Tristan unscrewed the sample box from the floor using a tool he drew from his utility harness. He'd switched the power source to the backup pack, and the box was secured on the scooter.

There was so much she needed to say to him, to ask him, but there was no time, no chance. The world around them was exploding in an undulating wave of blinding heat and destruction, and they needed to get the hell out of here with the samples.

Tristan wove in a sharp zigzag pattern to avoid the hail of plas-shot and debris that rained down on them. Ward's troops fought on though their leader was dead. Not that they had a choice. The Reavers would kill them regardless.

Plas-shot ate the ground directly in front of them, leaving a huge blackened gouge in the tundra. Tristan cut the scooter hard right to avoid sending them directly into the pit.

Flattening both her palms on the saddle, Tatiana lifted her weight on her arms, splayed her legs and did a quick repositioning—arm, then leg, then arm, then leg—until she was back to back with Tristan, facing the oncoming hoard, yanking out her AT450 and her Setti9 to fire them double fisted.

The wind was so cold, it scraped her throat like diamond-bright shards as she sucked in each breath. Then the waves of burning heat from the plas-shot slapped at her.

Slagging hell. It wasn't just Ward's troops after them. A cadre of Reavers had broken off from the main group and were closing on them, fast.

The ground beside them exploded in a glittering fountain of icy chunks, big enough that they bruised when they came down again. Tristan wove the scooter hard left, then right, taking an evasive pattern.

"Slag," she snarled as heat exploded in their wake, a shimmering wave. The plasma shot was too close. Too slagging close.

She fired back, hit the lead scooter with enough force to knock it out of the race.

But she was worried, damned worried. If something hit the sample box, then everything they'd done here was for nothing.

The tissue samples could be replaced; Tristan could take new samples from her. But the viral samples, and

Ward's genetically mutated, virally infected bacteria . . . those were irreplaceable.

Damned stupid Reavers.

Why the hell did she have to be right? Just this once, couldn't her instincts have proven wrong?

Then she heard it, the boom of a plascannon, so close and so loud it drowned out the sounds of battle and the hum of the engine and the pounding of her heart.

An expanding bell of blue fire reached a yuale into the sky, taking the lead Reaver out, incinerating his body and melting his scooter into a twisted, blackened blob.

At her back, she felt Tristan twist to look over his shoulder, knew he saw what she saw.

A plascannon rig had fired on one of their own. Someone was attacking the ones shooting at them. The Reavers were divided, some pursuing, some holding back.

And then she saw him, Belek-ool, standing atop the plascannon rig, his chest bare, the three gouges he'd cut in his flesh illuminated by the glow of a dozen plasma fires.

Her own cuts were almost healed, but in that moment, she felt them again, felt the bite of her blade and Belek-ool's, felt her blood drip, hot and red, buying their freedom.

The luxury of sensation overwhelmed her. The water of the underground hot spring was warm and smooth, gliding over her limbs, her back.

Tatiana closed her eyes, let her head fall back against the stone, and felt every muscle in her body relax.

This was decadence.

She didn't open her eyes when she heard him, the soft sound of his footfalls, nearly imperceptible. Tristan. She knew when he drew near, when he paused and stood looking down at her. She heard the sharp inhalation and the thud of his heart, faster now than it had been.

"How are you?" she asked, opening her eyes.

"I've been working all night, and I made some good progress. Kalen and Lamia's viral loads have decreased significantly." He laughed. "But I'll be better in a moment."

Shucking his clothes, he left them where they dropped and dove into the pool, sending a geyser of water pluming upward.

Her heart tripped as he surfaced, and she stared at him, at the breadth of his shoulders where they extended above the water, and his long, damp hair, thick and glossy. Droplets caught the glow of the lumilight, refracting light in a rainbow of color.

Slowly, slowly, he turned his head, his eyes midnight dark, heavy lidded.

Emotions swirled and tangled, and it was impossible to separate her physical longing from the longing of her soul. She swam toward him, loving the feel of the water against her skin.

"What do you want of me?" she asked, recognizing even as the words left her that it was she who had come to him, she who wanted to touch his warm skin, to lick the water from his lips, to taste him.

"All of you, my heart. I want all of you."

It was asking for little enough, she supposed, given all he had offered in return.

They had shared days in the lab these past weeks, and nights in each other's arms. Whispered confessions and promises.

He told her about his childhood. She pulled things out of him. About his brothers. His parents.

She knew now the ghosts that haunted him.

"I can't help wondering if some greater force designed our meeting, our union," she murmured now.

He was what she was. A genetic anomaly. The discovery of that had been mind-boggling for her—though, in retrospect, she could see now that there had been so many clues. His references to living through events that had taken place decades past. His unusual strength and stamina. The fact that he was immune to a pathogen that killed everyone else it contacted.

The clues coalesced now in clear definition.

Oh, his origins were different than her own. Whereas she and her siblings had been engineered before birth in a laboratory, Tristan's genes had been enhanced during adulthood.

Longevity. Advanced immune response. Decreased need for sleep.

There were differences between them, along with their similarities, and each day they discovered new things.

And they would have endless days and nights to discover more, to understand why the modifications had worked on Tristan but none of his comrades. He had survived both the First and Second Noble Wars, and the plague that had stolen his entire family while he struggled in helpless desperation to save them.

He had survived so many years alone.

He was alone no more. And neither was she.

"Tell me again of neighborhoods and Rollerblades and street hockey," she murmured, pressing her lips to his neck, nipping the skin behind his ear. "Tell me again of the Little League that involves a stick and a ball." Things she had never heard of, and when he tried to explain what they were, she couldn't imagine a place in the world where such things existed.

"First, you must tell me again that you love me," he growled.

Reaching up, she stroked the damp hair from his forehead and stared into his eyes. This, too, he had given her. The strength to love him, to accept herself with all her damage and failings, and to understand that she deserved to love and be loved.

She was not whole. She would likely never be whole or completely healed. But she could love.

She did love.

"I love you," she said.

And with a growl, Tristan came upon her, his kiss filled with promise and passion as they sank together into the warm depths, limbs entwined. One.

EPILOGUE

They rode into the camp from the southeast. An endless saucer of night sky stretched above them, bright with the glitter of myriad stars. Blown-out buildings, remnants of a city long dead, reached twisted metal fingers and jagged shards of broken concrete to the heavens. Between the building were scattered huts, and to one side, a pen for the dogs.

They snarled and barked and threw themselves against the mesh of their cage.

All around the perimeter were paired guards.

Reaching up, Tatiana adjusted her lip-com. "On the buildings," she said, noting the snipers in case Tristan had missed them.

He hadn't. His head was already tilted to check their positions, and then he spread his index and middle fingers, pointed them first to his own eyes, then to shattered buildings at two o'clock and ten o'clock.

"I see them," she said, noting the faint hint of movement, almost invisible in the shadows that wreathed the camp.

They slowed, and Tristan pulled his scooter slightly ahead, making himself the more likely target should it come to it. Tatiana shook her head. Some things just . . . were.

"You sure they're expecting us?" she asked, noting the number of weapons that were trained directly at them.

"They are." Tristan's voice crackled through the com. "But they are careful by necessity."

Now wasn't that the understatement of the year. Pretty much everyone would like to get their hands on the Northern Waste Settlers Committee, a fancy name for the rebels who fought against the New Government Order.

"Let's hope they aren't so careful that they kill us before you have a chance to say your piece." She still had no idea why Tristan felt it was so important to meet with the rebels. Surely whatever business he had with them could be carried out through satellite link and holo-vid.

But he'd insisted it couldn't be, so here they were, riding into a camp full of people who looked like they would prefer to shoot now and ask questions later.

Ahead of them was a shattered shell of a building, illuminated by two bright beams of light, and in the center was a dark hole that appeared to be a recessed doorway.

She followed Tristan to the left, parked her Morgat and climbed off.

Flipping her Setti9 from her wrist holster, she watched warily as several figures moved in the shadows, phantoms draped in ragged swaths of cloth, similar to the garb Tristan had worn the first night she met him.

These rebels were trained. She saw it in the way they moved.

She stepped in front of Tristan, angling her body for his protection. From the corner of her eye, she saw him reach for her and take a half-step forward.

Turning her head, she shot him a look.

"Old habits," he said with a shrug and a smile.

She smiled back. She couldn't help it.

One of the shadows separated itself from the others. A woman. Tall. Sleek. Her ragged garb hung on her frame as though it were the most elegant of clothing, shipped from Neo-Tokyo. Her head was bowed, her face shadowed, her dark hair—cut in a ragged crop to her shoulders—fell forward to obscure her features.

A man took a step forward, made as though to accompany her, but she made a half turn back toward him and held up a hand in negation.

"It's them, Trey."

At the sound of her voice, a sense of unreality fogged Tatiana's thoughts. She shook her head, feeling as though each stride the woman took toward her was both too fast and too slow.

"Tristan," she whispered, feeling him step up beside her. His hand slid to hers, his gloved fingers intertwining with her own.

The woman was before her now, and two other people joined her, one beside her and the other slightly behind. Reaching up, they dragged back their hoods, baring their features, and the world spun away as Tatiana stared at them.

Gray eyes. Black lashes. Features so similar to her own.

And there, behind them, a blond woman with her hair pulled back in a ponytail, and a ten-inch blade strapped to her thigh.

They were all exactly as she remembered them, and not at all as she remembered them. Wizard. Yuriko. Raina.

And it was impossible that they were here.

"No," Tatiana croaked, her throat so tight she could barely speak. Tristan's fingers tightened on her own, offering silent comfort and support. "It isn't possible. You're—"

"Alive," Yuriko said, reaching out, but stopping short of touching her, as though afraid she would disappear. "Alive and looking for you for so long." Her voice broke, and she drew a shuddering breath, and finally she did touch her, dragging her into a tight embrace. "We have been searching for you for so long, Tatiana, my beloved sister."

COUNTDOWN

MICHELLE MADDOX

THREE

Kira Jordan wakes up in a pitch-black room handcuffed to a metal wall. She has 60 seconds to escape. Thus begins a vicious game where to lose is to die.

TWO

The man she's been partnered with—her only ally in this nightmare—is a convicted mass murderer. But if he's so violent, why does he protect her? And stranger still, what is it behind those haunted sea-green eyes that makes her want to protect him?

ONE

No one to trust. Nowhere to run. And the only hope of survival is working together to beat the *Countdown*.

AVAILABLE AUGUST 2008

ISBN 13: 978-0-505-52755-4

To order a book or to request a catalog call:
1-800-481-9191

This book is also available at your local bookstore, or you can check out our Web site **www.dorchesterpub.com** where you can look up your favorite authors, read excerpts, or glance at our discussion forum to see what people have to say about your favorite books.

✂ # ☐ **YES!**

Sign me up for the Love Spell Book Club and send my FREE BOOKS! If I choose to stay in the club, I will pay only $8.50* each month, a savings of $6.48!

NAME: _____

ADDRESS: _____

TELEPHONE: _____

EMAIL: _____

☐ I want to pay by credit card.

☐ **VISA**   ☐ **MasterCard**   ☐ **DISCOVER**

ACCOUNT #: _____

EXPIRATION DATE: _____

SIGNATURE: _____

Mail this page along with $2.00 shipping and handling to:
Love Spell Book Club
PO Box 6640
Wayne, PA 19087
Or fax (must include credit card information) to:
610-995-9274
You can also sign up online at **www.dorchesterpub.com**.
*Plus $2.00 for shipping. Offer open to residents of the U.S. and Canada only. Canadian residents please call 1-800-481-9191 for pricing information.
If under 18, a parent or guardian must sign. Terms, prices and conditions subject to change. Subscription subject to acceptance. Dorchester Publishing reserves the right to reject any order or cancel any subscription.